The You Say Which Way Collection

THIS SET CONTAINS THREE ADVENTURES

Dungeon of Doom

The Secrets of the Singing Cave

Movie Mystery Madness

Published by:
The Fairytale Factory,
Wellington,
New Zealand.

ISBN-13:
978-1726159807

ISBN-10:
1726159809

YouSayWhichWay.com

How These Books Work

These are interactive books with YOU as the main character. You say which way the story goes. Some paths will lead to trouble, others to discovery and adventure. Have fun and follow the link of your choice at the end of each chapter. For example, **P34** means to turn to page 34.

Your first decision is to choose which book to read first. After that, it gets a bit trickier.

Dungeon of Doom	**P1**
Secrets of the Singing Cave	**P98**
Movie Mystery Madness	**P253**

The You Say Which Way Collection

1

DUNGEON OF DOOM

Secret Bonus Level

On Saturday morning, you're sitting around the kitchen table with Jim and Tina, playing *Dungeon of Doom* together on your laptops.

"Gotcha." Jim taps his keyboard to launch another fireball at the Nine-Headed Dragon's eleventh head. (One head grew back. Twice.)

"Yee ha!" Tina's onscreen avatar, Tina Warrior Princess, finally chops off the dragon's last head.

Level Completed appears in giant sparkly letters. The floor of the dungeon room fills with gold coins, gems, roast chickens, healing potions, and other end-of-level bonuses. Your avatar, Velzon the Elven Archer, runs around the room collecting them. Tina Warrior Princess and Jim's avatar, Wizard Zim, do the same.

"Warriors don't say 'yee ha'," Jim complains.

Tina grins. "I'm a *cowgirl* warrior princess, and I'll say 'yee ha' if I want to."

While they're arguing, you spot a weird shimmering circle on the wall by the Nine-Headed Dragon's tail, and walk over to it. "Um, guys," you say.

They're not listening.

"Try to take the game seriously, Tina," Jim says. "There's no such thing as cowgirl warrior princesses."

"Great advice, from a wizard wearing sunglasses," she sneers.

"They're not sunglasses, they're Enchanted Shadow Crystal Lenses. They give a plus 10 bonus when detecting and deciphering magic."

"Yeah, right, and they just happen to look exactly like sung–"

"Hey, Tina Warrior Princess and Wizard Zim!" you interrupt. "What's this mysterious round thingy on the wall in front of me?"

"Huh? What are you jabbering about?" Tina walks around, frowns at your laptop screen, then checks her own again. "My screen just shows ordinary wall there. Weird."

"Mine too," Jim says. "Can't be a magical artefact, coz I can't see it through my Enchanted Shadow Crystal Lenses. So it must be something Elvish."

"Well, duh." Tina rolls her eyes and returns to her chair.

They both look at you expectantly.

Huh! Just because Velzon is a 400-year-old elf, that doesn't make you an expert on mysterious shimmering walls.

You have an idea. Onscreen, you pick up a gold coin and toss it at the shimmery wall. As you'd half-expected, the coin vanishes. At the same moment, the edge of the circle flashes like a camera, and…were those letters?

"The wall flashed on my screen," Tina says. "What is it, a booby trap?"

She could be right.

"It was on my screen too. Might be just a program bug," Jim grumbles. "Remember that level in *Monkey Maniacs*, where jumping on the giant banana made the whole game crash?"

He could be right too.

"I think it's a portal." You toss another coin at it, watching the circle carefully. The letters reappear, and this time you can read them. "It says 'Secret Bonus Level' in Klodruchian runes."

"Cool," Tina whispers. "Whatever a Klod-whatsit is."

Jim sniffs. "I haven't seen anything on the internet about a secret bonus level in *Dungeon of Doom*."

"That makes it even cooler," Tina says. "Maybe we're the first players to find it. We'll be famous. Especially me."

"Why you?" you ask suspiciously.

"Coz I'll be first." Onscreen, Tina Warrior Princess leaps into the shimmering portal.

But you and Jim had the same idea too, and Velzon and Zim leap into the portal at the same time. Everything turns really bright, then really dark, then…

Huh? The whole kitchen's gone, and you're lying on a stone floor. Next to you are a tall woman covered in muscles and scars and battered armor, and a bearded guy in a purple robe and a pointy hat – Tina Warrior Princess and Wizard Zim, looking just like they do in the game, but…now they're real.

Impossible. Totally impossible.

"What happened?" Wizard Zim asks.

You look down. You're wearing Velzon's leaf-embroidered jerkin, spider silk trousers, and lizard-leather boots. Just to be sure, you reach up, and…yup, elf ears. On your back is a bow and quiver. On your belt is a long dagger of finest Kargalin steel. Exactly like in the game.

"We're inside *Dungeon of Doom*." Tina Warrior Princess stands up, a huge grin on her scarred face. "Cool!"

Zim tugs at his beard. "Don't be stupid. We can't be. What is this, some new virtual reality thing?" He turns to you. "I don't like it. Make it stop. Turn it off. Now!"

"How?" you ask.

He runs around the room, yelling, "Reset! End game! Escape! Power off! End simulation! Exit!" Nothing happens.

"Try to take the game seriously, Zim," Tina says with a smirk.

"I have to be home soon for lunch, or Mom will be angry."

"I don't think the great wizard Zim's mommy makes him lunch," you say, trying to make him laugh, but it doesn't work.

"Let's explore!" Tina shouts, and runs out the room's only doorway.

"We might as well. We can't just stay here," you tell Zim.

He crouches beside a pillar. "Why not? This room is nice and quiet, and there are plenty of roast chicken bonuses if I miss lunch."

"That's not how the game works, remember? If we stay in one place for too long, monsters attack us, more and more, until it's wall-to-wall fangs and claws. So we have to explore, to find this level's exit, and… get back to the real world." Well, you hope so.

"Mmm," he says reluctantly, and follows you out the doorway.

Tina's only a few steps away, frowning as she looks up and down a corridor. "This better not be a maze. I hate mazes. Always get lost." She says it like she's joking, but it's the truth – she has a terrible sense of direction, in real life and in games.

Left and right look the same – generic stone-walled dungeon corridors, lit by burning torches, with more doorways in the distance. This level's exit could be either way. Or both ways – some levels have more than one exit.

Zim peers both ways through his Enchanted Shadow Crystal Lenses, then shrugs and looks at you. "Well, pointy ears?"

After listening and sniffing in both directions, you point left. "Goblins. Lots of them." You point right. "Ogres. Coming this way."

Tina and Zim look at you expectantly.

"What, you want *me* to decide?"

5

Tina grins. "Yeah, Velzon, you're good at that elfy scouting stuff. That's the only reason we let you play with us."

Zim nods. "Let's play this level the same way we usually do – you leading the way."

"So I get shot first, and stabbed first, and zapped first?" you ask.

"No worries, we'll be right behind, ready to rescue you," Tina says.

"And I've got a zillion healing potions if you get injured," Zim says.

"Thanks, you two are so helpful."

It's time to make a decision. Do you:

Go left, towards the goblins? **P7**

Or

Go right, towards the ogres? **P54**

6

You need to go back and make a decision.

The Goblins

You turn left, because goblins are the least scary creatures in a dungeon.

But the goblin smell (like a mixture of wet dog and broccoli) gets stronger with every step you take. Maybe there are hundreds of goblins down this way. Or thousands. A thousand goblins together can kill just about anything, even a giant or a dragon. They'd easily wipe out an elf, a warrior princess, and a wizard. Maybe this direction wasn't such a good idea after all.

You hear the usual goblin sounds too – bickering and growling and grumbling that never stops, even in battle.

At the end of the corridor is an archway flanked by two big statues of frowning demons, one of them fallen. You crouch behind the fallen stone demon and peer through the archway.

Goblins. Hundreds of them, which explains the smell and noise.

What's surprising is that they're clambering up and down a tall rickety platform, and painting a huge mural that covers the entire far wall. Since when have goblins been artistic?

What's even more surprising is that the half-finished mural shows an elf, a warrior princess, and a wizard, who look a lot like the three of you.

"Is this a goblin joke, and they're about to turn and point at us and laugh, before attacking?" whispers Zim.

"Nah, a goblin isn't smart enough to think of that. Their idea of comedy is giggling while they bite off someone's fingers and toes," Tina whispers.

"I think it must be a magic mural that looks different to anyone who sees it," you whisper. "The goblins don't seem

8

to know they're painting us – or at least, they're paying no attention to this doorway."

Zim nods. "Yeah, don't get close to the mural. That whole wall's crawling with magic. I'm pretty sure the goblins are under a spell. But look over there." He points past the mural and the goblins to a doorway framed by ivy.

"So what?" Tina asks.

"Ivy doesn't grow underground. I think there's daylight through there. It could be this level's exit."

"Or just an outdoorsy part of it," you say. "Remember the outdoorsy part of Level 49, where we were attacked by wolves and struck by lightning and nearly eaten by a tree? Sometimes it's safer to stay indoors. Besides, we've got no way to sneak past the goblins."

"Actually, we do. I found a cool Invisibility spell in my Big Book of Spells, and I've been dying to try out."

Tina snorts. "Yeah, 'dying' – as in, we usually die whenever you try a new spell."

Die? Oh. "Hey, that's a really good point. What happens if we die?" you ask.

"Huh?"

"If we die here inside the game, what happens? Are we just sent back to our last Save Point? Or," you shiver, "do we die in the real world too?"

Zim whimpers.

Tina looks serious for once. "Yeah, but, um…" She grips her sword and looks around again. "How about that doorway there instead?"

You take a closer look at the shadow she's pointing to. She's right. Within the shadow is a narrow doorway. And it's close. You could probably sneak through it without the goblins noticing, even without an Invisibility spell.

"Yeah, that way is okay too, I guess, but it's not as…ivy-ish as the other way," Zim says, sounding embarrassed.

Obviously, he hadn't noticed the narrow doorway either. "But someone's scratched 'Beware' on the wall next to it."

"Beware of what?" you ask. "Beware of the dog? Beware of wet paint? Not very helpful."

"'Beware' is always good advice in a dungeon," Tina says.

It's time to make a decision. Do you:

Turn invisible and sneak past the goblins to the ivy doorway? **P10**

Or

Go through the narrow doorway? **P28**

Invisibly Sneak Past the Goblins

"Okay, Zim, let's try your Invisibility spell and see what's through that doorway with the ivy," you say.

Zim hums, makes a gargling noise, shakes his fingers, and spins his wand from hand to hand.

"Didn't work. We're still totally visible," Tina says.

"I haven't cast the spell yet. That was just my stretching exercises."

She rolls her eyes.

Zim pulls a leather-bound book from his robes and opens it. He mutters, wriggles his fingers, and twirls his wand, faster and faster.

Just as Tina opens her mouth, probably to make another sarcastic comment, she vanishes. So do Zim and you.

"Wow, it actually worked," comes Tina's voice from the empty air. "I take back all the mean things I was going to say about you, Wizard Zim."

"Thanks a lot, Princess Mean-er."

"Let's go. Quietly," you say, before they can start arguing again.

Within seconds, you discover the downside of being invisible – you can't see where you're walking, and can't see each other.

Tina stubs her toe on your boot heel and swears under her breath.

A few seconds later, Zim drops his wand. It clatters on the stone floor and is visible for a moment before he snatches it back up. Luckily, you all stay invisible, and the goblins don't seem to notice.

Or did they? Some of them lower their paint pots and brushes, look around as if puzzled, and sniff with their long pointy noses.

11

"Smelly!" squeals one. "Bad smelly! Peoples!"

What? They think *you're* smelly? It's surprising they can smell anything except themselves.

The goblins look around everywhere but can't see you.

"Magics!" squeals another goblin.

They glance towards the ivy doorway, whine and whimper to each other, then start painting faster than before. Who or what are they scared of?

Tina collides with you again. She grabs your shoulder, then nudges you forwards. Good idea. Maybe Zim is holding onto her too. Or maybe not. As quietly as possible, you shuffle forwards.

By the time you're halfway past the mural, the goblins are sniffing suspiciously again.

One goblin flings its paint pot and splatters blue paint over the floor, missing you only by a few feet. Other goblins get the same idea, and soon there's paint flying in every direction. They haven't hit you yet, but it's only a matter of time before…

"Wooooh!" A goblin points at the floor.

Oops. You've stepped in wet paint and are leaving a trail of multi-colored footprints.

"Run!" you yell.

The three of you race for the ivy doorway. Well, you do – hopefully Tina and Zim are following.

Dozens of goblins scamper down from the platform and give chase. Luckily, you have a head start, and have longer legs than goblins, and they still can't see more than your footprints.

They're right behind you, but the moment you reach the ivy doorway, they screech to a halt. There's lots of whispering and pointing and shoving, but not one of them is brave enough to step through the doorway, or to touch the ivy.

12

Good. Although now you're more and more worried about what's in here.

"Master, he sort them out," one says at last.

The others agree and repeat this to each other, nodding and giggling. Then they run back to the mural, leaving hundreds more painty footprints.

"Weird," whispers Tina's voice beside you.

"Totally weird," whispers Zim's voice. "So, we may as well explore and see if this is the exit, right?"

Something rustles in the ivy. You look around. No people or animals are in sight. The walls and floor are covered in thick ivy. It blocks the corridor a bit further along, although maybe you could push or cut a path through. The high ceiling looks like glass blocks, with sunlight shining through them. An indoor garden? Nice, but…in a dungeon?

"Yeah, we might as well look for the exit," Tina says. "I'm not going back out there while those goblins are around. Nasty little creatures. One of them tried to bite my foot. While giggling."

"But why didn't the goblins follow us in here?" you ask. "They must be terrified of this 'Master', whoever he is. Zim, can you make us visible again? Being invisible isn't nearly as much fun as I expected."

There's no reply.

Tina sighs. "Please, o mighty Wizard Zim, we humbly beg thee to remove thy super cool spell, yeah, thanks."

Still no reply.

"Not funny, Zim, just—"

Just what? Why'd Tina stop talking mid-sentence?

Something rustles in the ivy. Maybe the same something that rustled before. Maybe not.

"Tina? Zim?" You draw your dagger. "Hello? Anyone?"

More silence. You hope this is some stupid joke they're playing, because if not, it's something far worse.

13

Ivy wraps around your legs, and pulls you towards the deep green shadows. Perhaps it's trying to help you. Or kill you.

It's time to make a decision – and fast, while your arms are still free. Do you:

Cut yourself free with your dagger? **P14**

Or

Follow the ivy? **P15**

Chop the Ivy

You slash at the ivy with your dagger. The green tendrils part and fall away, but more replace them. You slash again, but your dagger's not much of a pruning knife. Soon, ivy wraps your hands and feet, squeezing in a deadly embrace. It sprouts into your nose, your ears, your eyes, until…

Suddenly you're back in the real world, alone, scrunched up on the kitchen floor and gasping for breath.

On the table above you, the words *Game Over* sparkle on your laptop screen. Huh? Why are you on the floor? Weren't you playing with your friends? Where are they, and…why can't you even remember their names?

On the far side of the room, a pot plant's leaves quiver in a draft. For some reason that you can't explain, you shiver.

Sorry, this part of your story is over – you were squeezed to death by angry ivy. If you'd made different choices, things might have gone better (or even worse). Have you met the Emerald Sage? Gotten lost in the maze? Been attacked by the bone army? Run from the giant rolling head? Helped the extremely wet queen? Said hello to the Reverse Dragon? Avoided the Zenobian Snapper?

It's time to make a decision. Do you:

Go back to the previous section? **P10**

Or

Go to the beginning of the story and try another path? **P1**

Or

Go to the great big list of choices and find a different path to read? **P364**

Follow the Ivy

A forest of ivy pushes and pulls you through its tangled vines. Your bow and quiver are ripped from your back, but you desperately hold on to the dagger with both hands, determined not to be left defenseless. Eventually the ivy dumps you into an empty room. Instead of hitting the hard stone floor, you land on something soft and invisible.

"Ow," says Zim's voice.

"Wasn't me," says Tina's voice.

"It's me, Velzon," you say. "Zim, invisibility's really annoying – can you cancel the spell?"

"No, I lost my wand in the ivy. Along with my healing potions, my wizard's hat, and my left boot. I even lost my Big Book of Spells."

"Big Book of Spells?" sneers a deep voice.

You turn. A tall green figure stands in a dark doorway.

"No proper wizard needs to carry a book of spells. Show yourselves, worms!" He waves a wand. Actually, it looks more like a twig, but it must be a wand, because you, Tina and Zim are suddenly visible again. Zim looks miserable, and Tina's lost her weapons in the ivy too.

You try to hide your dagger behind your back, but…it's been magically transformed into a daffodil.

The tall figure moves out of the doorway, revealing he's actually a short figure wearing a very tall green hat, so tall that the tip scrapes along the glass ceiling. His robes and boots are also green. Even his long white beard's a bit greenish – moss or mold, perhaps.

Scowling, he looks you all up and down, then turns to Zim. "Pathetic. More pathetic than my goblin watchdogs out there. A third-rate wizard like you thought you could march in here with your bodyguards and steal her from me?"

"Third-rate?" Zim sounds insulted.

"You think we're Zim's bodyguards?" Tina sounds even more insulted.

"Steal who?" you ask. "We don't want to steal anyone from anyone. We're just looking for the exit, sir."

"Oh really? What a coincidence – my last so-called visitors said the same thing. And claimed they'd never heard of me, the world-famous Emerald Sage. Hah!" He gestures with his wand at an ivy-covered wall, and the vines obediently shrink back, revealing a corridor. "Move."

You've never heard of a wizard called the Emerald Sage, but you aren't going to tell him that. As an elf, you've seen enough plant magic to realize this guy must be a powerful hortimancer, and you don't want to be turned into a daffodil.

Tina gets to her feet, clenching a fist while twitching her nose, which is her secret signal for *How about I punch this guy's face off?*

You shake your head – you don't want her turned into a daffodil either.

Zim stands uncomfortably in one boot and one bare foot. "Um, could I please have my other boot back, Mr. Sage, sir?"

The Emerald Sage waves his twig wand, and suddenly Zim's bare foot is a boot-sized block of solid wood. "Any more complaints?" he sneers.

"No, sir," you all chorus, and march down the corridor in front of him, Zim going step-thud-step-thud-step-thud with his wooden foot.

"What sort of name's Emerald Sage?" Tina mutters. "Sounds like an ingredient in my dad's spaghetti sauce recipe."

"Shush," you whisper.

The ivy ends, replaced by what look like Venus fly-traps, except these have eyes and turn to stare at you.

"Keep your distance," the Emerald Sage warns. "They're hungry."

Another part of his security system, apparently. He sure is paranoid.

The next corridor has daffodils growing everywhere. You tip-toe through them, trying not to step on any, just in case they're magically transformed previous adventurers.

The corridor leads to an untidy workroom, lined with shelves of pot plants and cobwebbed leather-bound books. Above a mantelpiece is a painting of busy goblins with paintbrushes. The picture's moving! Oh, that's the room you were in before. The painting must be some sort of magical security video monitor. Several long tables and the floor are stacked with more books, crumpled pages of parchment, quill pens, bottles of ink, and three rusty watering cans.

The far wall has an archway with words carved into it. Beyond is a large room, full of tangled thorn bushes, except for a stone platform with a bed on it.

In the bed, someone's snoring. "Sleeping Beauty," you, Zim and Tina say at the same time. This isn't the first weird fairytale you've encountered in *Dungeon of Doom*. There were three grumpy porridge-loving bears on Level 82.

"Yes," the Emerald Sage says dreamily. "Princess Valeria is the most beautiful woman in the world."

Um, that's not what you meant, but never mind. As far as you can see through the thorns, the sleeping princess is in her seventies. About the same age as the Emerald Sage. Oh.

"Is she your one true love, sir?" you ask.

"Not yet," the Emerald Sage says. "But when I release her from the spell, she'll be so grateful that she'll fall in love with me."

Is he really that dumb?

Tina rolls her eyes. She hates kissy stuff.

18

"And for how long have you been trying to free Princess Valeria, sir?" you ask, still in your politest voice.

"Fifty-two years."

Wow. Zim gasps, and Tina lets out a strangled giggle. You glare at them.

The Emerald Sage raises his wand, as if he's about to turn you all into daffodils or worse. "Back when my beloved Valeria was enchanted, I was just a young apprentice royal wizard, and I couldn't do anything against such a powerful spell. But I've been studying ancient tomes and arcane lore ever since, and now I'm very close to breaking it."

Uh-oh. You're not sure what arcane lore is, but he's definitely doing a Super-Villain speech and explaining his evil plans, which probably means you're about to die horribly.

Sure enough, he gives a creepy smile. "Now I need some volunteers to walk into the thorns when I cast my counter-spell."

You peer through the thorns again. Dozens of skeletons are intertwined in the branches, and more litter the floor. Probably previous "volunteers".

Tina and Zim sidle up to you.

"Let's make a run for it," Tina whispers. "I don't trust his stupid counter-spell."

"No, this must be a logic puzzle, like on Level 59," whispers Zim. "If we can help him solve it, that will break the spell, and the Sage will give us a huge reward. Besides, the level exit's probably behind those thorns."

It's time to make a decision. Do you:

Make a run for it? **P19**

Or

Try to break the spell? **P20**

Run for It

The Emerald Sage turns towards the princess for a moment. You nod to Tina and Zim, and the three of you run for the doorway. Not as quietly as you'd hoped – Zim's wooden foot thumps on the floor with every second step.

Something behind you zaps, and…

Suddenly you're back in the real world.

But something's wrong. Very wrong. There's the kitchen, and the table, and three laptops, looking perfectly normal. Except…you're in a bath? With two giant yellow flowers next to you? Oh, you're a giant yellow flower too. No, this isn't a bath, it's an ordinary vase on the window sill, which means…

"He turned us into daffodils," you tell the other two flowers – presumably Jim and Tina.

Or at least, you try to speak, except you don't have a mouth. Whoever heard of talking flowers? That makes you want to laugh, except you can't laugh either. Then you can't remember what was funny, and then you can't remember anything at all. Everything turns a beautiful shade of emerald green. Forever.

Sorry, this part of your story is over. If you'd made different choices, things might have gone better (or even worse). Have you gotten lost in the maze? Been attacked by the bone army? There are many paths to try.

It's time to make a decision. Do you:

Go back to the previous section? **P15**

Or

Go to the beginning and try another path? **P95**

Or

Go to the great big list of choices? **P364**

Break the Spell

"Okay, Zim, let's try to break the spell," you whisper, hoping he knows what he's doing.

He turns to the Emerald Sage. "I'm nowhere near as great a wizard as you are, sir, but I might be able to help. What type of spell it is? Hyper-dimensional Glass? Daemonic Vortex Wall?"

Is he making this stuff up?

"Curse of Eternal Thorns," the Emerald Sage snaps. "Isn't that obvious? Why else would I spend fifty-two years studying hortimancy?"

Okay, apparently all wizards really do talk like this. What a pair of nerds.

Zim nods. "Of course, I should have thought of Curse of Eternal Thorns. That explains the, um, thorns. What's the spell's thaumaturgical constriction?"

The Emerald Sage snorts and points to the words carved around the stone archway. "A cryptic prophecy. Such a cliché."

The words read:

Below the earth, in caverns deep,
the princess shall forever sleep,
bewitched, until a worthy mind
can slay the thorns, not thorns, and find
beneath these words, the truth. Or else

The last stone is blank.

"Or else what? Why's the final line missing?" Zim picks up a long parchment page from a table. It's the words from the archway, copied out a dozen times, with words underlined or circled or crossed out or translated into other languages. The whole page is marked with arrows and scribbly diagrams and notes in terrible tiny handwriting. "Hmm. What does the prophecy mean, sir?"

"Nothing," the Emerald Sage snarls. "I wasted years trying to decipher it, but it's just a red herring, a distraction. Forget it. I've spent the last few years researching a rare counter-spell called Botanical Discombobulation. I'm fairly sure I've got it right this time."

Only "fairly sure"? That's not reassuring.

"Zim's great at deciphering prophecies," you say, hoping to gain some more time.

"Um, yeah." Zim looks uncertainly at the parchment and back to the archway.

"Yeah, totally," Tina adds. "He's an ace at prophecies, crosswords, and Sudoku."

The Emerald Sage furrows his brow. "Cross Words? Sudoku? I've never heard of such spells. Perhaps you are wiser than you seem, Zim. Or perhaps you're trying to trick me, just like all those others over the years. Let's find out."

He waves his wand, and all three of you take a step towards the archway. Then another step.

"What's happening?" Tina asks. "My feet are moving by themselves."

"He's cast Inexorable March on us," Zim moans. "We'll keep walking, no matter what."

She tries punching her legs, but that doesn't stop her taking another step. "We're headed for those sharp thorns."

The Emerald Sage giggles. "This is your chance to demonstrate the power of Sudoku. Or die. Good luck, I want you to succeed, I really do. I'll be right here, casting Botanical Discombobulation." He waves his wand again and begins chanting. Beyond the gateway, the thorny branches start to bend out of the way, creating a path towards old Sleeping Beauty.

Great, except that the bent branches are quivering, as if only held there by invisible hands, ready to spring back at you at any moment.

"Any ideas about the prophecy, guys?" You try to hold onto a table, but the spell's too strong.

Tina shrugs. "Don't ask me, I hate poetry."

"Think of the lines as song lyrics," Zim tells her. "Prophecies always mean something important. There must be a clue in there somewhere."

"Below the earth, in caverns deep," she warbles, off-key, while playing air guitar. "Yeah, I can imagine my favorite death metal band thrashing out a song like that. But what does 'thorns, not thorns' mean anyway? And who goes around slaying thorns? Doesn't make sense."

Behind you, the Emerald Sage continues chanting. Another step. You're at the archway.

"That's the whole point, it's a paradox," you say, then realize what you just said. "Um, yeah, perhaps the thorns aren't really thorns."

"They're not cuddly teddy bears!" Zim snaps.

You try but fail to hold on to the archway. Your next step gives you an uncomfortably close look at the quivering thorns.

If the Emerald Sage's Botanical Discombobulation spell fails now, you'll be skewered.

Hmm, why are the thorns in pairs, like…tiny fangs? Ah. "Zim, do you have any spells that slay snakes?"

His eyes widen. "Probably, in my Big Book of Spells, but I don't have that or my wand anymore."

"Anything that could work on a room full of snakes? Anything at all? Think fast!"

"Well, there's Serpentine Snooze, I suppose. Every junior wizard learns to cast that. It doesn't even need a wand. But no, that's far too easy."

You take another involuntary step, and a pair of thorns (or maybe fangs) presses into your arm. Ouch, they really hurt. And what if they're poisonous? "Try it, Zim, now!"

He waves his arms like the world's worst disco dancer, while chanting something that sounds like a drain unblocking.

The thorny branches shudder and drop to the floor, falling apart into, yes, snakes. Great, now you're surrounded by a roomful of hissing snakes.

But before you can make an Indiana Jones joke, they slither into the room's corners and…fall asleep. Maybe from Zim's spell, or perhaps they're exhausted from pretending to be thorns for fifty-two years.

"What have you done?" the Emerald Sage squeals. "Don't you dare kiss her, she's mine." He dashes past, heading for the bed on the platform.

"Ew, I wasn't going to kiss anyone," Tina mutters.

Zim giggles.

Before the Emerald Sage reaches the old woman, she wakes and sits up.

"Took you long enough, Norman," she says. "Partly my own fault, I admit. I had such fun writing that prophecy, even though I couldn't think of a good rhyme for 'Or Else', so I never finished it. And then I had to cast the spell in a mad rush, and it was my first spell ever, and I think I mispronounced a few words."

"You cast the spell on yourself?" squeaks the Emerald Sage (apparently also known as Norman). "But why? How? You're a princess, not a wizard."

"Being a princess was so boring. Mom and Dad were trying to marry me off to every second prince who walked past, and I hadn't met even one I liked. Such a bunch of fools." She pulls a thick book from under her pillow. "One day, I found this old book in the library, full of exciting spells. I thought, why not create a magical puzzle and see which prince is smart enough to solve it? I expected someone would work it out in a few days or weeks at most. But none of them did. Everyone gave up after a month or so. Except you, not-prince Norman."

He blushes.

"But, still, fifty-two years?" she continues. "And then these three solve it for you?" She points at you, Zim and Tina, still slowly marching towards her platform.

Norman's mouth opens and closes as if he's a goldfish.

"Just a lucky guess," you say, feeling sorry for him.

Tina and Zim nod.

"Well, at least you never gave up on me, Norman," she says kindly. "I appreciate that. I'm terribly thirsty. Let's have a chat over a nice cup of tea. People still drink tea, don't they? Good. Come on, dear." She takes his hand, walks over to a doorway in the far wall, and leads him up a flight of stairs.

Leaving you here?

"Excuse me!" you shout. "Emerald Sage? Sir? Could you cancel your Inexcusable March spell, please?"

There's no reply.

"Inexorable March," Zim corrects.

Tina turns to the doorway and yells, "Hey, Emerald Parsley, cut this marching stuff and give us our huge reward for breaking the snakey spell for you!"

Silence. They've gone.

"Ungrateful sod!" she yells.

All of you take another step and stub your toes on the platform for the hundredth time. Splinters fall off Zim's wooden foot.

"Princess Sleepy Head was no better, just walked off and left us," Tina continues. "Princesses are awful, can't be trusted."

"But you're a princess," Zim points out.

"No, no, us warrior princesses are okay. Obviously. It's those non-warrior princesses you have to watch out for."

Another step. Ow. Why are Zim and Tina wasting time yacking about princesses?

"Can't you do something to break this marching spell?" you ask Zim.

He shakes his head. "Not without my Big Book of Spells."

"How about that one?" Tina points to the book left by the old princess.

"Oh, yeah, didn't think of that." He stretches out, manages to grab the book by its corner, and flicks through the pages. "Hey, this is a cool book, much better than my old one."

"Hurry, my toes are getting sorer and sorer. I'm sure I've broken a toenail."

Your toes hurt too.

"Okay, okay, I found a Mystical Dispellation spell that should work," Zim says, "but I don't have a wand. Even a twig or a pencil would do."

You point to the splinters by his wooden foot. "What about one of those?"

He picks up a thin sliver of wood and frowns. "A bit small. But here goes." He waves the "wand" and recites something that sounds like a goat arguing with a dolphin. Suddenly you can move your own feet again. What a relief.

"My poor toes." Tina sits on the floor, pulls her boots off, and rubs her feet. "Hey, look under the bed."

You crouch down and see *Level Exit* carved on the flagstones.

"Great, let's get out of here," you say. "Give me a hand moving the bed out of the way, guys."

It's a strangely heavy bed. Lumpy too. Together, you heave it to one side. The mattress clanks and tinkles as it hits the floor. Hmm, that's no ordinary mattress. You undo a row of buttons, and out fall two crowns, a bracelet and a diamond necklace, followed by a stream of gold coins.

Zim grins. "We got a huge reward after all."

Five minutes later, weighed down with treasure, you step onto the *Level Exit* flagstones, and…

Suddenly you're back in the real world, sitting at the table with Jim and Tina. *Bonus Level Completed* is in big sparkly letters on your laptop screen.

"We won!" Jim says. "That was cool. Wow, is that the time? I'd better get home for lunch. See you guys back here next Saturday to play Level 101." He folds up his laptop, grabs a walking stick and limps out the door, going step-thud-step-thud-step-thud.

"Um," you say to Tina. "Was Jim's foot always like that?"

She frowns. "Can't remember. It…must have been, right?"

You go to the window and look out. There's Jim, going step-thud-step-thud-step-thud along the pavement.

On the other side of the road is an old couple in their seventies, out for a stroll. They're both dressed in green and look familiar somehow. They see Jim, and the woman says something to the man. Reluctantly, he waves something twig-like. Jim's walking stick vanishes, and he walks away normally, not even noticing the magical change.

"You have weird neighbors," Tina says. "See you next week."

Congratulations, you've finished this part of your story. Then again, if you'd made different choices, things might have gone even better (or much worse).

Have you gotten lost in the maze? Been attacked by the bone army? Run from the giant rolling head? Helped the extremely wet queen? Said hello to the Reverse Dragon? Avoided the Zenobian Snapper?

It's time to make a decision. Do you:

Go back to the beginning of the story and try another path? **P95**

Or

Go to the great big list of choices? **P364**

The Narrow Doorway

No, you don't trust Zim's Invisibility spell. Not enough to trust your life on it. (Or Zim and Tina's lives.)

You point to the narrow doorway. "We'll run there, one at a time, as quietly as possible."

They nod.

You go first. The doorway's only a dozen steps away, but it feels like running a mile. Luckily, the goblins don't notice you. Crouched in the doorway's shadow, you turn back to the archway you came from. Zim and Tina are still behind the fallen statue, pushing and shoving each other and arguing in loud whispers. Idiots.

A goblin looks around, spots them and shrieks an alarm. They make a mad dash towards your doorway, chased by dozens of goblins.

"It's all her fault," Zim shouts.

"It's all his fault," Tina shouts, at the same time.

They're *still* arguing? With the goblins in pursuit, you sprint along a twisty-turny corridor and through an open red door. Tina and Zim follow you, then you slam the door shut behind them. Just in time – seconds later, muffled pounding and kicking and screeching come from the other side.

"What sort of room is this?" Tina gasps, out of breath. "Looks sort of steampunky."

True. The room's circular, with tarnished brass walls, floor and ceiling, and is lit by gas lamps. No one's running around wearing goggles and a bowler hat and talking in a bad British accent though.

"What's holding that door shut?" Zim asks. "There's not even a handle or knob, let alone a lock or bolt."

"And no other exits." Tina draws her sword, clearly expecting the red door to burst open any moment. "It's a trap!" she adds in her Admiral Ackbar voice (which is pretty bad – her Chewbacca impersonation is much better).

You draw your bow. Zim pulls his wand from his robe.

From somewhere above comes a metallic clunk, followed by squeaking and whirring. The circular floor quivers under your feet, then rotates, while the walls spin in the opposite direction. Dizzy, you fall to your knees. What next? Will the ceiling descend and crush you? Will giant spinning saw blades come out of the walls?

A few seconds later, the spinning slows and stops with another clunk. The goblin noises have gone. The red door has vanished – instead, now there's a white door, a yellow door, and a purple door.

"I feel sick," Zim moans, lying on the floor. "That was worse than a roller coaster."

"You've never ridden a roller coaster," Tina snaps, getting back to her feet. "Riding a plastic horsey on a carousel with your seven-year-old brother doesn't count."

He sits up. "That horse was a public safety hazard! I complained to the manager!"

"Guys!" you interrupt. "Concentrate. Look, the doors have changed. There's three now, and none of them are red."

"Impossible. Doors don't just appear from nowhere." Tina glares at them as if trying to scare them into disappearing. "This better not be one of those stupid magic mazes. I told you before, I hate mazes."

"Yeah, yeah, we know." Zim staggers to his feet and looks around the room. "No sign of magic, so it must be a *non-*magic maze. Better?"

She scowls at him.

"I reckon we're inside a giant mechanical puzzle," you say. "Perhaps it's a security system to guard a treasure room.

30

Now we have to pick the right door to find the treasure and the level exit."

Tina sniffs. "And behind the other two doors are horrible gory deaths, no doubt."

Zim agrees with her. Those two agreeing on anything is a bad sign.

"There must be clues if we're smart enough to spot them," you insist. "Look there, a line of scraped red paint – that's probably from the red door that disappeared. And every yard or so, there's a vertical line that's scraped shiny. I think these walls are panels which slide up and down when the room spins, and some of the panels have doors in them. Make sense?"

Neither Tina nor Zim look like they believe you, but neither has any better suggestions.

You take a closer look at the three doors.

The white door is plain and smooth, and hums like a refrigerator. Maybe it really is a refrigerator, with milk cartons, eggs and carrots inside? Nah, that seems too weird even for this place.

The yellow door has a brass button at knee level. Below it, "Don't Press Me" is engraved in Dwarvish. If the door's for dwarves, why is it normal height? And why would anyone have a doorbell with a "Don't Press Me" sign?

The purple door is lined with rows of silver rivets shaped like little skulls. With fangs. Charming.

None of that's any help, but Zim and Tina are waiting for you to make a decision. Do you choose:

The white door? **P31**

The yellow door? **P50**

Or

The purple door? **P51**

31

The White Door

"This way," you say, trying to sound confident, and open the white door. To your relief, it's not a refrigerator – that would have been so embarrassing – instead, it's another twisty corridor.

Three turns and two curves later, you all stop at another white door.

Tina opens it.

Inside is an empty circular room, with brass walls, floor and ceiling.

She sighs. "Surprise, surprise, another round room with a white door and a yellow door and a purple door. Have we doubled back to the same room, or are there a million identical rooms? Did I mention that I hate mazes?"

As soon as you walk in, the white door slams itself shut. From above comes a familiar clunk, followed by squeaking and whirring.

For a few seconds, the circular floor spins one way while the walls spin the other way, just like last time.

Zim lies curled on the floor (again), groaning (again). "I'm dying. Dying, I tell you."

Tina looks around, then turns to you. "The room didn't change this time. There's still a white door, a purple door, and a yellow door."

You shake your head. "Before, it had a white door, a yellow door, and a purple door."

"Huh?"

"The same color doors, but their order's changed."

"Very observant, smarty pants. Doesn't help us, though. If you're right about walls and doors sliding up and down when the room spins, then this might be the same room. Or not." She growls. "We can't even trust the door we came through.

There could be a big bucket full of zombie piranha behind it now. Mazes aren't fair."

"Would you please stop telling us every five seconds how much you hate mazes?" Zim asks from the floor. "I'm going to–" Mid-sentence, he stops and stares at the purple door.

"Going to what?" Tina asks suspiciously. "Barf on the floor? Don't you dare. Use your wizard hat as a barf bag if you have to. Zim? Are you listening?"

Apparently not. He points at the purple door. "In the last room – actually I think we're still in the same room – I said there's no magic in here. True. But from down here, I can see a tiny gap under that door. Something's glowing violet through there, just like under the purple door in the last room. And through my Enchanted Shadow Crystal Lenses, the glow isn't just violet, it's ultra-violet."

"Violet, lavender, whatever," Tina says. "Who cares what shade of purple?"

"In this game, ultra-violet is a super-powerful magical color. As you'd know if you were a magic user like me." He checks around the room, especially under the other two doors. "Nope, no other magic. I think this is a clue – the same ultra-violet glow under a purple door, either in two rooms or the same room twice. It's the only thing we know definitely hasn't changed."

"Yeah," you say, "but not much of a clue by itself."

"Better than nothing." Tina strides towards the purple door.

"No, stop!" Zim shouts as he scrambles to his feet. "Ultra-violet is the color of necromancy."

"Necro Nancy?" She shrugs. "Never heard of her." She's lying – she just loves winding Zim up.

"Necromancy! Death magic!" he squeals.

Death magic sounds scary.

Although Zim could be wrong – he's not the smartest wizard around.

It's time to make a decision, and fast. Do you:

Stop Tina opening the purple door? **P34**

Or

Let her open the purple door? **P46**

Don't Open the Purple Door

"Tina, no!" you shout. "Zim's our magic expert. We have to trust him. Just like he and I trust you about warrior stuff. Please."

She stops, her hand an inch from the purple door, and glares at you both. For a moment, you think she's going to open it anyway just to be annoying, but then she sighs and drops her hand. "Okay, scaredy-cats. Which door – white or yellow? Anything to get out of this maze."

"Any other magical clues?" you ask Zim.

"No. Do the other doors look the same as they did before?"

"Exactly the same," Tina says.

"Yep," you say, looking around. "Hey, no, look at the label below the brass button on the yellow door. It has 'Press Me' engraved on it in Dwarvish. Before, it said, 'Don't Press Me'.

Zim crouches down and stares at the label. "So, this is a different room. Or a different door. Or it has a sneaky doorbell that can change labels, like James Bond's car license plates."

"Or Velzon can't read Dwarvish properly," Tina points out.

"Thanks," you say. Not that she could read one word of Dwarvish.

"So, it's your fault if you pick the wrong door now," she adds.

"Thanks again."

It's time to make a decision. Do you:

Pick the white door? **P35**

Or

Pick the yellow door? **P36**

The White Door

"Let's try the white door," you say.

Zim and Tina grunt unenthusiastically, but follow you through it.

Three turns and two curves later, you stop at another white door. Inside is an empty circular room, with brass walls, floor and ceiling, and a white door and a yellow door and a purple door. Exactly like the last one. Sigh.

As soon as you walk in, the white door slams itself shut. There are the usual noises, then the circular floor spins one way while the walls spin the other way. Just like last time.

"I hate mazes," Tina grumbles.

"We know," Zim grumbles. "I hate spinning rooms."

"We know."

"Let's get out of here," you say. "Any ideas?"

Nope. They've both given up.

You check all three doors, but they look the same as last time. The label below the brass button on the yellow door reads "Press Me."

It's time to make a decision. Do you open:

The white door? **P35**

Or

The yellow door? **P36**

Or

The purple door? **P51**

The Yellow Door

"Okay then, the yellow door." You try to open it, but it won't budge.

Zim leans over and presses the "Press Me" doorbell.

"Good thinking," you tell him, embarrassed at not thinking of that yourself.

Something behind the door clicks and whirs. "Not more spinning," Zim groans, and slumps to the floor.

But the floor doesn't move.

You'd expected the yellow door would open. Instead, a much smaller yellow door – not much taller than your knees – opens inside it.

"Maybe it's a doggy door," says Tina.

"With a doorbell?" you ask.

"Dogs are smart enough to use doorbells."

"Not smart enough to read Dwarvish, though."

"Isn't it more likely to be a dwarf-sized door, built by dwarves, so that dwarves can read the doorbell label, press the doorbell, then walk through the dwarf-sized door?" Zim asks.

Tina rolls her eyes. "Wow, listen to Mister Sensible."

"Good one again, Zim." You're embarrassed at not thinking of this either. "So, I guess we have to crawl through?"

As the three of you get down on your knees and peer through the small yellow door, a grumpy dwarf appears, holding an axe. "Mmmph. Thought you might be goblins for a moment."

"No, sir," Tina says.

"I'm a woman!"

"Sorry, ma'am. Nice beard."

"Mmmph. You're late. Well, don't stand around cluttering up the place. Come in."

Late for what? "Thank you, ma'am," you say, afraid to ask. Never make a dwarf angry, especially when she's holding an axe.

"And close that door," she says. "There's an awful cold draft out there sometimes."

The three of you squeeze through the small yellow door, closing it behind you, and follow the dwarf down a corridor. The corridor's dwarf-height, so she can walk fine, but you have to keep crawling.

Nice corridor otherwise. The walls are blue stone, intricately carved with runes and bearded faces. Probably this dwarf clan's ancestors from the last thousand or so years.

"Magnificent stonework, ma'am," you say, partly to be polite and partly because it's true.

"Mmmph."

"My hands and knees are getting sore," whispers Tina.

"Shush," Zim whispers back.

The dwarf overheard. "Ceiling not high enough for you, missy? I can fix that in a jiffy – come here and I'll chop your legs off." She roars with laughter.

That's a very old dwarf joke, probably older than this corridor. You all pretend to laugh.

To your relief, the next door (carved with more runes and bearded faces) leads to a larger room with a ceiling high enough to let you stand, although Zim has to carry his tall wizard hat.

A dozen worried-looking dwarves line the room. They stare at you, frown, and mutter to each other.

"Is that them?" one asks.

"Must be. They don't look the type, do they? Won't last five minutes."

"Well, they can't do any worse than the last lot, can they?"

And so on. You glance at Tina and Zim, who shrug.

The female dwarf leads you onwards. The next door is even grander – polished oak, inlaid with strips of gold, spelling out the clan name Grash'klrgl.

She waves you through the door.

Wow. It's a throne room, the most magnificent room in any dwarf citadel, and normally only seen by honored guests. In your years of gaming, you've never seen one so luxurious, with stone pillars that glitter like opals, and furniture of oak and precious metals, sparkling with gemstones. On a high marble platform with steps on three sides is a throne of turquoise and silver, topped with a pearl-like jewel the size of a football.

Something's wrong, though. Where is everyone? Looks like they left in a hurry, too. Furniture's been knocked over, and a goblet's lying on the floor in a puddle of wine.

"Mmmph. Best of luck." The dwarf leaves, locking the three of you inside.

"Um, I'm confused. What's happening?" Zim puts his hat on and looks around.

"There's only one logical explanation," Tina says. "They think we're the three glorious tall emperors foretold by ancient dwarven prophecy. Any moment now, they'll be back with our coronation feast of spicy fried chicken, strawberry smoothies, and chocolate brownies dipped in chocolate sauce."

"Did you just make that up?" you ask.

"Yup. Good, wasn't it?"

"Makes as much sense as anything I can think of. We're missing something important. Why would dwarves invite us in, then lock us in their throne room surrounded by their treasure?"

"What's that?" Zim points across the room.

Huh? Sticking out of the stone floor is a grey triangular wedge. It glides along the floor, occasionally bumping into furniture, then turns, sinks down into the floor and disappears. A few seconds later, it reappears, and circles the marble throne platform. Oh, that's no wedge, it's a fin.

"Stone shark!" all three of you say at the same time.

Zim looks at you in astonishment. "How do you two know about stone sharks?"

"We elves know and respect elemental creatures," you say. "Especially really dangerous ones like stone sharks – them, we prefer to respect from a distance."

"I read this cool graphic novel where an evil queen used stone sharks to destroy her enemy's fortress," Tina says. "Great plan, until the sharks accidentally crushed her to death during her victory parade. Stone sharks are totally bad-ass. No one tells them what to do."

"Only senior lithomancers can control them," Zim says. "And before anyone asks, no, I'm not even a junior lithomancer. All the advice I've read about stone sharks says to hide somewhere far from any stone and hope they'll swim away." He climbs onto a wooden table – not that that would be much protection.

The stone shark shows no interest in him or anyone else, but also doesn't look like it's about to swim away. It circles the marble throne platform again, "swimming" through the stone floor like a normal shark through water.

"I think it wants something from the platform." You look up the marble steps to the throne. "Food, maybe? What do they eat? Gems?"

Tina shakes her head. "There are gems everywhere in this room. The shark's not gobbling them up."

"What about that giant pearl thingy over the throne? If it is a pearl. It doesn't look like any I've ever seen. Not that I'm an expert on giant pearls."

"Oh. Mmm. Yes." Zim runs back to the door, and knocks. "Excuse me, dwarves. That huge pearly gem on top of your throne – did you dig it up recently?"

"Yes, the Moonstone was unearthed just six days ago, in our new Krlb'zgrb mine," comes the female dwarf's muffled voice through the door. "It is our finest treasure. No other clan has anything to match it."

"And did the stone shark appear soon afterwards?"

"Mmmph."

Zim looks smug. "That pearly gem isn't a gem. It's a stone shark's egg, and the shark wants it back."

"Then kill the shark! What kind of magical pest exterminators are you?" she snaps.

Oh, perhaps she invited you in by mistake?

"We're not exterminators," you say. "We never said we were."

"Mmmmmph."

The dwarves argue amongst themselves. The door's too thick for you to hear their words, but they sound angry. With each other, or with you?

"The only way out of this room is through that door," you whisper to Tina and Zim, "so we have to get the dwarves to open it. First, we need a bargaining chip to stop them killing us."

After dodging the stone shark, you lead Zim and Tina up the marble platform and onto the throne. Removing the egg from its silver mounting is hard work, even using your dagger as a lever. Tina helps with the point of her sword. The egg unexpectedly pops free, and bounces on a step before Zim catches it.

"I hope you know what you're doing, Velzon." He hands the heavy egg back to you.

"So do I. You guys ready?"

They nod. Tina draws her sword and Zim raises his wand.

"Okay, let's give the shark its egg back," you say, loudly so the dwarves will hear.

As hoped, the door opens. A dozen heavily armed dwarves rush in, but stop when they see the egg in your arms.

"Give that back now," growls the largest dwarf, twirling axes in both hands.

It's time to make a decision. Do you:

Distract the dwarves by throwing them the egg? **P42**

Or

Throw the egg to the stone shark? **P44**

42

Throw the egg to the Dwarves

"Sure," you tell the dwarves. "Catch it if you can."

You toss the egg down the steps to your left, not directly towards the dwarves. As you'd hoped, it bounces unpredictably, and the dwarves chase after it. Meanwhile, the three of you race down the other side of the throne platform, heading for the open door.

It was never a great plan, just the best you could think of at the time. And it almost works…until two snarling dwarves block your path. They raise their throwing axes, but are interrupted by shouting and screaming from other dwarves.

A dwarf runs past, holding the egg, but is hit by a grey blur – the stone shark – and becomes a long red bloodstain. The egg bounces twice, is caught by one terrified-looking dwarf who quickly tosses it to another, who in turn tries outrunning the shark, unsuccessfully. The egg bounces away again. The enraged shark headbutts a stone pillar, then the throne platform, which both creak and collapse into rubble. You can't see the egg any more, and apparently neither can the dwarves – they're running in all directions. Hopefully they've forgotten about you.

"Let's get out of here before the shark destroys the whole place!" Tina drags you towards the door.

"Where's Zim?"

She points back to where Zim lies on the floor, a dwarf axe in his head. "We have to go, now!"

The shark rams a wall, huge granite blocks tumble all around, and everything turns black.

Suddenly you're all back in the real world, sitting at the kitchen table. On your laptop screen are the words *Game Over.*

"I've got a splitting headache," Jim says, rubbing his forehead. "What were we playing? I can't remember a thing."

Tina shrugs. "Something about eggs? No, that doesn't sound right."

"I'm sure there was a shark," you say. "Fairly sure. It's all fading. Hey, does anyone else have sore knees?"

Sorry, this part of your story is over. If you'd made different choices, things might have gone better (or even worse). Have you met the Emerald Sage? Been attacked by the bone army? Run from the giant rolling head? Helped the extremely wet queen? Said hello to the Reverse Dragon? Avoided the Zenobian Snapper?

It's time to make a decision. Do you:

Go back to the previous section? **P36**

Or

Go back to the beginning of the story and try another path? **P95**

Or

Go to the great big list of choices? **P364**

Throw the egg to the Shark

The dwarves don't have any right to steal the stone shark's egg. It's not a jewel, no matter how pretty it looks.

Hoping this isn't a huge mistake, you wait for the stone shark to glide back into view, then toss the egg towards it.

Stone sharks are eyeless, but somehow it senses the approaching egg. It changes direction, leaps into the air and swallows the egg whole, then disappears into the floor.

"Just like I said, you can't trust elves and humans. Kill them!" yells the largest dwarf, and raises the axes in his (or her) hands.

"Look!" Zim points to the throne's seat, where the words *Level Exit* have suddenly appeared.

An axe flashes past your head. Ouch, what happened? You reach up and discover half your left ear is gone. Tina collapses with an axe in her helmet, and Zim's bleeding too – he's lost two fingers. You and he drag Tina onto the throne, and–

Suddenly you're back in the real world, sitting at the kitchen table, staring at the words *Bonus Level Completed* on your laptop screen.

"I've got a splitting headache." Tina rubs her unmarked forehead. "My knees hurt too. I'm out of here."

"My knees hurt, and my hand hurts." Jim counts his fingers carefully.

"My pointy left ear hurts," you say. "As well as my knees."

"You don't have pointy ears."

"Um, yeah, right. What were we playing? I can't remember a thing about it. Something about knees and eggs? Doesn't make sense."

He shrugs. "See you next week. I'm going home to feed my fish. Don't know why I just thought of that."

Congratulations, you've finished this part of your story. Then again, if you'd made different choices, things might have gone even better (or much worse). Have you met the Emerald Sage? Been attacked by the bone army? Run from the giant rolling head? Helped the extremely wet queen? Said hello to the Reverse Dragon? Avoided the Zenobian Snapper?

It's time to make a decision. Do you:

Would you like to:

Go back to the beginning of the story and try another path? **P95**

Or

Go to the great big list of choices? **P364**

The Purple Door

"Okay, scaredy-cats, here goes." Her sword at the ready, Tina tugs the purple door open.

You draw your bow.

"We're going to die," Zim whimpers, raising his wand.

There's an icy blast of air from the other side of the door, but nothing horrible leaps out.

"It's just a purple floor covered in dusty old bones." Tina sounds disappointed.

"Ultra-violet, not purple," Zim corrects. "But you can't see that without Enchanted Shadow Crystal Lenses."

"Whatever. So then, use your super magic sunglasses and tell us what nasties are waiting in there."

"No idea, coz the whole floor is glowing ultra-violet. That could mean we drop dead the moment we step in. Or there could be dozens of monsters hiding amongst the bones. Or it could mean the room's harmless, and some necromancer's favorite interior decorating color is ultra-violet. Us magicians are weird."

"Yeah, I've noticed." Tina pokes her sword and then a foot through the doorway. Nothing happens.

"There's a door in the far corner." You point. "See it? The black door in the black frame, with the black symbols carved in it."

She peers across the room. "Where?"

Zim can't see it either, until he casts an Owl Sight spell on his Crystal Lenses. "Good spotting, Velzon. Must be your elven eyes. That's not just any old door, that's a Sanctuary Portal, like we found back on Level 44."

"I remember that." Tina grins. "Sanctuary Portals are awesome! Full restore of health points and armor points. That's bound to be the level exit too."

"Probably," Zim says. "If we can get to it without getting killed. This will take careful planning."

Too late. Tina's already jogging across the room, kicking bones aside as she goes.

"We'd better help her," you tell Zim.

"So much for careful planning," he grumbles, following you into the room.

Wow, it's cold in here. Like a walk-in freezer.

"Slow down," you call to Tina.

Surprisingly, she does, and turns back, frowning. "As well as a million dusty broken skeletons, there are also a zillion or so broken weapons and rags. I'm guessing they're from the last million people to try to walk through here, so, um…yeah, let's play safe and do this together. What's your plan, Zim?"

"Plan? What plan?" He mutters, points his wand in various directions, and shrugs. "The only thing I'm sure of is that we three are the only living creatures in here. And I'm cold."

"Join us," whisper hundreds of voices around you. Bones twitch and rattle, then rise and connect to form nightmarish mutant skeletons – some two-skulled or three-legged, some walking on six arms, some crawling like giant snakes on dozens of human ribcages. They all have glowing violet eyes. "Join us forever."

"Run for the portal!" you yell.

Tina takes the lead, swinging her sword at skeletons that come too close.

They shatter and fall. More quickly replace them.

Zim zaps skeletons with his wand, but the death magic is too strong – they just stagger and pause, before resuming a zombie-like march towards you.

Your arrows whoosh harmlessly through skeletons' ribcages. You karate-kick a three-headed skeleton as it reaches out a bony hand, and run faster, dodging anything that moves.

The Sanctuary Portal is close now, mostly thanks to Tina smiting skeletons out of the way.

Thousands of bones rattle, dance into the air, and form a hideous octopus-shaped bone monster as tall as the ceiling. "Join us," it whispers.

Tina lops off one bony tentacle, but is knocked to the floor by another.

"Your mortal blades and arrows cannot kill me," the monster whispers.

Okay, that gives you an idea. You grab a long straight bone from the floor, and shoot it like an arrow into the monster's glowing eye, hoping that death magic can be hurt by more death magic.

It works – sort of. The monster shrieks and collapses, thrashing its tentacles.

"Run for your lives!" you yell, sure this is your final chance. You dodge a dozen snapping jaws, stomp on one bony tentacle, and stumble the last few steps to the warmth and safety of the Sanctuary Portal.

Someone screams. You whirl around. Zim and Tina are dangling from the monster's tentacles.

"No!" you scream.

In a flash of violet light, they both turn to skeletons, and fall to the floor amongst the millions of other bones.

Level Exit appears on the Portal's floor under your feet. Suddenly you're back in the real world, sitting at the kitchen table and shivering, staring at the words *Game Over* on your laptop screen.

You're alone, but weren't you playing with…um, a wizard and warrior? They saved you, didn't they? What were their names? It's fading fast, like waking after a nightmare. Something about a skeleton octopus? No, that doesn't make sense, octopuses don't have skeletons. Maybe you imagined the whole thing.

Onscreen, words flicker. *Dungeon of Doom. Game Over. Try again?* Again? You don't remember playing it at all.

Congratulations, you've finished this part of your story. Then again, if you'd made different choices, things might have gone much better (or much worse). Have you met the Emerald Sage? Run from the giant rolling head? Helped the extremely wet queen? Said hello to the Reverse Dragon? Avoided the Zenobian Snapper?

It's time to make a decision. Do you:

Go to the beginning and try another path? **P95**

Or

Go to the great big list of choices? **P364**

The Yellow Door

"Okay, let's open the yellow door," you say. But when you try, it doesn't budge, not even when the three of you try together.

Zim presses the "Don't Press Me" doorbell.

"Can't you read?" shouts an angry voice in Dwarvish from somewhere inside.

"Sorry," he says back.

"We could smash the door down," Tina suggests.

"How? Using your head as a battering ram?" Zim asks.

"This must be a dead end," you say hurriedly, before they can start another argument. "Let's try another door."

It's time to make a decision. Do you open:

The white door? **P35**

Or

The purple door? **P51**

The Purple Door

"Let's try the purple door." You try not to worry about its rows of silver rivets shaped like skulls. After all, lots of things in dungeons have skulls on them. Wallpaper, toothbrushes, teddy bears probably. It's traditional. Old school.

You pull the heavy purple door open. An icy blast of air blows into your face.

"Whoop-de-do. A big empty room with a purple floor covered in dusty old bones." Tina sounds disappointed.

"Urp." Zim peers through his Enchanted Shadow Crystal Lenses. "That's not purple, it's ultra-violet. The color of necromancy."

"Necro Nancy? Never heard of her."

She's joking. A month ago, she complained about "neck romance" just to annoy him.

Zim falls for it, again. "Necromancy! Death magic! That whole room's incredibly dangerous."

Tina smirks.

The cold air stops blowing and starts sucking instead.

"That's quite an air conditioner they've got in there," she says.

"It could be a huge monster breathing in and out?" you say.

"Someone or something could be trying to suck us in there," Zim says. "We should stand back, just in case."

Tina grins nervously. "Nah, I agree with Velzon – it's a humungous monster doing some heavy breathing. Hopefully a gigantic ice dragon, guarding an even more gigantic horde of diamonds. We'll wait until we hear snoring, then sneak in and steal the lot."

52

The sucky breeze becomes a sucky wind. Her grin disappears and she takes a step back.

"Let's close the door," you say.

But the open door won't budge an inch, not even with the three of you pushing and pulling it.

The white and yellow doors blow open, and the sucky wind becomes a sucky hurricane. Two squealing goblins blow past and vanish into the room.

"It's a Deadly Doom Vortex," Zim yells over the howling gale. "Hang on for your lives!"

Great advice, except there's nothing to hang on to. Within seconds, all three of you are pulled off your feet and sucked into the room.

The wind stops, the purple door slams shut, and you fall to the floor.

"Ow," Tina says. "Skeletons are terrible landing pads. Wow, it's really cold in here."

"We're doomed," says Zim.

The floor's almost hidden beneath millions of bones, presumably from everyone who's ever died in here. Humans, elves, dwarves, trolls, even a couple of suspiciously new goblin skeletons a few yards away.

"Join us," whisper hundreds of icy voices around the room. Thousands of bones rattle and connect into nightmarish mutant skeletons with too many heads or limbs. Their skulls' empty eye sockets glow purple. "Join us forever," their voices whisper.

"No, thanks." Tina beheads a skeleton with her sword before it can grab her.

Zim waves his wand and zaps a few skeletons. They don't fall, just stagger then resume a zombie-like march towards you.

53

Your arrows are useless, whooshing through skeletons' ribcages. How are you supposed to kill something already dead?

The three of you fight back to back, but are surrounded. The last thing you see is an eight-tentacled bone monster looming over you, then a flash of icy violet light.

Suddenly you're all back in the real world, sitting at the kitchen table and shivering. The words *Game Over* sparkle on your laptop screen.

Tina hugs herself. "Why is it so cold in here? What happened?"

"Weren't we playing a computer game?" Zim asks. "Something about a giant purple octopus skeleton?"

"Something like that, I think," you say. "No, that can't be right. Octopuses don't have skeletons."

"Stupid game, whatever it was. See you guys next week." Tina leaves, carefully walking around the purple rug on the floor.

Sorry, this part of your story is over. If you'd made different choices, things might have gone much better (or even worse). Have you met the Emerald Sage? Run from the giant rolling head? Helped the extremely wet queen? Said hello to the Reverse Dragon? Avoided the Zenobian Snapper?

It's time to make a decision. Do you:

Go back to the previous section? **P28**

Or

Go to the beginning of the story and try another path? **P95**

Or

Go to the great big list of choices? **P364**

Ogres, Rock and Roll

You turn right, towards the ogres. Sure, ogres are scary, but they're also dim and predictable.

The three of you advance down the corridor, passing several closed doors.

The ogres' footsteps get closer, echoing down the corridor.

You stop and listen. "Four, maybe five of them, around the next corner. Get ready."

Tina raises her sword.

Zim summons a sparkly green fireball.

You draw an arrow from your quiver and raise your bow.

Four huge ogres burst around the corner and…thunder straight past.

"They didn't even notice us," Tina grumbles. "How rude."

"One stepped on my foot," Zim says. "Ouchies."

"Maybe they were running from something," you say.

"Like what?"

"Something worse than four ogres. So maybe we should run too."

Zim and Tina aren't convinced, until a head rolls around the corner – a head as wide as the corridor and nearly touching the ceiling.

It rolls straight towards you, grinning and waggling a long purple tongue.

"Run!" You take off down the corridor, not checking whether Zim and Tina are following. Well, they told you to lead the way, right?

The first door you reach is locked, and there's no time to try your elven lock-picking skills.

The next one's locked too. And the one after that.

55

Finally, gasping for breath, you reach an open doorway, but inside is pitch black.

You glance back. Zim and Tina are close behind. Close behind them is the rolling head.

It's time to make a decision, and fast. Do you:

Enter the dark room? **P56**

Or

Keep running? **P85**

Dark Room

You run into the dark room, and immediately hit a wall. "Ow!"

Tina and Zim run into your back.

"Double ow!"

The ceiling starts to glow, revealing that the room's only a few feet deep and wide.

"Stupid elf! This is a dead end!" Tina snarls.

Outside, the giant head rolls to a stop. Luckily, it's too big to fit through the doorway, but its long purple tongue snakes out, grabs your leg and pulls. The room's metal door starts to slide closed by itself – no idea why, but a door between you and that giant head sounds great.

The door hits the tongue, and stops.

"Stab it!" Tina shouts.

You draw your dagger from your belt.

"No, tickle it! Trust me, Velzon!" Zim shouts.

It's time to make a decision. Do you:

Stab the tongue? **P57**

Or

Tickle the tongue? **P59**

Stabby Stabby

You stab the purple tongue.

Its end falls off, and the room's door slides closed. Outside, the giant head roars in pain or rage or both. It batters at the door, but can't get through.

The tongue end stretches and swells and keeps growing, thicker and longer, like a large snake. Tina stabs it with her sword, but that just makes more bits fall off, and they grow into more snakes.

"I told you not to stab it," Zim moans. "It's Orzkedryle's Endless Legion of Tongue Serpents. We're doomed."

"Orzka what?"

Dozens of tongue serpents wrap around the three of you, squeezing, crushing.

With your last breath, you scream, not that it helps. Everything turns black, and…

Suddenly the three of you are back in the kitchen, wrapped together in a pile on the floor.

"Gross!" you say, and Tina says "Blurgh!" and Jim says, "No one's allowed to cuddle me except Mom," all at the same time.

Blushing, you look at each other, then stare at the floor.

"I'm late for lunch. Bye." Jim grabs his laptop and rushes out the door.

"I'm late for…something too." Tina leaves, almost running.

You stare at your laptop screen. *Game Over. Try Again?*

Sorry, this part of your story is over. If you'd made different choices, things might have gone better (or even worse). Have you met the Emerald Sage? Gotten lost in the maze? Been attacked by the bone army? Helped the extremely wet queen?

58

Said hello to the Reverse Dragon? Avoided the Zenobian Snapper?

It's time to make a decision. Do you:

Go back to the previous section? **P56**

Or

Go back to the beginning of the story and try another path? **P95**

Or

Go to the great big list of choices? **P364**

Tickly Tickly

Feeling silly, you tickle the purple tongue. The giant head giggles, then roars helplessly with laughter. It laughs so hard that its tongue loosens its hold on your leg. You push the tongue back out of the room, and the door slides shut.

"How did you know that tickling would work?" you ask Zim. "Is that some sort of wizardly secret magic trick?"

He looks embarrassed. "Um, not really. That head out there is the infamous Orzkedryle and her Endless Legion of Tongue Serpents, and I've heard she's unbeatable in combat. But…my tongue's ticklish, so I thought maybe her tongue would be too."

"How do you know your tongue's ticklish?" Tina asks.

"Haven't you ever tickled your tongue?"

"No! What kind of weirdo are you?"

"The kind who's just saved our lives," you point out.

She scowls. "Maybe, maybe not. We're still trapped in this stupid tiny little room."

You look at the mysteriously glowing ceiling, the sliding metal door, and a row of dwarven runes next to the door. Oh. "I don't think this is really a room."

"Then what is it? A chocolate cake?"

You press one of the runes. As you'd suspected, the whole room quivers and hums and starts to move.

Zim squeals. "It's a trash compactor, like in Star Wars. We'll be crushed to death!"

"The whole room's moving – this is an elevator," you say. "You watch too many movies."

Tina snorts. "An elevator in a dungeon? Don't be ridic–"

The door opens, revealing…no giant head, to your relief. Just an empty stone-walled corridor, dimly lit by thousands of glowing blue dots on the walls.

60

"Lucky guess," she mutters.

The three of you step out, and immediately bang your heads on the low ceiling.

"Looks like a dwarven mine tunnel." Zim rubs the top of his head and picks his tall wizard hat off the floor. "I don't mind dwarves, except they're too short."

"Well, yeah, but if they were taller then they wouldn't be dwarves," Tina says. "What are these little blue glowing thingies?"

"Slumberworms," you say. "Don't touch them."

"Poisonous?"

"One bite sends you to sleep in seconds."

"Doesn't sound so bad."

"While you're asleep, the worms eat you alive."

"Gross!" She steps back. "Okay, worm nerd, which way do we go to get away from them?"

You look and listen and sniff again in both directions. "Less worms if we go left, but only because it's cold and damp. They don't like cold and damp."

"There's strong magic that way too, I can feel it," Zim adds. "Can't tell what it is."

"To the right is warmer, and I see a faint golden glow," you continue. "Fire, maybe, but I don't smell smoke. And I don't smell dwarves in either direction – dunno where they've gone."

"Let's go right," Tina says.

"Let's go left," says Zim.

Sigh. It's time to make a decision. Do you:

Go left, towards the cold and damp? **P61**

Or

Go right, towards the warm glow? **P76**

So Cool

The three of you turn left. The corridor floor slopes downwards, occasionally passing empty rooms. Around a corner, a wide puddle blocks the corridor, and moisture glistens on the walls and drips from the ceiling. On the far side of the puddle, the floor slopes upwards again.

"Why are we stopping?" Tina asks. "It's only a puddle of water. Isn't it?"

Zim chews his lip and squints through his Enchanted Shadow Crystal Lenses. "Water, sure, but…there's something else here too. Something magical. And powerful. What do you think, Velzon?"

You shrug, equally puzzled. "Yeah, my pointy elven ears are twitching. There's elemental magic close by. Don't know exactly what or where, though."

Tina pokes her sword into the puddle, and taps the stone floor below. "Maybe you two are scared of a puddle, but I'm not. It's too wide to jump over, and I'd rather not get my feet wet – that's all that bothers me. Zim, could you magic us up some rubber boots, or fly us over the puddle or something?"

He shakes his head. "The magical something is suppressing my wizardly powers. This might be a trap."

Tina pokes the puddle again with her sword, and then with the toe of her boot. Nothing happens again. She takes a few steps back, runs through the puddle, then turns and pokes her tongue out. "Come on, you big babies."

You follow her through the puddle. Your feet get wet too – elven boots aren't any more waterproof than warrior princess boots – but nothing else happens.

Zim frowns. "My mom says never to walk in wet shoes or you'll get blisters."

Tina snorts. "This is a dungeon. Blisters are the least of our problems. Don't worry, I promise I won't tell your mommy."

Grimacing and muttering to himself, Zim wades through the puddle, then the three of you squelch up the corridor.

"My left heel's getting a blister already," Zim whines.

"You'll feel much better after a nice warm bath," says a cheerful voice.

The three of you stop and look around, but see no one.

"Who said that?" you ask.

"It is I, Queen Moist, beloved ruler of the water spirits. Thank you, brave heroes, for rescuing me from that horrid puddle."

"You're a queen?" Tina asks. "I'm royalty too – Tina Warrior Princess. Pleased to meet you."

"Mmm." The queen doesn't sound impressed.

"Sorry to interrupt your royal majesty, but...are the three of us carrying you in our wet boots, Queen Moist?" Zim asks, staring suspiciously at his feet.

"Of course, we water spirits don't have silly boring bodies like you. We can live in any water. I wasted half an hour last week ordering a rat to rescue me from that puddle, but rodents are so stupid. You three look much cleverer."

"Thanks," Tina says.

"Forward!" orders the queen. "I must return to my palace immediately. My adoring subjects will be frantic with worry."

You, Tina and Zim look at each other.

"Is there a reward, your majesty?" You remember playing Level 84 a few weeks ago – after the three of you rescued a prince from a dragon, his grateful parents rewarded you with an enchanted carrot to get past the end-of-level giant rabbit.

"You will have my eternal royal gratitude," she says. "And as I said before, a nice warm bath."

"Oh." Whoop-de-do.

"And all the gold you can carry," she adds. "We'll be glad to get rid of it. We don't have much use for metal."

Oooh, gold, lots of gold. You, Tina and Zim look at each other again, and nod.

"Okay, your majesty, we'll take you home."

You continue squelching up the corridor. Wet boots are horrible to walk in. Zim (and his mom) might be right about blisters.

"It's not far," the queen says. "Next left, up the stairs, past the wall of screaming skulls, around the corner and second doorway on the right."

Wall of screaming skulls?

A few minutes later, you discover it's an actual wall made of hundreds and hundreds of skulls, all screaming at each other nonstop.

"Bone-face!"

"You're skinny!"

"Your nose has fallen off!"

"So has yours! And your eyeballs!"

"Don't you bare your teeth at me, cheeky!"

And so on, endlessly, shrieking at the top of their skeletal voices. They don't even notice you passing by.

"Such dreadful neighbors," Queen Moist says, as you turn a corner and their voices fade a little. "Always screaming, day and night. That's why my loyal subjects sent me on a special mission to find us a quieter new home."

"And did you?" Zim asks.

"No, I got stuck in that boring puddle. Blah, who'd want to live there?"

Ahead, more voices echo along the corridor. These ones are laughing and chattering. A wall of happy skulls? Probably not.

"Hear that? My loyal subjects must have heard news of my rescue," the queen continues. "And now they're preparing a surprise welcome-back party to show how much they adore me. How lovely."

A surprise party? Seems unlikely, but admittedly, you've never been to a water spirit party.

"Did you say second doorway on the right?" Tina asks. "There are no more doorways, just that little hole."

"That's the entrance to my royal palace. Hmm, you're big lumpy creatures – do you think you can squeeze through?"

You crouch down and peer through the narrow waist-high hole where the happy voices are coming from. On the other side is a wide stretch of water like a swimming pool, its surface rippling and splashing as if full of swimmers having fun. Invisible swimmers, that is. Oh, water spirits' bodies must be made of water. Although maybe it's not a swimming pool. The water looks too deep, and…why so many bubbles? There's a weird soapy smell too. "We can fit through the hole. It doesn't look dangerous, but—"

"Dangerous?" The queen sounds insulted. "Of course it's not dangerous. You're my honored royal guests. Hurry up and take me through, that's an order. I'm queen, so you must obey me. That includes you, Princess Tina, because queens outrank princesses."

Tina rolls her eyes.

Zim shrugs. "Let's drop off Moist, collect the reward, and get out of here. Anything to be out of these wet boots."

A good plan, except…why's the queen's so bossy? Can you really trust her?

It's time to make a decision. Do you:

Go through the hole to the 'swimming pool'? **P65**

Or

No way, this must be a trap. **P73**

Swimming Pool (or is it?)

The three of you crawl through the hole and onto a wide white ledge at the water's edge.

This swimming pool, if that's what it is, is the biggest you've ever seen. Hey, why are the ends rounded, and… no, unbelievable, are they…taps?

This is no swimming pool, it's a giant bathtub! Hmm, where's the giant?

The water spirits see you, and suddenly stop laughing and chattering and splashing. The surface of the tub water goes still. You feel Queen Moist wiggle out of your boots.

She splashes into the water. "Greetings, my adoring loyal subjects. I have returned safely. Let the celebrations begin!"

But celebrations don't begin. Instead there's silence, so quiet that you can hear the screaming skulls down the corridor.

The water ripples, and lots of voices start talking at once.

"I thought we'd finally got rid of her."

"You said she'd never find her way back!"

"I'm not putting up with her again."

"Should have boiled her into steam. That's the only way to get rid of unwanted royals."

"How dare you?" the queen snaps. "Royal guards, arrest these traitors immediately!"

"We are your royal guard, your royal snobbiness, or rather, we *were*. After we tricked you into leaving, we voted to become a democracy, so you're no longer queen, and you can go stick your—"

"Excuse me," interrupts Tina. "Terribly sorry, I can see you guys are really busy, so if we could just collect our reward, then we'll be on our way."

"What reward?" asks a grumpy voice from in the water.

66

"The queen promised us all the gold we can carry."

"Well, um, yes." The ex-queen sounds embarrassed. "And far more importantly, my eternal gratitude and a nice warm bath."

"Queeny tricked you," says the grumpy voice. "The only gold around here is those taps. If you can carry them, then sure, take them."

The water spirits roar with laughter.

The golden taps at the end of the bathtub are taller than you.

Even if you could somehow get them off the wall, it would take a dozen trolls to lift even one of them.

"Let's get out of here," you tell Zim and Tina.

"No, please, two-legs, stay for your nice warm bath," the grumpy voice sneers. "Stay forever, we're so grateful."

Hundreds of water spirits hurl themselves at you. They're only water and don't hurt – it's like getting soaked by a horizontal rainstorm. Together, you, Tina and Zim inch backwards to the hole you came through. Slowly and carefully, because the ledge of the bathtub is now wet and slippery.

Zim's foot skids, and he nearly falls. He reaches out to you. "Help!"

Quickly now, do you:

Help Zim? **P67**

Or

No, you're not brave enough? **P71**

Help Zim

You grab Zim's hand to save him. Unfortunately, he grabs at Tina and she loses her balance too, and you all fall into the bathtub water together.

Your wet clothes and weapons drag you down. Zim, who can't swim, flails helplessly. Tina's normally a great swimmer, but she's weighed down by her steel armor and weapons.

Far below, an enormous chain glints in the water. Oh, of course, this is a bathtub, so that must be the chain for the plug. Just maybe it's also a way out of here.

You point down at the chain, and Tina nods.

Zim's in bad shape, coughing and spluttering.

You grab him and hold his head above water. "Take a deep breath," you tell him. "The only way out is down."

Looking confused, he nods.

After you all take a few lungfuls of air, you dive, towing him.

As hoped, at the bottom of the chain is a huge plug, wider than you are tall. You jam your dagger in one side of the plug and Tina jams her sword in the other side, together trying to lever it out of the plughole. It's hard work, and you're running out of breath fast. Zim's eyes are closed, and he looks half-dead.

At last, the plug jerks upwards, and bathwater pours down the plughole, washing you with it.

Down you go, through dark pipes, occasionally passing glowing eyes and grasping tentacles. At least you can catch a breath now and again, although some of the awful smells make you cough and choke.

Finally, the current slows in a dimly lit cavern. Battered and bruised, you crawl onto a low stone ledge at the water's edge.

68

Where are Tina and Zim?

Is that Tina's cloak floating past? You grab it, and her hand grabs you.

"Help," she cries weakly.

You pull her out, wondering why she's so heavy, then discover she's still holding on to Zim.

"Is he dead?"

"Yes," Zim croaks, and coughs up some water. "Worse than dead."

The three of you rest for a while.

Until you hear something in the distance. "Rats, coming this way. Lots of them."

Tina shrugs. "So what? I'm not afraid of rats, even without my sword."

"We were in a giant bathtub, then washed down a giant sewer, so maybe they're giant rats? I lost my bow and dagger."

"My wand's broken," Zim says. "I lost my magic potions and my Big Book of Spells, and my magic sunglasses."

"Hah! I knew they were just sunglasses," Tina says.

"*Magic* sunglasses."

While they argue, you look around.

The only doorway is in the direction the rats are coming from. Back into the stinky water? No thanks, not if there's any alternative.

The wall on the other side of the ledge is covered in carvings, including a picture of three adventurers fighting off giant rats – someone's idea of a joke?

Not funny.

There's also a huge carved face with a creepy smile, and "Say the Magic Word!" carved on its forehead. Another unfunny joke? Or…

"Zim, is that a magic door?"

He nods. "Standard wizardly protection, sealed with a binding spell, and will only open to the correct password. If I still had my Crystal Lenses and my wand, I might be able to break the spell and open it. But I don't, so I can't." His lip trembles.

"Then we'd better start guessing magic words. Those rats are getting closer."

The three of you try every magic word you know. The old classics like "Open Sesame" and "Abracadabra" and "Hocus Pocus" and "Alakazam," then some of your favorite Ancient Elvish Words of Power. Zim tries lots of wizardly words, although to be honest, you suspect he's making some of them up. Nothing works.

A swarm of rats bursts from the far end of the cavern. Yeah, giant rats. Fast runners too.

"Got it!" Tina walks up to the carved face and says, "Please."

The face's mouth opens wide, revealing a small brightly lit room.

Tina grins. "Wow, Mom was right. 'Please' really is the magic word."

The three of you walk through the open mouth, and it snaps shut behind you.

"Great, we're safe from the giant rats, unless they're very polite talking giant rats," Zim says. "But now we're trapped again."

Or so it seems, until you notice *Level Exit* carved on the back of the mouth door.

You reach out and touch it, and suddenly you're back in the real world, soaking wet, sitting around the kitchen table with Jim and Tina. *Bonus Level Completed* is in big sparkly letters on your laptop screen.

"We won!" Tina says.

70

Jim snorts. "Won? I nearly drowned! My clothes are sopping wet, and I stink. Mom's going to yell at me."

"Remember to say 'please' and 'thank you' to her," you remind him as he squelches out.

"Not funny!"

"I'm serious. You too, Tina – your mom saved us."

"Yeah, sort of, maybe, I suppose. I'd better get home and out of these wet clothes. Back here next Saturday to play Level 101?"

Congratulations, you've finished this part of your story. Then again, if you'd made different choices, things might have gone even better (or much worse).

Have you met the Emerald Sage? Gotten lost in the maze? Been attacked by the bone army? Said hello to the Reverse Dragon? Avoided the Zenobian Snapper?

It's time to make a decision. Do you:

Go back to the beginning of the story and try another path? **P95**

Or

Go to the great big list of choices? **P364**

Don't Help Zim

Sure, Zim's your friend, but not good enough a friend that you'd risk drowning.

He grabs at Tina, and she loses her balance too. Both of them fall into the bathtub water and sink without trace.

"Tina? Zim?"

Nothing. They're gone.

"Two down, one to go!" yells a watery voice from the tub.

The water spirits' splashes now get three times as bad, as they're aimed at you alone. Every time you take a step towards the hole you came through, the splashing gets worse, and you're nearly washed into the tub twice.

You look around, and spot another hole higher up the bathroom wall. Surely the water spirits can't splash that high? It's worth a try. Better than staying here, anyway.

So you start climbing, as fast as you can, holding on for dear life when the splashing gets too bad. As you climb out of range, they stop splashing and start yelling and cursing at you instead. Ignoring them, you concentrate on the hole above you, one handhold and one step at a time.

"Good riddance, two-legs, say hello to eight-legs!" is their final insult, as you clamber into the hole.

What did that mean?

Inside the hole, eyes stare at you, then long hairy legs grab you. Eight legs. Just as you finally realize (far too late) that it's a giant spider, it bites your arm. Everything turns black, and…

Suddenly you're back in the real world, sitting alone at the kitchen table, with a really sore arm. The words *Game Over* sparkle on your laptop screen. Huh?

Weren't you playing a computer game with someone, maybe two someones? Something about a giant bathtub?

72

No, that doesn't make sense. Maybe you just imagined the whole thing.

Behind the table, a spider abseils down the wall, and you shiver.

Sorry, this part of your story is over. If you'd made different choices, things might have gone better (or even worse). Have you met the Emerald Sage? Gotten lost in the maze? Been attacked by the bone army? Said hello to the Reverse Dragon? Avoided the Zenobian Snapper?

It's time to make a decision. Do you:

Go back to the previous section? **P65**

Or

Go back to the beginning of the story and try another path? **P95**

Or

Go to the great big list of choices? **P364**

Sorry, Your Majesty

No, you'd rather not go through that hole – it could be a trap by Queen Moist.

"Sorry, your majesty, this is as far as we can take you," you tell her, very politely. She seems the sort to have a bad temper, and who knows what an angry water spirit might do.

"Obey me this instant, my minions!" she shrieks.

Your wet boots grow icicles. So do Zim's and Tina's boots.

"Quick, boots off before she freezes our feet solid!" shouts Tina.

You frantically fumble with your boots but can't unbuckle them.

"Impudent two-legs," the queen squeals. "Obey me while you can still walk!" She turns your wet boots scalding hot.

You're close to screaming in pain when suddenly your boots vanish. Tina and Zim are barefoot too. Through the hole comes splashing and yelling.

"What happened?" you ask.

Zim grins. "My super wizardly magic."

"I thought you couldn't fight elemental magic."

His grin gets wider. "I can't. That was the cleverest part – the queen was dragging us by the water in our boots, so I just cast Instantaneous Disintegration on the boots, and whoosh, she went with them before she realized my cunning plan."

Tina nods. "Thanks, Zim, smart move. Although now we've got no boots."

"Moan, moan, moan. Anyone like a healing potion for their frozen blistered feet?"

He must be in a good mood – usually he won't hand out his precious potions unless someone gets an arm chopped off or worse.

The three of you sit and rub purple fizzy healing potion on your poor feet. Feels great.

Through the hole comes lots of shouting, mostly Queen Moist yelling orders, and lots of other voices yelling rude watery insults back.

"She doesn't sound like a very popular queen," Tina says. "Did you believe her 'all the gold you can carry' promise?"

"Nah," you say. "Had to be a scam. Let's get out of here. Unless you can cast us an Instant New Boots spell first, Zim?"

He sniffs. "Don't be silly, there's no such thing. I'm a wizard, not a shoe shop. Anyway, I've got a feeling that we're close to an exit."

So you all walk barefoot along the corridor and back past the wall of screaming skulls, trying to avoid the pointy gravel and spiders and rat poo on the floor.

Unfortunately, you're too busy avoiding stepping on yucky things, and so are totally surprised when a trapdoor opens beneath you.

You fall into a very deep dark hole, so deep that you keep falling, and falling, and falling. So deep that there's time for a long argument, all three of you blaming each other for not spotting the trapdoor. So deep that Zim has time to try casting various spells, none of which help in the slightest.

You point down. "I see the bottom. There's something there."

"Unless it's an enormous pile of soft cushions, I don't think it's going to help us," Tina says.

"Stop distracting me," Zim grumbles. He waves his wand again and turns into a giant chicken, but only for a few seconds. "Nearly had it that time!"

You look down, trying to work out what's below. Oh. It looks like a floor. A hard stone floor. The last thing you ever see is a ring of happy goblins looking up. The last thing you ever hear is "Here comes lunch!"

Sorry, this part of your story is over. If you'd made different choices, things might have gone better (or even worse). What would have happened if you'd helped the queen through the hole? Have you met the Emerald Sage? Gotten lost in the maze? Been attacked by the bone army? Said hello to the Reverse Dragon? Avoided the Zenobian Snapper?

It's time to make a decision. Do you:

Would you like to:

Go back to the previous section? **P61**

Or

Go back to the beginning of the story and try another path? **P95**

Or

Go to the great big list of choices? **P364**

So Hot

The three of you turn right and stroll up a gently sloping corridor for several minutes. It's deserted, and the only sign of danger is when you pass a small glowing blue pile on the floor – a goblin corpse, being nibbled by a swarm of slumberworms.

"Yuck," Zim says, and accidentally hits his head on the ceiling for the fifth time. "Ow."

"You should wear a steel helmet like me. Doesn't hurt at all." With a grin, Tina head-butts the ceiling.

The clang echoes up and down the corridor. The distant golden glow dims and flickers for a few seconds.

Her smile fades. "What was that?"

"A coincidence?" Zim whispers.

"Then why are you whispering?"

"In case it's not a coincidence."

The flickering has stopped. Whatever it was.

"Let's carry on," you say. "But be careful. The dwarves wouldn't have abandoned these tunnels without good reason. We're playing *Dungeon of Doom*, not *Ultra-Peaceful Happy Underground Walk of Absolutely No Danger*. Lots of nasty things are down here."

"What if it's something really, really dangerous?"

"Then it's probably the end-of-level monster guarding the exit. Isn't that what we're looking for?"

"Oh, yeah, I forgot."

You pass another glowing blue corpse. This one's a spider, bigger than your head, covered in wiggling slumberworms.

Around a corner, the corridor slopes downwards towards an open doorway, the source of the mysterious golden glow.

An equally mysterious rumble comes from the same doorway, as does a breeze of warm air and an odd smell.

"Maybe it's a fire demon," Tina says.

"Or central heating?" Zim suggests with a weak smile.

"Or a volcano," you say. "Hardly any slumberworms along here. Not sure whether that's good or bad."

You pass a side corridor blocked with rubble, then a couple of short charred skeletons. One's holding a dwarven axe and a fire-blackened gold necklace.

"This must be a trap," Zim says, looking around nervously. "I told you we should have gone the other way, down that nice damp cold corridor."

Tina snorts. "Yeah, yeah, maybe. After I get a good look through that doorway."

"Nice and slowly," you say. "In case we have to run."

Together, weapons drawn, you peer through the doorway. Inside is a steep narrow stone staircase with no handrail, leading downwards. From far above, beams of sunlight illuminate a room the size of a tennis court. The floor's heaped with gold and silver and jewels – the biggest treasure hoard you've ever seen, and the source of the golden glow.

Tina gasps, her eyes wide. "Wow. I mean…wow!" She starts down the staircase.

"Wait!" you say. "Like Zim said, this might be a trap. I mean, who's going to leave a mountain of treasure lying around? Certainly not dwarves."

Zim frowns. "My Enchanted Shadow Crystal Lenses don't detect any magical traps. Do your elfy super-duper trap-detecting senses?"

"I haven't spotted any traps, no, but…come on, guys, there has to be something or someone guarding all that gold. And this room has no other exits, unless you can grow wings and fly up through that big hole in the ceiling. It's too dangerous."

"I'm ready for anything." Tina draws her sword and carries on down the stairs.

Zim looks longingly down at the treasure. "Sorry, Velzon, but…you know that old TV cartoon where the billionaire duck had a swimming pool full of money? I always thought that was so cool, and this is the closest I'll ever get." He follows Tina.

It's time to make a decision. Do you:

Follow them down the stairs? **P79**

Or

Leave them and escape? **P84**

Down the Stairs

For a moment, you're tempted to stay up here and let them be eaten or exploded or squashed or turned into purple bunny rabbits or whatever horrible fate must be waiting below.

But…you can't, coz they're your friends. They need you. And, to be really honest, swimming in money does sound like fun. So you follow them down the stairs.

Partway down, you realize the mysterious rumbling has stopped. Whatever it was.

"Look, I'm making a money angel," Zim says, lying on his back amongst the coins and waving his arms and legs back and forth.

"A what?" You're only half paying attention, still looking around for danger and still not spotting anything.

"A money angel – like a snow angel, but in money!"

"Oh, right."

"Wish I had my phone to take a selfie," Tina says, playing money angel too.

Giggling, she and Zim throw handfuls of diamonds at each other, causing a small avalanche in a nearby hill of treasure.

"So nice to see visitors enjoying themselves," says the deepest voice ever. The hill disintegrates as a huge dragon rises from underneath.

Oh, of course. Far too late, you notice bones scattered amongst the treasure.

"I so rarely get visitors, and when I do, they usually run away when they see me," the dragon continues, sounding offended.

It must be one of those talkative dragons. Good – maybe you can talk your way out of this. And it's not a fire breather

– there's no gust of scorched air when it speaks – that's good too. Unless it just likes chatting with people before eating them.

"It's a great honor to meet you, your magnificence," you say, hoping your voice isn't shaking.

Tina and Zim take the hint.

"You're even more gloriously terrifying than I'd imagined," Tina says, bowing.

Zim bows too and takes off his hat. "Yeah, you're totally awesomely…um…awesome. Your majesty. Sir. Or ma'am." His knees are shaking.

The dragon smiles. "Such lovely manners. You're very kind, little wizard, but I'm not royalty. I do have eighty-seven crowns, though. Would you like one each as souvenirs?"

A dragon giving treasure away? You've never heard of that before. No, actually, there was something you read online last year, what was it again…

The dragon lashes out at Tina, so fast she doesn't have time to duck. But instead of killing her, it just knocks her helmet off.

"Erk," she says in a small voice.

The dragon gives her a spikey golden crown, shaped like an angry skull with giant rubies for eyes. "This was the favorite battle crown of the mighty warlord Quoznar the Undying. Until he died."

"Cool!" She admires her reflection in a nearby silver tray. "Thanks heaps."

"It suits you, my dear," the dragon says. "Now, something suitable for a wizard and an elf, hmm, yes, perfect, where did I leave them?" It turns away, revealing an alarmingly large butt, and sifts through a hill of glittering jewelry.

Suddenly, you realize what's happening, and run over to Tina and Zim, holding a finger to your lips. "That's a Reverse Dragon. Zim, remember the Bright Shadow spell you used in Level 87?" you whisper, hoping the dragon doesn't overhear.

"What's a Reverse Dragon?"

"No time to explain! Cast Bright Shadow on us all, right now. It's our only chance."

He frowns and shrugs, then recites several lines of ancient Cobolese while waving his wand in weird spirals. Suddenly another Velzon, Zim and Tina stand next to you, or at least three fairly good imitations.

The dragon wiggles its butt. "Perhaps you could stay for lunch?"

"Thank you, your magnificence," you say, then race for the stairs, risking a quick glance back to confirm that Zim and Tina are following – the real Zim and Tina, that is.

The three fake yous, magical Bright Shadow mirages, stay where they are. The dragon wiggles its butt again and farts orange flame over them. "Barbequed adventurers for lunch. My favorite," it roars happily.

You run up the stairs, not stopping, not even when something below clangs and Tina yells.

By the top of the stairs, you're out of breath, and so exhausted that you fall to the corridor floor when something pushes you from behind. Oh, it's Tina and Zim, both gasping for breath too.

"I dropped my beautiful scary battle crown," Tina wails.

"Good. It looked like a skull dipped in glitter," Zim mutters.

"Forget the stupid crown – where's the dragon?" You peer over the stairway, hoping to stay out of sight.

No such luck.

The dragon's climbing the wall with long sharp claws. It spots you and speeds up. "Come back, my tasty, tricksy little snacks."

"Farty McFlameButt can't possibly squeeze through this little doorway," Tina says. "We're safe. Aren't we?"

"We're not out of fiery fart range yet."

Wearily, you all jog up the corridor slope. You pass the charred dwarf skeletons and fire-blackened gold necklace again. The dragon's previous victims? So, still not out of range.

"I can see you." The dragon's voice echoes up the corridor.

Glancing back, you see it maneuvering its butt to point through the doorway.

In desperation, you drag Zim and Tina into the short blocked side corridor. It's only a few yards deep, but it's the best – and only – cover available. "Maybe we can use the rubble to shield ourselves."

The three of you start heaving rocks and stones towards the main corridor, then drop to the ground as a jet of orange flame shoots past. It doesn't hit you, but Zim's tall wizard hat bursts into flame.

He squeals, pulls the hat off and bashes it against the wall, trying to extinguish the flames. Then stops, looks up and frowns. "Um, guys? Look."

Level Exit is carved on a stone ceiling slab.

He pulls out his wand and casts a Jackrabbit Jump spell. You all leap up and through the exit, just in time to avoid another jet of orange flame.

Suddenly you're back in the real world, sitting around the kitchen table with Jim and Tina, staring at *Bonus Level Completed* in big sparkly letters on your laptop screen.

"Did we win?" asks Tim.

"We survived," you say.

"My wizard hat was ruined," he grumbles.

"I lost my steel helmet," Tina mutters. "And that cool crown."

"We survived," you repeat.

She shrugs. "Anyone for Level 101?"

Congratulations, you've finished this part of your story. Then again, if you'd made different choices, things might have gone even better (or much worse). Have you met the Emerald Sage? Gotten lost in the maze? Been attacked by the bone army? Helped the extremely wet queen? Avoided the Zenobian Snapper?

It's time to make a decision. Do you:

Go back to the beginning of the story and try another path? **P95**

Or

Go to the great big list of choices? **P364**

Leave Them and Escape

No way are you following Zim and Tina down there. If those two fools want to die over some gold, that's their problem.

You head back up the corridor.

The sound of voices stops you. Tina, Zim, and an incredibly deep voice. You turn and look back at the glowing doorway.

If they're having a nice chat, then whoever it is can't be dangerous, right?

More talking, and the deep voice laughs. Not a nice laugh. Then there's screaming, horrible screaming, that stops suddenly, which is somehow even more horrible. A puff of warm air reaches you, smelling like a barbeque gone wrong.

Part of you wants to run away as fast as you can. Another part wants to go back and find out what happened. Yet another part of you has already guessed the worst.

Something passes the glowing doorway, then something else blocks it. Huh? Looks like…a huge scaly dragon butt? That makes no sense. The last thing you ever see is the butt farting a long jet of orange flame up the corridor, heading straight for you.

Sorry, this part of your story is over. If you'd made different choices, things might have gone better (or even worse). What would have happened if you'd followed Zim and Tina? Have you met the Emerald Sage? There are many paths.

It's time to make a decision. Do you:

Go back to the previous section? **P76**

Go to the beginning and try another path? **P95**

Or

Go to the great big list of choices? **P364**

Keep Running

No, absolutely anything could be in that dark room. Far too risky. So you race past the doorway, around a corner, then screech to a stop in front of a gate of thick wrought iron bars. The bars are bent, and the gate's been torn off one of its hinges. Behind the gate is a short corridor, ending in two doors facing each other. The three of you squeeze through the gap around the broken hinge, then run up the corridor, past a dented "Do Not Feed the Animals" sign on the floor.

"What animals?" Tina asks.

"Maybe they escaped," you say. "I hope so. I don't want to meet whatever was strong enough to break that gate."

"Judging by the stinky smell, something's still here," Zim says.

The giant head thuds into the gate behind you, and pokes its long purple tongue through the bars. Clearly disappointed it can't reach anyone, it repeatedly rams the gate, which creaks and starts to bend.

"I reckon we've got maybe a minute before Big Head smashes through and licks us to death," Tina says. "What's through those doors?"

Both are solid oak, barred with stout ironwood beams, and have barred windows. These are serious doors, for keeping dangerous things in. Hmm, they'd also be good for keeping giant heads out.

Whatever's inside the left door is clucking like a deep-voiced chicken with a head cold, but is almost certainly far nastier. You cautiously peer through the door's window and jump back as a barbed talon stabs at you and misses by an inch. "That's a Zenobian Snapper. Seven legs, all with talons like that. Super-fast and super-aggressive. Oh, and the talons are poisonous."

86

Zim and Tina frown.

Even more cautiously, you peer through the right door's window. Nothing. No, there in the shadows, a row of unblinking black eyes, silently watching, waiting. "It's a Nammering," you continue. "Completely harmless at a distance. It waits until a victim gets too close, then grabs them and bites their head off. And it has four mouths – enough to bite all our heads off and still have a spare mouth to laugh at us at the same time."

Tina sighs. "Not much of a choice, is it?"

"I just had a crazy idea," Zim says. "What if I cast an Invisibility spell on us, then we open both doors at once, and let the Zenobian Snapper run over and attack the Nammering?"

Tina sighs again. "You're right, that is a crazy idea."

Or is it? Behind you, the giant head rams the gate again.

It's time to make a decision, and fast. Do you:

Open both doors and hope the monsters fight each other? **P91**

Or

Open the left door and fight the Zenobian Snapper? **P87**

Or

Open the right door and fight the Nammering? **P89**

The Zenobian Snapper

You turn to the left door. "Zim, what magic do you have to help against a Zenobian Snapper?"

He pulls a tiny glass flask from a pocket inside his robe. "Negastic Sleeping Powder. Won't actually put a Snapper to sleep, but should slow it down. Then I can throw a few imploding fireballs."

Tina draws her sword. "And I can smite it lots. That'll help too."

"Well, yeah, I should hope so," you say, trying not to sound sarcastic. "I'll, um, shoot it with an arrow."

"Ooh, scary," Tina says, sounding extremely sarcastic. But you can tell she's just as scared as you are.

So's Zim. His hands shaking, he throws the flask through the door's window.

It smashes on the floor inside.

The weird clucking slows and stops. So far, so good.

Behind you, the giant head rams the gate yet again, and another hinge squeals and breaks. There's no time to lose.

Together, you lift the ironwood beam barring the door. Zim summons two silvery fireballs. You open the door, hoping to see a Zenobian Snapper yawning on the floor.

But the floor's empty, other than Zim's broken flask and a scattering of glittery powder.

Suddenly, a very awake Snapper drops from the ceiling, clucking happily.

Before you have time to even scream, long talons lash out and stab you. The last thing you ever see is the inside of its jaws.

Sorry, this part of your story is over. If you'd made different choices, things might have gone better (or even worse). Have

88

you met the Emerald Sage? Gotten lost in the maze? Been attacked by the bone army? Helped the extremely wet queen? Said hello to the Reverse Dragon?

It's time to make a decision. Do you:

Go back to the previous section? **P85**

Or

Go back to the beginning of the story and try another path? **P95**

Or

Go to the great big list of choices? **P364**

The Nammering

You turn to the right door. "Anyone fought a Nammering before?"

"Yeah, a few months ago," Tina says. "Well, I think so. Can't be one hundred percent sure. Whatever it was, it grabbed me and bit my head off before I had time to ask it any questions."

Zim rolls his eyes. "Thanks, that's so helpful."

"Are you a Nammering expert?"

"Well, I do know Nammerings like to hide in the dark, and they have great night vision. So how about a Sun Flash spell to dazzle it while we run past?" He rummages in his Big Book of Spells.

Behind you, the giant head rams the gate yet again. Another hinge squeals and breaks. There's no time to lose.

"Faster," you tell Zim.

"Okay, found it. Ready when you are." He raises his wand.

You and Tina lift the ironwood beam barring the door, then push the door open and stand back.

"Cover your eyes!" Zim warns.

Something flashes so brightly that you see a silhouette of the bones in your hand.

You lower your hand and open your eyes. The room looks empty. Has the Nammering been frightened away?

Keeping her distance from any shadows, Tina leads the way into the room. She stops mid-step. "Um, I just thought of an itsy-bitsy flaw in our plan. There can't be an exit in this room, coz if there was, the Nammering would have escaped through it long ago. So how exactly are we going to get out?"

Oh. Hadn't thought of that.

90

From outside comes the sort of noise you imagine a giant head would make when finally smashing through a wrought iron gate.

"Can we barricade the door?" you ask, pushing it closed.

It's a real fancy door – its inside is covered in elaborate carvings of strange animals. Why would someone go to the trouble of carving all over a door, and then use the room to keep a monster in? Although maybe this room was never designed to hold monsters.

Too late, you notice the door's looking back at you with a row of black eyes. That's no carving, it's the Nammering lying in wait. The last thing you ever see is it lunging at you, mouths wide open.

Sorry, this part of your story is over. But have you met the Emerald Sage? Gotten lost in the maze? Been attacked by the bone army? Helped the extremely wet queen? Said hello to the Reverse Dragon?

It's time to make a decision. Do you:

Go back to the previous section? **P85**

Or

Go back to the beginning of the story and try another path? **P95**

Or

Go to the great big list of choices? **P364**

Open Both Doors

"Let's try Zim's crazy idea," you say. "Like they say in eighties action movies, it's a million-to-one chance, but it just might work."

Zim grins, and Tina sighs.

Behind you, the giant head rams the gate yet again, and another hinge squeals and snaps. There's no time to lose. As risky as this plan is, you have to do it right now.

Zim flicks through his Big Book of Spells and hurriedly casts an Invisibility spell on all three of you.

Together, you lift the ironwood beams barring the doors.

Tina opens the Nammering's door. There's no reaction from inside.

You open the Snapper's door, hoping you're completely and totally invisible – otherwise the Zenobian Snapper might decide to kill you instead of the Nammering.

The plan works perfectly. Ignoring you, the Snapper charges into the other room and attacks the Nammering. You can't see who's winning, and judging by the horrible noises they're making, you don't want to see.

Seconds later, the giant head smashes through the gate, and races into the same room to join the "fun". Even better.

You close and bar the Nammering's door, just in case. Zim dispels the Invisibility spell. High fives all around.

"You're not as crazy as you look, Zim," Tina says.

"Thanks." He smiles.

That's the nicest thing she's said to him in weeks.

"Hmm, there can't be an exit in the Snapper's room – if there was, the Snapper would have used it ages ago." You look back down the corridor and the gate wreckage. "So I guess we'll have to go back the way we came. At least we don't have to worry about the giant head any more."

Something in the Nammering's room roars, as if agreeing.

"Let's at least have a look in the Snapper's room. There could be treasure or something." Tina goes in, not waiting for you and Zim.

"Or hundreds of baby Snappers," Zim grumbles, but follows her anyway.

The room stinks. The stone floor is littered with well-gnawed bones, some of them fresh, and dented armor and broken weapons. No baby monsters, though.

Zim toes some glittery powder by a tiny broken glass flask. "Looks like Negastic Sleeping Powder. Someone thought they could put a Zenobian Snapper to sleep. Very risky."

Tina's more interested in a small alcove. "Hey, guys, maybe there is an exit after all."

It doesn't look like much, just a round narrow tunnel sloping gently downwards. Far too small for the Snapper, but you three could squeeze through on your hands and knees. A gentle breeze of fresh air blows out of it – well, fresher than the other air in here.

Zim frowns. "Crawling through an air vent? Like in one of Velzon's eighties action movies?"

"Why not? Even Zenobian Snappers need to breathe." You climb into the tunnel and start crawling. Tina and Zim follow.

A few yards in, the whole tunnel suddenly tilts. You tumble down a steep slope and fall onto a stone floor. Tina falls on you. Zim falls on Tina. Ouch.

It's a generic stone-walled dungeon corridor, lit by burning torches.

Seems familiar somehow. Very familiar.

After listening and sniffing in both directions, you sigh. "This is the same corridor we started from. Goblins to the left. Ogres to the right."

93

Tina swears under her breath and kicks the wall. "Left. We went right last time, and look how that turned out."

"No, we should go right again," Zim insists. "It'll be easy this time – we've already cleared out most of the monsters."

They look at you. It's time to make a decision. Do you:

Go left, towards the goblins? **P7**

Or

Go right, towards the ogres? **P94**

Ogres Again

You turn right and advance down the corridor.

Just like last time, the ogres run past, followed by a giant rolling head. Just like last time, you run.

"Is that the same giant head or a different one?" Zim asks, puffing as he follows you.

"Who cares?" Tina says. "Where's that dark open doorway we didn't try last time? Has it disappeared?"

"There it is!" You run through it, and smash into a wall. "Ow!" Tina and Zim thud into your back. "Double ow!"

The ceiling suddenly glows, showing that the room's only a few feet deep and wide.

"This is a dead end!" Tina snarls. "I told you we should have turned left!"

Outside, the giant head rolls to a stop. It can't fit through the doorway, any more than the other giant head could fit through the wrought iron gate, but its long purple tongue grabs your leg and pulls. The room's metal door starts to slide closed by itself, hits the tongue, and stops.

"Stab it!" Tina shouts.

You draw your dagger.

"No, tickle it! Trust me, Velzon!" Zim shouts.

It's time to make a decision. Do you:

Stab the tongue? **P57**

Or

Tickle the tongue? **P59**

Back at the Beginning

On Saturday morning, you're sitting around the kitchen table with Jim and Tina, playing *Dungeon of Doom* together on your laptops.

"Gotcha." Jim taps his keyboard to launch another fireball at the Nine-Headed Dragon's eleventh head. (One head grew back. Twice.)

"Yee ha!" Tina's onscreen avatar, Tina Warrior Princess, finally chops off the dragon's last head.

Level Completed appears in giant sparkly letters. The floor of the dungeon room fills with end-of-level bonuses. Your avatar, Velzon the Elven Archer, runs around the room collecting them. Tina Warrior Princess and Jim's avatar, Wizard Zim, do the same.

"Warriors don't say 'yee ha'," Jim complains.

Okay, you know what happens next – you see the weird shimmering circle on the wall, and finally the others stop bantering and see it too.

Onscreen, you pick up a gold coin and toss it at the shimmery wall. As you'd half-expected, the coin vanishes. At the same moment, the edge of the circle flashes like a camera, spelling out words.

"It says ' Secret Bonus Level' in Klodruchian runes," you say. Cool.

Onscreen, Tina Warrior Princess and Velzon and Zim leap into the shimmering portal at the same time. Everything turns really bright, then really dark, then…

Huh? The kitchen's gone, and you're lying on a stone floor. Next to you are a tall woman covered in muscles and scars and battered armor, and a bearded guy in a purple robe and a pointy hat – Tina Warrior Princess and Wizard Zim, looking just like they do in the game, but…now they're real.

Impossible. Totally impossible.

"What happened?" Wizard Zim asks.

You look down. You're wearing Velzon's leaf-embroidered jerkin, spider silk trousers, and lizard-leather boots. Just to be sure, you reach up, and…yup, elf ears. On your back is a bow and quiver. On your belt is a long dagger of finest Kargalin steel. Exactly like in the game.

"We're inside *Dungeon of Doom.*" Tina Warrior Princess stands up, a huge grin on her scarred face. "Cool!"

Zim tugs at his beard. "Don't be stupid. We can't be. What is this, some new virtual reality thing?" He turns to you. "I don't like it. Make it stop. Turn it off. Now!"

"How?" you ask.

He runs around the room, yelling, "Reset! End game! Escape! Power off! End simulation! Exit!" Nothing happens.

"Let's explore!" Tina shouts, and runs out the room's only doorway.

"We might as well. We can't just stay here," you tell Zim.

"Mmm," he says reluctantly, and follows you through the doorway.

Tina's only a few steps away, frowning as she looks up and down a corridor. "This better not be a maze. I hate mazes. Always get lost." She says it like she's joking, but it's the truth – she has a terrible sense of direction, in real life and in games.

Left and right look the same – generic stone-walled dungeon corridors, lit by burning torches, with more doorways in the distance.

This level's exit could be either way. Or both ways – some levels have more than one exit.

Zim peers both ways through his Enchanted Shadow Crystal Lenses, then shrugs and looks at you. "Well, pointy ears?"

After listening and sniffing in both directions, you point left. "Goblins. Lots of them." You point right. "Ogres. Coming this way."

Tina and Zim look at you expectantly.

"What, you want *me* to decide?"

Tina grins. "Yeah, Velzon, you're good at that elfy scouting stuff. That's the only reason we let you play with us."

Zim nods. "Let's play this level the same way we usually do – you leading the way."

"So I get shot first, and stabbed first, and zapped first?" you ask.

"No worries, we'll be right behind, ready to rescue you," Tina says.

"And I've got a zillion healing potions if you get injured," Zim says.

"Thanks, you two are so helpful."

It's time to make a decision. Do you:

Go left, towards the goblins? **P7**

Or

Go right, towards the ogres? **P54**

SECRETS OF THE SINGING CAVE

The stronghold

While chewing a strip of dried meat, you stare at the brightly-colored hunting scene painted on the cave wall. A herd of massive vootbeests with tough, wrinkled hides and razor-sharp horns lumber beside graceful zeeboks. A stealthy pack of zegar trail behind, waiting for a chance to pounce. Off to one side, swarming shredders devour an unlucky havera caught outside its burrow. In the center of the mural, a triumphant hunt master in white robes walks alongside a contingent of spear bearers carrying slabs of meat back to the cave.

At the other end of the great chamber, young hunters practice the teamwork required for success on the grasslands. It reminds you of last season when you went through the same drills.

In mid routine, the trainer yells "Shredders!"

The apprentices dive for cover.

"Well done," the trainer says. "But I'm sure you can do better. Remember, there are the quick and the shredded. Let's do it again."

Filtered light streams through a large crack high in the cave's vaulted ceiling. Compared to the searing heat above ground, the air is cool.

At the center of the great chamber is 'the pit', a massive sink hole with stairs that spiral around its outer wall to the living spaces and other chambers below.

Your friend, Thamus, sits in the flickering light of a small fire entertaining children by making shadow animals on the wall. His long thin fingers dance in the air. The animals prance back and forth, mesmerizing his audience as he tells his tale. You quietly join the group.

Thamus' face is pale from living most of his twelve seasons underground—his skin nearly translucent, emphasizing the fine bone structure of his cheeks and his large blue eyes.

A childhood accident damaged his knee, rendering it stiff and useless. So, instead of becoming an apprentice hunter, or novice water guardian, cook, or herb gatherer, he's studying to become a storyteller and keeper of the tribe's history.

As you watch the show, a shadowy zeebok stretches its long neck to pick sweet crackleberries from the top of a bush.

"And forever more the zeebok's neck stayed long enough to reach any berries he found," Thamus tells his wide-eyed audience. "And that is why the delicious fruit is so rare today."

Boom, ba-boom, ba-boom. The drums echo up from the pit. A water ceremony is about to begin. Instinctively you pat the water skin slung at your back. The children run off down the stairs to join their families.

Thamus banks the fire and smiles up at you. "Are you coming to the ceremony?"

"It's either that or hunting," you say, thinking again of the cave painting and how much you'd like a break from dried meat.

Thamus grabs your forearm and hoists himself up. "I hear rumors there will be less water distributed today."

"Why do the water guardians always decide how much we get?" you ask.

Thamus turns up his palms and shrugs. "Hmmm … That's the way it's always been. They are the guardians of the well. The stories tell us this."

100

You walk towards the pit and stare into its depths. Small fires flicker. Tendrils of wood smoke rise and dance like disembodied spirits. Drops of condensation seep down the stone walls and disappear into the darkness below where they collect in a pool of life-giving water. The *Well of Tears*, lifeblood of the stronghold.

Ahooooooooooo, calls a longhorn from the citadel far below.

Down near the bottom of the pit, where the water guardians live, bucket boys chant in time with the drums as they hoist the sacred water, hand over hand, from the *Well of Tears* in preparation for the ceremony.

A hunt master, Manaria, and six of her spear bearers march up the steps from their chambers deep in the stronghold, their footsteps slapping in time to the drums.

Boom, ba-boom, ba-boom. Boom, ba-boom, ba-boom.

The stark white of Manaria's robes gives her a ghostly appearance in the dim light. Beads of bloodstone adorn her neck, signifying her many triumphs. Hand-crafted armor of thick leather protects her torso. Her dark pupils, flecked with amber, glow in the light of her flaming torch.

Ahoooooooo!

What should you do? Do you join Manaria and her spear bearers in the hope of obtaining fresh meat and glory? Or do you stay for the ceremony and top up your water skin?

The water ritual is a temptation. Those that take part get extra. But if the hunt is successful, you will be first to share in the choicest meat, a great treat after a winter of dried food.

It is time to make your first decision. Do you:

Go to the ceremony for the extra water ration? **P105**

Or

Go hunting with the hunt master in the hope of obtaining fresh meat? **P101**

The hunt

You jog down the pit stairs to level three and duck into a narrow passage. Below the stronghold's great chamber, light barely penetrates. You have no fear of the dark, though. Your hand slides along the wall, feeling for the carved symbols that mark the entrance to each chamber. When you feel three V-shaped grooves, you step inside your cave. Edging past your sleeping pallet, you grab a spear and slip a long knife into a leather sheath at your waist, then run back up the steps towards the great chamber.

Training to become a hunter is tough. Although apprentices aren't expected to hunt every day, being above ground is exciting despite the heat and risk. You sprint to catch up with Manaria before her hunting party leaves.

There's safety in numbers. Predators target stragglers. Alone, you could be dragged off by a pack of zegar, or captured by roving bands of slavers lying in wait along the escarpment.

You leap up the last few steps.

At the top of the pit, the great chamber slopes gently to the cave's opening. Long spear-like vootbeest horns are stacked along the wall, ready to be shaped into knife handles or used as weapons if the stronghold needs defending.

The opening is protected by a massive grid of branches interlaced with strips of leather. Guards protect the entrance at all times to keep predators or slavers from entering. A longhorn leans against the wall on either side of the gate. Three short blasts and all but the youngest children will come running to defend the stronghold.

You fall in behind Manaria and her spear bearers.

Hinges creak as a guard opens a gate set into the barrier wall.

A spear bearer peers through the greenery concealing the entrance and down the lightly forested slope of the escarpment to the grassland far below. "Toooo-wit. Toooo-wit."

All is clear.

Your group moves cautiously down the slope towards the grassland. A clear blue sky sits above the dusty-brown landscape. Small clumps of stunted trees and thorn bushes dance in the shimmering heat.

By the time the sun is directly overhead, everyone except the thick-skinned vootbeests will be hiding from its burning rays.

Manaria whistles once, signaling a halt, and moves to the head of the group. Holding her head high, chin thrust forward, she sniffs the air, her leather breastplate rising with each intake of breath. You do the same, hoping to catch the scent of vootbeests crossing your tribe's territory during their annual migration north in search of fresh feed. But all you smell is dust.

Manaria's stance changes. She leans towards the south, nostrils flaring. She's caught the scent of something!

"Voot! Voot!" She's off—spear tucked under one arm, feet pounding a steady rhythm over the slightly undulating ground.

The rest of you rush to keep up.

At regular intervals, Manaria stops and sniffs the air. Now you smell it too. The acrid scent of animals on the move.

As your group crests a slight rise, you see a dust cloud in the distance.

Vootbeests. Thousands of them. Only dots in the distance, but their reddish color is unmistakable, even from where you stoop, hands on knees, gasping for breath.

Before you've recovered, Manaria is running again.

Finally the hunters stop, close to the herd. The aroma of vootpoo is stronger and makes your nose tingle. If you get nothing else today, at least carrying home some vootpoo will make you popular with the herb gatherers.

Manaria turns to her spear bearers. You and an apprentice named Rooth hover nearby, wondering what happens next. You've hunted numerous times, but you've never found vootbeests before. Usually it's just a few slow-moving havera that have wandered too far from their burrows.

Tales of these massive migrations are common, but the stories haven't prepared you for the sight before you. You turn to Rooth. "Look at them!"

Rooth's eyes are wide, her mouth ajar. She is about to reply when Manaria thumps the base of her spear into the hard ground, demanding everyone's attention.

"Teamwork is needed to take down a vootbeest," she says, looking at you. "The animal's hooves are capable of crushing your skull with one kick."

You swallow.

"Its horns can skewer you with ease," she continues. "And the barbs on its tail are almost impossible to remove."

"By the waters," Rooth says, shivering a little.

Manaria thumps her spear. "Quiet, apprentice!"

Rooth's hand covers her mouth as Manaria's glare burns a hole in her.

"We'll split into two groups." Manaria points to a small grove of trees in the distance. "I'll take half the group and lay an ambush behind those trees. You others, circle around behind a vootbeest and split it from the herd. Then drive it towards us."

Both tasks are dangerous.

A fully grown vootbeest is heavily muscled and stands taller than you at the shoulder. Its thick hide deflects stone-tipped spears easily. The vootbeest's neck, just under its jaw, is its only weakness.

But will the chasers be able to separate one from the herd and drive it towards the ambushers without being injured?

The ambushers' task is to take a position near the path of the onrushing vootbeest, get a decent shot at its neck, while dodging the animal's lethal horns.

You and Rooth have only been hunting a short while. Rank amateurs in comparison to the others. These spear bearers are accustomed to hunting together. They know each other's strengths and weaknesses and automatically split into two groups. Without another word, the biggest and strongest throwers turn and walk towards the trees.

Manaria's eyes bore into you. "Well?" she says. "Are you a chaser or a thrower?"

It's time to move out. You must make a decision quickly. Do you:

Go with the chasers? **P110**

Or

Go with the throwers? **P112**

The ceremony

"I'm off to the ceremony," you tell Thamus. "I'm thirsty and my water skin is nearly empty." You hold it up for him to see.

It's barely a quarter full. The water guardians don't realize how thirsty a hunter gets. And you've been out hunting three of the last four days.

"Don't you get extra water when you're hunting?" Thamus asks.

"Not enough."

"Hmmm … Then why do it?" Thamus asks.

"If I have to chew another piece of dried vootbeest, I'll go crazy."

Thamus nods. "But you can't catch animals that aren't there, can you?"

Your friend has a point. Until the migration starts, the chance of success is slight. Apart from catching a few unwary havera outside their burrows, the last few hunts have been a waste of time.

As you start down the steps, you raise your eyebrows at Thamus. "Well, are you coming?"

The pit's steps spiral deeper and deeper into the stronghold. Condensation drips down the stone walls. In places, the rock is so moist you feel like licking it. Not that you'd ever perform such an act. You'd be caged if anyone caught you doing that! Only the water guardians can allocate water. Steal from the tribe, and you'll be left to rot.

As you and Thamus descend further, flaming torches appear on the walls. More people join the throng. Everyone needs water.

The drumbeats get louder. Again the longhorn blows. Eight levels down, you reach a large tunnel. Ornate carvings surrounding the opening depict the family symbols of current and previous water guardians. This is the entrance to the citadel. The tribe's most sacred place.

As you walk along the tunnel, torches cast an eerie light. Shadows dance along the walls. At the end of the tunnel, a large chamber opens out.

Huge stalactites hang from the ceiling like the teeth of a giant shredder. You shudder at the thought. Those horrible creatures are bad enough being the size of your hand.

Terraced seats, carved by previous generations into the chamber's walls, provide places for the whole community.

Thirteen water guardians, dressed in pale blue robes, sit on a platform where everyone can see them. Their eyes are closed and their hands rest on their thighs palms up. Their skin is so pale they look like statues carved into the walls.

Before them, balanced on a trivet of round stones, sits a basin filled to the brim with clear, cool, sparkling water. The surface of the water dances in time to the drumbeats.

To the left of the basin, a dozen bucket boys kneel on the ground. Their white robes symbolizing the purity of the water they've drawn from the *Well of Tears*, their heads bowed to honor its life-giving properties every resident of the stronghold relies on.

A drummer beats a final *ba-boom!*

The sudden silence is startling. You hold your breath, not wanting to spoil the effect. Thamus isn't breathing either.

It's then that you hear the singing. Soft, like rain falling. Words you can almost make out, but not quite. The singing continues as the thirteen water guardians open their eyes and rise to their feet.

The guardians are dressed identically, except one. The prime guardian stands in centre position. In addition to his blue robe, he wears a crown of thirteen bloodstones shaped like teardrops woven together with mintwort vines. The prime guardian's skin is so pale you can see veins and the shape of his skull and jaw beneath it. He is stooped with age, but his dilated pupils shine with inner fire.

He steps forward before the hushed community. "By the waters," he begins. "Our ancestors grace us with their song. It will be a good season. May you never thirst."

"May you never thirst," repeat the gathering.

"As you know, this is the season when we wait for the rains to come, and our blessed *Well of Tears* is at its shallowest. Thankfully, due to the expert leadership of my fellow guardians we should make it through the long dry. But because of the current scarcity, everyone here today will only be allocated half a skin."

Your heart sinks. Half a skin isn't very much water. Less than normal. You were hoping for a full skin. How are you meant to hunt without water?

A murmur runs through the crowd. Others expected more too.

A hunter in the back of the crowd stands up. "How are we meant to survive on so little? It's easy for you. You guardians get all the water you want."

The hum of the crowd increases. The prime guardian nods towards the drummers. *Ba-boom!* It is a drumbeat that demands silence.

Then he shakes his head and raises a finger, wagging it at the hunter as if he were a naughty child. "Do you think I don't feel your disappointment? This decision was not made without great deliberation. Do the ancestors not sing to tell us all will be well?"

The other guardians nod their heads in unison.

Another member of the crowd stands. It's Zenan, one of the tribe's three hunt masters. He wears a white robe made from fine zeebok skin and has a full necklace of bloodstone beads signifying his triumphs.

"Many hunters are discouraged," Zenan says. "How am I to lead them out of the safety of the stronghold and onto the parched grasslands where they run so far, at great risk, if they don't have sufficient water? Shredders are plentiful, yet water is scarce."

There is more murmuring in the crowd.

"It's time the hunters have more say in the distribution of water," Zenan continues. "It's time the guardians share this responsibility with those of us who supply the stronghold with meat. It's time the guardians became servants of the tribe, not their masters."

The crowd sits in stunned silence. Did this hunt master just challenge the authority of the water guardians? Will they respond to this challenge?

You only have to wait a moment to find out.

Heavy footsteps pound down the tunnel towards the citadel.

You watch agog as twenty members of the citadel's elite guard enter the chamber, spears at the ready, long knives on belts at their waist.

The prime guardian raises a gnarled hand and points towards Zenan. "Cage that man!"

Thamus leans towards you. "Why were the guards nearby? Were the guardians expecting trouble?"

"The stronghold has ears," you say. "I've heard grumbling about water among the hunters, but never expected someone to speak out in the citadel."

Zenan pulls a knife from his robe, glowers at the prime guardian, and then turns to the crowd. "Enough of this tyranny! Hunters, to me!"

While on the grassland, whatever the hunt master says, you're obliged to do. But here in the citadel, you're unsure.

You agree that the hunters need a larger share of water. They spend more time in the heat above ground and risk their lives every time they leave the stronghold. They need to keep strong and alert.

Other hunters leap to Zenan's defense, their weapons at the ready. But you're only an apprentice. What should you do? Do you dare rebel against the water guardians?

Quickly, there is not much time.

You must decide. Do you:

Go and support Zenan? **P163**

Or

Stay seated and allow Zenan to be caged? **P159**

The chase

Rooth has also decided to chase. The two of you join three spear bearers as they trot towards the herd. The group approaches in a looping arc so the vootbeests aren't spooked before the ambushers get into position.

The most experienced spear bearer leads the chasers. He is tall, lean, and has a graceful stride. His skin is dark brown and his robe flows behind him as he runs.

Near the edge of the herd, the lead spear bearer stops behind a clump of thorn bushes and looks to see if the ambushers are in position.

A raised spear with a piece of white fur fluttering on its tip indicates they are.

Now an animal must be chosen. A young one is best, but not so young that an over-protective mother will fight to keep it safe when you attempt to separate it from the herd. Nor do you want an animal that is in the prime of life because of its strength.

The lead chaser points to a medium-sized animal wandering a short distance from the edge of the herd. Its head swings low, with horns almost brushing the ground, as it chomps on a dry clump of vootgrass. The animal is oblivious to your group. Perfect.

"Get ready," the lead chaser says, giving you and Rooth a quick glance. "And watch out for the tail when it's your turn."

The spear bearers crouch, ready to move.

If the chaser can't force the beast further away from the herd towards the ambushing party, they will have no chance.

"Voot! Voot!" the lead chaser calls as he dashes from cover and circles to the far side of the vootbeest. He jabs the animal in its haunch.

The beast kicks its hind legs and starts trotting, its meal forgotten. The next chaser sees her opportunity and does the same, ducking under a tail of flailing quills in the process.

By now, the rest of the herd is shying away from the strange creatures attacking one of their members. After another prod from the third spear bearer, it's your turn.

The vootbeest is nearly to the ambush point. Just one more poke, and Manaria and her crew can pounce.

But the animal snorts, digs in its hooves, and skids to a stop.

Not sure of what to do, you skid to a stop too.

The vootbeest turns in your direction. Twin horns glint in the sunlight. Snot flies as it shakes its head and stamps a front hoof. It looks right at you, its eyes an angry red.

Your knees tremble as you wave your spear. "Voot! Voot!"

The beast takes another step in your direction, raises its head and roars.

You've been told not to challenge a vootbeest on your own, but here is your big chance. Should you throw your spear? But what happens if you only wound the animal and enrage it further? Vootbeests have been known to chase down hunters and skewer them with their horns. Even at full speed, you'd have no chance of outrunning it.

The beast raises its head and roars again. Its neck is exposed.

What do you do? Do you:

Throw your spear at the vootbeest's neck? **P118**

Or

Run and hope the vootbeest follows you closer to the hunt master? **P123**

The ambush

Manaria leads the ambushers towards the clump of trees. Her courage when hunting vootbeests is legend throughout the tribe, and her necklace of bloodstone beads is testament to her supreme skill.

Rooth, the other apprentice, has gone with the chasers.

You rate yourself as a spear thrower—a skill practiced ever since you could walk. You finger the lone bloodstone bead hanging on the leather thong at your neck. Your first—proudly won in competition against others your age last season.

Not far from where you wait is a steady parade of vootbeests. Occasionally one lowers its head and rips a mouthful of vootgrass from the ground as it passes. And while there is little nutrition in this dry, stalky meal, it will have to do until they reach the rich feed further north.

What enables the vootbeests to make such a trek is their ability to store water in a spongy hump on their chest between waterholes.

Manaria takes a piece of white fur from a pouch in her robe and ties it to the end of her spear and waves it above her head—a signal for the chasers to start.

"Apprentice," she says, looking in your direction. "The spear bearers and I will rush into position once the chasers have separated a beast from the herd. Your job is to stay between the vootbeest and these trees to keep the vootbeest from veering into them in an attempt to escape.

Manaria waves her signal flag until she's sure the chasers have seen it, and then stuffs the fur back out of sight. "Everyone, get ready. On my command."

The hunt master and her three spear bearers crouch with one knee on the ground, their spears pointing forward. You do the same a pace behind them. A trickle of sweat runs off your forehead and plops into the dust. Nerves jangle.

The snuffling of vootbeests and the steady thud of their massive hooves hitting the baked ground is a constant rumble. Glints of light reflect from a thousand sun-bleached horns.

Manaria leans forward and peers around a tree trunk. Timing is everything. Rush out too soon, and the vootbeest will swerve before their spears are thrown.

"Voot! Voot!" The calls of the chasers are getting closer.

Your heart thumps, and your nostrils sting as you breathe the acrid scent of the herd.

"Soon," the hunt master says.

With muscles coiled, ready to spring, you wait for her command.

Plop goes another drop of sweat.

"Ready …" Manaria leans slightly forwards, her muscles tense.

Your fingers tighten around the shaft of your spear. Legs tremble.

"Now!"

In a flash, the hunt master and her three spear bearers are in a line directly in the path of the onrushing vootbeest, their spears raised, arms back. You rush to your position.

The vootbeest sees the hunters in its path and turn its head in your direction. The beast's eyes lock with yours, its deadly horns point right at you. A blast of hot breath shoots a clump of dust and snot from the vootbeest's nostrils. Your legs wobble.

Will it swerve in your direction?

"Voot! Voot!" You scream at the top of your voice. You throw your spear. The throw isn't perfect, but its glancing blow off the animal's tough hide is enough to keep it on track towards the hunt master and her team.

"Throw!" Manaria cries, letting fly with her spear.

As soon as the spears leave the hunters' hands, the throwers dive left and right.

There is a thud as one of the spears finds its mark, but still the beast runs on.

At first, you think it can't have been a killing blow, but then the vootbeest slows. Its front legs buckle and it crashes to the ground.

"Voot! Voot!" the spear bearers cheer.

"Voot! Voot!" the chasers cheer.

"Voot! Voot!" you shout, just happy to be alive.

It takes the strength of the whole group to turn the vootbeest onto its back. The spear embedded in its neck bears the mark of the hunt master. Knives are drawn and the animal is quickly butchered. Special care is taken while cutting around the water hump so it can be used to transport its precious contents back to the cave.

The largest share of the liver is given to Manaria. Spear bearers get the next largest, and you and Rooth get smaller pieces. You waste no time in sinking your teeth into the still-warm treat. Juice runs down your chin as you savor the first fresh food you've tasted in quite some time.

Rooth smiles at you, her teeth red and dripping. This meal will provide the energy you'll need to carry the meat back to the cave.

After the hunting party have finished eating and carving up the beast, Manaria distributes the loads.

You are given one of the vootbeest's forelegs to carry. It weighs nearly half of what you do. The larger spear bearers carry slabs of rump and sirloin.

Manaria carries the water bladder and, having made the kill, straps the two massive horns to her back. These trophies, and the rich marrow they contain, will be presented as tribute to the water guardians. In exchange, the guardians will award the hunt master another bloodstone bead to add to her collection.

Manaria passes the water bladder around to lighten her load. "Drink quickly. Zegar will be here soon. We must go."

Zegar have the keenest noses on the grassland. They can smell blood for miles on the wind and run in packs of twenty or more. A fully grown zegar weighs as much as you do and can run all afternoon. Packs of zegar working together can bring down an adult vootbeest, although they usually attack weaker members of the herd.

But even a pack of zegar fears the swarms of shredders that populate the grassland.

Shredders are a flying nightmare. They're small, but have razor-sharp claws and a lust for blood. When an animal is caught in the open by a swarm of these horrid creatures, it can be stripped to the bone in no time. The only defense against them is to shelter in a cave, where they are disorientated by the dim light, or to dive under the thickest thorn bush you can find and hide until the swarm leaves.

Vootbeests have little to fear from shredders. Their hide is too tough for the tiny teeth to penetrate. Instead, the shredders will often sit on a vootbeest and devour the many parasites that attempt to burrow into its leathery hide.

"Let's go," says Manaria. "If we hurry we'll avoid the worst of the heat."

"Oomph!" You heave the hunk of leg onto your back and secure the leather straps that will hold it in place during your trek back to the cave. You bend your knees and bounce up and down until the weight settles into a comfortable position.

It will take the rest of the morning to return to the stronghold. A hot, uncomfortable and potentially dangerous trek. As you walk, you scan the grassland for danger.

116

Unfortunately, a pack of sixteen zegar picks up your hunting party's scent. At first, the pack is just a collection of dots in the distance. But there is little doubt they'll be upon you well before you reach the safety of the stronghold.

Manaria picks up the pace. "Hurry! The closer we are to the cave when the pack reaches us, the less meat we'll have to sacrifice."

Rooth puts on a burst of speed and pulls away, leaving you trailing at the end of the line. Not an ideal spot when a pack of hungry zegar is on your tail. You clutch the straps holding your load in place, lean forward, and increase speed.

It's getting hotter. Your mouth is dry and your thighs burn. You continually glance over your shoulder to see how fast the zegar are gaining. Their loping stride is economical and effective. The zegar are getting close.

The leader of a zegar pack is usually the largest. Sometimes male, sometimes female. Always the toughest, cleverest, and deadliest.

You wonder how close Manaria will allow the pack to get before she tosses them some meat. You hope it's not long. The zegar are close enough for you to see their yellow eyes and black snouts.

Rooth is slowing down. The weight and heat are getting to her.

She isn't as fit as you are. Not enough hunting.

"Rooth!" Manaria yells. "Get ready to drop your load. On my command!"

You increase your speed a little. Rooth drops back to jettison her load.

The zegar are yipping in anticipation now. The scent of blood has them sprinting, gaining with every stride, a stone's throw away.

"Now, Rooth!" Manaria yells.

Rooth slips her shoulder straps and drops her load. With the weight gone, she sprints towards the rest of you. She looks back to see what the zegar are doing, trips, and slams to the ground. She struggles to her knees, and manages to regain her feet. But when she tries to run, she's limping and holding her side. Pain is reflected in her face and you hear her harsh breathing.

The alpha zegar yips a message to the pack. This sounds different from their normal yips of excitement.

Does the pack leader sense an opportunity? Are the zegar going to attack Rooth? It certainly wouldn't be the first time zegar have taken an apprentice while on a hunting trip.

What do you do? Do you throw the meat you are carrying to the zegar to save Rooth? Or do you keep running and let Rooth fend for herself?

Quick, the zegar are close! It is time to make a decision! Do you:

Help Rooth? **P140**

Or

Keep running and let Rooth fend for herself? **P142**

Throw the spear at the vootbeest's neck

As the vootbeest lifts its head and bellows at the sky, you whip the spear forward. *Thunk!* The beast's roar is instantly silenced and it drops to its knees momentarily before falling onto its side. You've done it! Your first kill. And as a chaser! Even better.

Surely you'll get a bloodstone bead for this triumph.

Rooth runs up and pounds your back. "What a throw! Did you see how fast it went down?"

You can't believe your luck.

Manaria trots over to your position. "Fool! You're lucky you weren't killed trying a shot like that!"

"But … but …"

"But what? You're better than everyone else just because you won a spear throwing competition last season?" Manaria shakes her head in disgust. "Apprentices!"

Not the reaction you expected.

"Get out of my sight! I'll deal with you later. Oh, and take Rooth with you before she does something stupid!"

Your mind reels as the two of you walk a short distance to a patch of thorn bushes and sit in the shade.

The spear bearers begin to butcher the vootbeest. To show her displeasure, Manaria is likely to give you an especially heavy piece to carry back to the stronghold.

You rest your forehead on your knees and wonder how your triumph turned to vootpoo so quickly. "That was harsh. And to take it out on you too …"

But Rooth isn't listening. She's on her feet pointing towards a black cloud swirling and twisting as it races towards Manaria and her spear bearers.

"Shredders!" Rooth screams. "Run!"

119

The hunting party takes one look at the approaching swarm, drops everything, and runs for their lives.

Rooth grabs the sleeve of your robe. "Don't just sit there, get under the thorn bush!"

You roll onto your belly and wriggle in under the lower branches. The thorn bush's long spiky needles will protect you from the swarm of shredders, who can only attack from above.

Rooth slides in beside you. From this position of safety, you watch the spear bearers run. But one by one, they are caught by the swarm. The lead chaser is fast. He almost makes it to the thorn bush before he too is taken.

"By the waters!" Rooth says. "There must be a thousand of those horrible creatures!"

Rooth is right. The hunting party didn't stand a chance. Had Manaria not sent you and Rooth away, the shredders would have eaten the two of you as well.

The shredders swarm around the fallen hunters. Then, as quickly as it arrived, the swarm is racing towards the horizon and its next victim.

The two of you lie in shocked silence, staring out at the scene. After a while, Rooth rolls onto her side and stares at you. "Do you think it's safe to get out?"

"I—I think so."

You wriggle out from under the bush and scan the grassland. Bones, tattered robes, and fallen weapons are all that remain of the hunting party. The herd of vootbeests marches on untroubled, their thick hides protecting them from attack.

Rooth clutches your arm. "So what do we do now?"

You reclaim your arm and approach the nearest pile of bones. "These weapons are valuable. We should gather them up and take them back to the stronghold."

Rooth nods. “Maybe we can salvage some of the vootbeest you killed too.”

You walk towards what’s left of the vootbeest, picking up the spears and knives of your fallen comrades as you go. Manaria’s string of bloodstone beads lie next to a pile of bones and a gleaming skull. You hold the beads up to show Rooth before slipping it into a pocket in your robe.

Insects buzz around the blood-soaked ground, a reminder that you and Rooth have no time to waste. Insects aren’t the only things attracted by the scent of blood. Zegar will smell it too. There are always packs following the herd.

“We need to salvage what we can and get moving,” you say.

The body of the vootbeest has been stripped to the bone. All that remains are the two hind quarters where the beast’s thick skin has stopped the shredders from getting to the meat below.

With a knife, you trim one of the hindquarters into a size you can carry. Rooth does the same with the other. You strap the meat onto your backs, pick up the spears and knives gathered from the fallen hunters, and start the long trek back to the cave.

Normally, you’d have taken the vootbeest’s horns to exchange with the water guardians for a bloodstone bead, but with the extra weapons, the horns are too much to carry. Besides, you and Rooth are sure to be rewarded for the return of the weapons and Manaria’s necklace.

On the trek back to the cave, you watch for shredders and take note where the nearest thorn bush is.

It takes most of the day to reach the edge of the grassland where the escarpment begins to rise towards the mountainous cliffs that run to the horizon in each direction.

Then it's up through a glade of yonobo trees, and you're back at the stronghold's entrance.

"By the waters," Rooth says in relief. "We've made it."

The vigilant guards have the gate open in a flash and, upon seeing your exhausted state, are quick to relieve you of your loads of meat.

Others in the great chamber have noticed your arrival and come over to investigate.

"Shredders," you mumble as you toss a collection of spears and knives onto the ground. The pile of weapons is a grim reminder of the above-ground dangers.

"All of them gone?" the shocked crowd asks, as they stare down at the pile. "And only the apprentices survived. How is that possible?"

You are exhausted and too parched to speak. Yet tribespeople still crowd in expecting an explanation.

Thamus squeezes through the throng and presses his water skin into your hand. After taking a long drink, you pass the skin to Rooth.

"Give them room," Thamus says. "I'm sure they'll tell us the tale of the hunt after we feast on the fresh meat they've brought back. Right now, they need rest."

You clasp Thamus' forearm and give him a weak smile.

Rooth wipes her mouth with the sleeve of her robe and returns his water skin. "By the waters, I needed that."

The crowd, satisfied with Thamus' promise of stories and feasting, return to their chores. Meanwhile, one of the tribe's cooks heaves the haunches of vootbeest onto his broad shoulders and carries them to the cooking area at the far end of the great chamber. There they are cut into smaller pieces, skewered with green yonobo branches and positioned over a bed of glowing red coals. Only the hunt master, Zenan, remains nearby.

122

He is a tall, imposing figure, well-muscled, and with white zeebok robes contrasting his suntanned skin. The string of bloodstone beads around his neck is even larger than the one nestled in your pocket.

Deep creases form around his eyes as he stares down at you. "Shredders, you say?"

You swallow the lump in your throat, the horrible memory of the attack still vivid in your mind. "So many of them. The others didn't stand a cha—chance."

Zenan nods in understanding and pats your shoulder. "It's okay. I know it's difficult. These shredder plagues occur when breeding conditions are just right. This will make a hunter's life much more dangerous."

He's right. A dozen or so shredders are bad enough. Every season a few hunters are lost to their sharp claws and veracious appetites. But a swarm like the one your hunting party encountered … well, that's something different.

"There must be something we can do to protect ourselves."

Zenan shrugs. "A few have died trying."

While walking back to the stronghold after the attack, you had plenty of time to think. Mainly about how the needles of the thorn bush protected you and Rooth from the shredder's claws, and what a perfect weapon those needles would make. You've had an idea and you're pretty sure it will work.

It is time to make a decision. Do you:

Tell Zenan about your plan to protect hunters from shredders? **P130**

Or

Talk to Thamus about your shredder protection plan first? **P135**

Run towards the hunt master

You wheel around and sprint towards the ambushers just as the vootbeest charges. Thankfully, your acceleration is faster than the lumbering animal, but you know when it reaches top speed, it will catch you easily.

A quick jink to the right. Hooves pound behind you. Your nerves tingle as you put on a burst of speed, expecting to feel the horns rip through your body at any moment.

There is a flash of white ahead. Manaria and her spear bearers leap out from behind the trees, their arms drawn back. Spears at the ready.

One last burst of speed. Your thighs and lungs burn.

Whoosh! Whoosh! Whoosh! Three spears zip past your head. You dodge right and dive to the ground, covering your head with your arms as you roll.

"Voot! Voot!" The spear bearers shout with excitement.

Hearing their celebration, you breathe a sigh of relief and drag yourself out of the dirt. Everyone is gathered around the fallen animal. Manaria's spear protrudes from the vootbeest's neck. She has proven herself yet again, most likely saving your life in the process.

She sees you approach. "Well done, apprentice. I thought you were going to freeze there for a moment," Manaria says before turning back to the spear bearers to organize the division of loads. The horns and the vootbeest's spongy water hump will be her responsibility.

The spear bearers make short work of the vootbeest, carving off the haunches and hind legs. The animal's liver is shared amongst the hunters, each receiving a piece. Manaria, being the hunt master, gets the largest piece, the apprentices the smallest. The still-warm slice you receive melts in your mouth and slides effortlessly down your throat. It's the first fresh food you've had in ages.

As each of the hunting party secures their designated load onto their backs with strips cut from the vootbeest's hide, Manaria passes the vootbeest's water hump around to lighten her load. "Drink quickly," she says. "We must get going before the zegar arrive. Zenan told me of a sizeable pack roaming this area."

Zenan is your tribe's most respected hunt master. You've been out with him a couple of times, but places on his hunts are hard to get due to his popularity.

"Okay, let's move out," Manaria says as she hoists the horns over her shoulder and starts back towards the stronghold. "Keep an eye out for shredders too. The zegar aren't the only ones with keen noses."

The mention of shredders gives you the jitters. Those blood-sucking horrors may be small, but a swarm can devour a zeebok or a hunter in no time. Only the vootbeest's thick hides save them from danger. Every other living creature must seek refuge, and dive under a thorn bush or head underground to escape the shredders' claws and razor-sharp teeth.

The trek back to the stronghold is long and hot. Manaria calls a brief stop under the broad leaves of a yonobo tree, providing temporary relief from the relentless sun.

In the distance, a zeebok family grazes on a thorn bush, their long necks enabling them to reach the tender leaves near the top.

While sitting in the shade, Manaria gives everyone another drink from the vootbeest's hump. Water is heavy to carry and, despite needing a drink herself, the hunt master is happy to lighten her load further. The water tastes slightly of mintwort, a sign the animal has been eating the herb recently. It's a pleasant change from the tepid water in your water skin.

Refreshed, the hunting party starts the last leg of the journey back to the stronghold. The section of the escarpment where the entrance to the cave is located rises distinctively in the distance.

Everyone's pleased to be off the grassland. Nearly home. It's cooler too. A glade of yonobo trees provides protection from the sun.

Not far up the hill, Manaria points towards a clump of bright green bushes. "Apprentices, grab some mintwort. The cooks will need it for the feast tonight."

Keen to get into the relative coolness of the stronghold, you and Rooth waste no time stripping handfuls of leaves off the plant. These you stuff into pockets in your robe. The scent of mintwort fills your nostrils as you make the final climb up to the cave.

The return of a successful hunting party is always a joyous occasion. To those who stayed behind, it means that friends and family members are safe, and that the tribe will soon feast on fresh meat.

For the hunters, it is the end of a long and dangerous trek—but there is a feeling of satisfaction too, especially when people are eager to hear stories of the hunt.

It is these tales that Thamus and other storytellers will repeat for generations to come.

During the feast, the spear bearers will tell of their experience, and the hunt master will present the trophy horns, and the sweet marrow they contain, to the water guardians. In return, the guardians will award bloodstone beads to those who did well on the hunt to mark their triumph.

Manaria is bound to get another bead. And depending on how well the others speak, they too may be rewarded. You have no doubt the tale of your near skewering will create a few chuckles amongst the crowd.

A while later, after a brief sleep in your chamber, you head back up the pit staircase. The mouth-watering aroma of food fills the great chamber. Standing at the fire, cooks rotate loaded skewers, occasionally tossing handfuls of herbs onto the embers to flavor the meat. On a stone bench nearby, Thamus tells stories to children eagerly awaiting food.

Tendrils of smoke rise towards the ceiling of the chamber, filtering the afternoon light through a blue-grey haze. Others gather too. Drawn to the great chamber by their desire for fresh food and storytelling.

You wander over, sit next to Thamus, and listen. It's a story you've heard many times about the Great Hunter who first found the stronghold many generations ago. It tells how this brave hunter followed a huge three-horned vootbeest into the cave and, armed only with a napstone blade, leapt onto the vootbeest's back and rode him around the great chamber, stabbing at the beast's massive neck until the vootbeest tired and fell with an almighty thud to the ground, collapsing the stone floor, and creating the pit.

Thamus finishes his story just as a cook picks up a longhorn and blows a long low note signaling that the food is ready.

Children rush to be first in line. They each pull a scrap of leather from their robes and hold it out. The cook places chunks of steaming vootbeest onto it and they rush back to sit and gnaw on the meat's crispy exterior.

Juice runs down their chins. Smiles and laughter breaks out throughout the great chamber. The first feast of the migration is everyone's favorite time.

When you get your share of meat, you pull your knife from your robe and cut it in half. Some you'll keep for later.

Age and a few stomach aches have taught you not to eat too fast.

After chewing his meat for a while, Thamus looks your way. "Hmmm … did you do well on the hunt?"

There's no point lying. When the feast is over, each spear bearer, and then finally the hunt master, Manaria, will tell their versions of what happened. Apprentices are not permitted to speak.

"I—I nearly got skewered," you say, feeling your face redden. "If it weren't for Manaria's excellent aim, I'd probably be dead."

"Really?" Thamus says. "Makes me glad I'm a storyteller. The thought of those horns jabbing through me gives me leakage."

"Yeah, I nearly leaked all right."

Thamus smiles. "Oh well, maybe next time you'll get some bloodstone."

"I'm just happy to be enjoying the feast. I've never run so fast in my life!"

After finishing his food, one of the spear bearers from the hunting party collects his spear from where it's leaning against the cave wall and starts banging it on the stone floor. The *clack, clack, clack* echoes throughout the great chamber. The sound of people talking and burping is replaced with an excited buzz of anticipation.

The stories are about to begin.

The first speaker is one of the chasers. She tells of her bravery in prodding the mighty vootbeest towards the ambush. How she had to duck its lethal tail and how the mighty hooves missed her by the narrowest of margins. She tells how the chase was long and difficult, the ground rough underfoot. There is no mention of your near-death experience.

The other spear bearers also tell of their bravery.

The ambushers downplay that their spears missed the target, but play up how they faced down the rampaging vootbeest and only dove out of the beast's path at the very last moment, risking life and limb.

Manaria is last to speak. She stands tall, her white robe flowing to the ground around her.

All eyes are upon her.

"Today was a triumph of teamwork," she starts. "My team."

Manaria looks around the room to make sure everyone is watching. "Everyone had to play their part so that we could enjoy this feast. The chasers were brave as they split the vootbeest from the herd. The ambushers stood firm as the mighty beast charged directly at them. But no one has spoken of the brave apprentice who stared into the eyes of the maddened beast. Who stood firm as the vootbeest stomped its massive hooves. Who refused to allow our quarry to escape into a glade of trees. Who locked eyes with the beast without fear until, in its rage, the beast charged after the apprentice, right towards our ambush."

Manaria lifts her hand and holds her thumb and forefinger a short distance apart. "An apprentice who came this close to having the horns of this mighty beast rip through their body so that I could get a shot at its neck."

Thamus nudges you with his elbow. "Is she talking about you?"

It takes you a moment to realize that she is.

Manaria walks over and grabs your hand. She leads you over to a flat rock and pulls you up on top of it with her. "My apprentice!" The crowd cheers.

Two water guardians approach, each with a bloodstone bead resting on a piece of white leather. One for you, and one for the hunt master.

"For skill and bravery, we, the keepers of the sacred well, present you, Manaria, and you, Apprentice, these awards. May you never thirst."

"May you never thirst!" the crowd echoes.

Congratulations, you've completed a successful hunt and been rewarded with a precious bloodstone bead.

But what would have happened if you'd taken a different path? In a *You Say Which Way* story, you can find out. There are many secrets to discover.

It is time to make your next decision. Do you:

Go back to the beginning and read a different track? **P98**

Or

Go to the big list of choices to find parts of the story you haven't read yet? **P365**

Tell Zenan your plan to protect hunters from shredders

You find Zenan in the great chamber.

"I have an idea that might protect us from shredders," you say. "Been thinking about it ever since the attack."

Zenan looks down at you with a smirk on his face. "You've been thinking, have you?"

You ignore his sarcasm. "I have an idea for a thorn thrower."

"A thorn thrower?" Zenan says. "How's that work?"

You explain your idea of cutting narrow grooves in a shortened spear handle and fitting fifty or so thorns into them. You tell him how the thorns are thrown by smacking the handle against an outstretched palm, causing the handle to stop with a jolt and flinging the thorns towards the approaching swarm.

"How do you know the thorns will fly straight?"

"Have you ever picked a thorn out of your robe and dropped it on the ground?" you ask Zenan.

"A few. Why?"

"How did it land?"

Cogs whirl in Zenan's mind. "You're right. They always land point first. The rounded end has more resistance through the air, which makes the point hit first."

"The same reason we put strips of leather on the butt of our spears. So that they fly true."

Zenan scratches his chin. "But even if the thorns fly straight and kill a few shredders, the rest of the swarm will get you."

You shake your head. "If the thorns kill enough shredders, those that aren't killed will stop to devour those that are. It won't stop the swarm, but it might give a hunter the extra time they need to dive under a thorn bush."

"That's true," Zenan says. "They are cannibals. Blood is what directs them."

"So, will you take me out to collect some thorns?"

"I can do better than that," he says. "Come with me. I've got something interesting to show you."

Zenan strides over to the pit and heads down the staircase. At level five, he turns into a narrow corridor. You feel for symbols carved into the walls as you walk. At the end of the corridor, he enters a chamber and lights a torch.

The chamber's walls are covered in holes. Big holes, little ones. High. Low. Everywhere there are holes.

"Wow," you say. "What is this place?"

"We call it the chamber of interesting things. Or should I say, a chamber of potentially useful things." Zenan does a quick search and then removes a large bundle of thorns from one of the holes. "Here you go. When you've finished your weapon, let me know and we can test its efficiency."

You are about to head back to the great chamber when you hear a familiar singing echo around the chamber. "So you hear singing down here too?"

Zenan listens for a moment and then nods. "The ancestors like this chamber. It's why it was chosen to store our history. Now off you go. I've got a hunt to organize."

You'd like to ask Zenan more questions, but now is not the time. Instead, you take the bundle of thorns up to the great chamber where the light is better, find a suitable piece of wood for the handle, and start carving.

After smoothing the wood, you make two grooves down half the handle's length. Then you fit the rounded ends of the thorns into the grooves. Occasionally a thorn is trimmed so its fit is snug, but not so tight that it won't fly out when the handle is given a jolt.

Once fifty thorns are fitted, you're ready to show Zenan.

He's probably down on a lower level where most of the hunters have their chambers.

Just as you enter the pit, three sharp bursts sound on the longhorns. The stronghold is under attack!

Who or what is attacking doesn't matter, everyone knows that when the horns sound, they must come immediately to defend the stronghold. Some residents bring their spears and knives, other grab vootbeest horns from those leaning against the wall by the main gate.

You are one of the first to reach the gate.

The attackers are a band of hairy men. Slavers. They are trying to cut their way through the bindings holding the gate together, grab a few captives, and flee.

The gate guards have other ideas and stab at the slavers through the gaps.

You stand back. You'd like to test your thrower against them, but others are in the way.

Then you see Zenan rush up the pit stairs with a dozen spear bearers. As he reaches you, he sees the item in your hand. "I see you made your weapon."

"I—I'd like to use it on the slavers, but I'm afraid I might hurt one of ours."

Zenan evaluates the situation. "Well, here's your chance. Get ready to throw. I'll order everyone back from the gate to give you a shot. But you'd better be quick. We can't afford to leave the gate unprotected for more than a breath or two."

Without waiting for an answer, Zenan rushes forward. "Back from the gate! Now, everyone! Back from the gate!"

Residents of the stronghold are trained to listen to the hunt masters in situations like this. They draw back from the gate, following Zenan's lead.

Now's your chance.

You step forward and lift the thrower as if you are going to throw a spear. Your free hand is out in front of you at shoulder height.

With a fast forward motion, you bring the thorn thrower forward and smack the fist holding its handle into the palm of your other hand.

The handle stops with a jolt, flinging the thorns forward. As the thorns fly, they spread slightly. At the same time, the slavers, having seen the retreat, move forward to crowd the gate. When the thorns hit, about half of the projectiles fly between the cross members and sink deep into the slavers' flesh. The rest stick into the timbers of the gate itself.

"Yeowwwwwww," cry the hairy men as the stinging thorns bury deep into arms and torsos.

"Forward!" yells Zenan.

Your tribespeople surge forward once more. Not that they have much opposition any more.

Many thorns have hit slavers, three of whom lie on the ground with multiple thorns sticking out of them. The hairy men shriek and dance about. Their bodies are on fire. They clutch at the thorns, trying to pull them from their burning skin. The damage is done. The slavers desire to fight is gone. Those lucky enough to be unharmed by the thorns help the injured retreat.

"Voot! Voot! Voot!" cheer the defenders.

Zenan rests his arm over your shoulder. "That's quite a weapon you've got there, apprentice. Would you like to look through the chamber of interesting things and see if you can come up with some more bright ideas? Or, if you'd prefer, you can come hunting with me tomorrow. Who knows, you might get a chance to try that thing out against shredders."

Both options sound interesting. Being invited to hunt with Zenan is an honor. But so is his offer to look around the chamber of interesting things. Imagine what could be in all those holes.

You scratch your head as you consider your options.

"Think about it," Zenan says, sensing your indecision. "Let me know what you decide."

When you run across Thamus, you mention the chamber of interesting things to him. He's never heard of it.

"Please, take me with you to the chamber. I love interesting things."

"But I've been invited to go with Zenan and try the thrower out on the shredders," you say. "It worked against the slavers."

"Hmmm … slavers are a bigger target."

"Yeah, but …"

It is time to make an important decision. Zenan will want an answer soon. Do you:

Go hunting with Zenan and try the thrower? **P194**

Or

Go with Thamus to the chamber of interesting things? **P199**

Talk to Thamus about your shredder protection plan first

"I'll see you later at the feast," you tell Rooth.

You walk to the edge of the pit and peer over its edge. Thamus is on level two and heading further down.

"Hey, Thamus! Wait for me!"

After sprinting down the steps, you pull him into an alcove, eager to tell him your plan.

As your words spill out, Thamus puts a finger to your lips. "Shhh … now, tell me again, only slower this time."

A sigh escapes your chest as you sink to the floor and lean against the wall.

The caress of cool rock on your back feels great after the burning heat of the grassland.

"First imagine the needle of a thorn bush and how it's wider where it joins onto the stem."

"Yes," Thamus says.

"Now imagine we pick a bunch of these thorns and place their rounded ends into a groove cut into a shortened spear handle."

"Okay," Thamus says. "But how is that going to help you ward off shredders?"

"The handle will act as a thrower for the thorns. A hunter will bring their arm back, as if they are going to throw a spear, but then, rather than throwing, they smack their hand into the palm of their other hand, and the jolt will send the thorns flying in the direction of the swarm."

"I think I see …"

"The fat end of the needle creates more drag through the air than the pointed end. That'll keep the needles heading straight at the target."

"Hmmm … a thorn would easily kill a shredder," Thamus says.

136

"And fifty thorns would kill lots more. Once the other shredders smell blood, they'll devour any injured shredders before moving on. That might give a hunter enough time to take cover, providing a thorn bush wasn't too far away."

Thamus is barely visible in the shadows as you wait for his reaction.

"It could work," he says. "But how do you test it without running the risk of getting shredded?"

"Yeah, that's the problem."

"And how do you carry a stick with thorns sticking out of it without jabbing yourself? Just a slight scratch will sting like crazy."

"A leather pouch would do the job. I'd sling it over my back with the handle just above my shoulder. That way I could grab the handle quickly. I can see it in my mind. I'm sure it'll work."

Thamus clambers to his feet, using your shoulder for support. "Hmmm … I wonder what hunt master Zenan would think of your design."

"Good question."

But do you want to talk to a hunt master before you've had a chance to try out your idea?

You'll need thorns, of course. Or maybe Thamus is right. What should you do?

It is time to make a decision. Do you:

Go and collect thorns from the nearest thorn bush to test out your idea? **P137**

Or

Go and tell Zenan the hunt master about the idea and see what he thinks? **P130**

Go and collect thorns from the nearest thorn bush

The best way to test your design is to construct a thorn thrower. To do that, you'll need to go above ground and find the nearest thorn bush. And that means going back onto the grassland.

It's too late in the day to join up with another hunting party, and you're too excited to get started to leave it until tomorrow, so you only have one option. If you want to get the thorns today, you'll have to go outside the cave on your own.

Thorn bushes are common on the grassland, so you won't need to go far. What could go wrong?

After a quick trip to your sleeping quarters, you grab your spear and head back up to the great chamber. You walk purposefully towards the gate.

"Where do you think you're going?" a large gate guard asks.

"The cook wants some mintwort."

"What? You're picking it by yourself?"

"I saw some nearby when we came back from hunting. I wish I hadn't mentioned it now."

"Well, be careful," a second guard says as he swings back the gate. "You don't want to run into those shredders again."

"Not wrong there," you say. "Let the cook know he'll have to get his own mintwort if I'm not back before sunset."

The smaller guard smiles and nods towards the open gate. "May you never thirst."

After stepping through the foliage hiding the mouth of the cave, you look down through the trees towards the grassland. No dangers in sight.

138

You take a deep breath and start walking. This is the first time you've been outside the stronghold on your own, and the idea sends shivers down your spine despite the heat. "No shredders and you'll be fine," you tell yourself. "Just keep your eyes and ears open."

On the way down the slope, you stop at regular intervals to cup a hand around your ear and listen for the distinctive zegar *yip* and to scan the sky for shredders. So far so good. The air is clear, and you can see the towering escarpment running off to your right, forming the eastern border of the vast grasslands.

Once on the flat, thorn bushes are plentiful. Nearby is a particularly large specimen, so you start plucking thorns off its lower branches. It's important not to jab yourself. The needles sting like crazy. Break one off under your skin and your whole hand will go red and swell up. Once picked, you lay the thorns on a scrap of leather. This you'll roll up for safe transport back to the stronghold.

It doesn't take long before you have a bundle of thorns neatly folded into a pocket of your robe. Time to get back to the stronghold.

About half way back to the cave, you spot a bright green patch. It's mintwort. Intending to grab a few handfuls so the guards don't get suspicious, you veer off the path. You've been above ground long enough. Every moment that passes puts you at risk.

As you pick handfuls of mintwort, there is a crunch of dried leaves behind you. You spin around and search the shadows for danger. A twig snaps. You drop the mintwort, clutch your spear with one hand and pull your knife from its sheath with the other.

A patch of brown and black circles around behind you. It's a mid-sized zegar.

There is another rustle behind you. More zegar.

Yip, yip. A signal from the pack leader.

When you hear replies from both sides, you understand the zegar have been stalking you.

Another twig snaps. It's closer this time.

You spin around. "Yahhhhhhhh! Get out of here!"

But the zegar are close now. Bolder. The pack leader steps out from behind a tree and stares at you. It licks its lips. Yellow eyes bore into you. *Yip, yip!*

There are too many to fight on your own. The alpha zegar growls and runs at you. You turn to flee, but there are zegar all around you.

Yip, yip, yip!

Sorry, but this part of your story is over. Unfortunately, you've left the stronghold on your own and run into trouble. If you were closer to the cave, you might have been able to make a run for it. But in the end, an apprentice is no match for a hungry pack of zegar.

Lucky for you, this is a *You Say Which Way* adventure and you still have options.

You have three choices. Do you:

Go back and make that last decision again? **P130**

Or

Go back to the beginning of the story and read a different track? **P98**

Or

Go to the big list of choices and pick another chapter to read? **P365**

140

Help Rooth

Most of the pack descends on the meat Rooth has dropped, their sharp teeth ripping into the tough skin to get to the juicy meat beneath. But the alpha zegar and three others keep coming, not satisfied with her sacrifice. They are a big pack. One leg won't go far.

Without thinking, you race back to Rooth, slipping off the leather straps holding the leg of vootbeest on your back as you run.

You must act fast. Rooth is struggling, clutching her ribs as she tries to escape. The zegar will be upon her at any moment.

After flinging your load towards the fast-approaching animals, you grab Rooth's hand and pull her along despite her grunts of protest.

The leg skids to a halt in the dust at the zegars' feet.

Yip! Yip! barks the alpha zegar. She has what she wants now.

You help Rooth towards the other hunters, and at the same time keep an eye on the pack. The alpha zegar gives you one last look, and then rips into the fresh meat.

By the time you and Rooth catch up to the main hunting party, they are nearly back at the cave.

"Why didn't you stop and help us?" you ask Manaria.

The hunt master smiles. "Because you are strong, and I knew you would cope with the situation."

Your eyes narrow. "But what if you were wrong? What if we were taken by the zegar?"

"Then the tribe would have two fewer mouths to feed."

"But …"

Manaria and her spear bearers laugh as they trot off towards the entrance of the cave.

You turn to Rooth. "Why are they laughing? You nearly got eaten."

"She only likes the apprentices when they make her look good," Rooth says, shaking her head. "She's not half the leader hunt master Zenan is."

It isn't long before the two of you enter the cave to find Manaria standing on a slab of stone in the great chamber. Around her, the crowd cheers as she holds the mighty vootbeest's horns aloft. Cooks have already taken the meat to an area beside the fireplace and are slicing it into shares. Some of it will be dried and distributed amongst the families. The remainder will be roasted immediately and eaten by everyone in a communal feast.

"The herds have arrived!" shouts Manaria. "Our bellies will no longer ache with hunger."

"Voot! Voot! Voot!" shouts the gathering.

You don't feel like cheering. Manaria doesn't care about her fellow tribespeople. She's just after more bloodstone beads and the adulation of the crowd. And to think you used to look up to her. Maybe you should tell the crowd how she left Rooth at the mercy of the zegar.

But do you want to cross her? Maybe you should just enjoy the feast.

Besides, Manaria is powerful and has many allies. But how would you feel if your silence resulted in the death of some poor apprentice in the future?

It is time to make a decision. Do you:

Stand up and complain about the hunt master? **P220**

Or

Enjoy the feast? **P245**

Keep running and let Rooth fend for herself

You're not proud of yourself for leaving Rooth to the mercy of the zegar, but the pack is too close to risk going back to help.

Ahead of you, Manaria and her crew are pulling further away. The weight of the vootbeest on your back is too heavy for you to keep up with them.

When you look back to see how Rooth is going, you see she is on her feet, preparing to throw her spear at the fast-approaching pack. Her only hope is to kill the pack leader. Unless she can shock the pack in some way, she has no chance.

Rooth takes aim and throws.

Thankfully, her spear hits its target. The pack leader cartwheels and skids to a stop. Rooth starts moving again, still clutching her side and limping. But at least she's left the zegar in confusion. For the moment, anyway.

You glance back as you jog, watching Rooth's drama over your shoulder. You never see the havera burrow ahead of you.

Your leg sinks to mid-shin, bringing you to a sudden stop. Momentum throws your upper body forward.

Crack! Woomph!

As you hit the ground, red-hot pain shoots up your leg from the break. "Arggggh!"

Rooth looks down at you with sad eyes. "Sorry, you're too heavy to carry," she says as she trots past.

A large male zegar nips the hindquarters of its slightly smaller rival. The rival yelps and cowers down on its haunches. It didn't take long. The pack has a new leader.

Yip, yip, yip.

You try to pull your leg from the burrow, but the pain is too great.

The new pack leader's eyes lock with yours.

Yip, yip!

I'm sorry, but this part of your adventure is over. Unfortunately, everyone has left you behind and the zegar are going to have you for lunch. Would things have worked out differently if you'd gone back to help Rooth? Possibly. Lucky for you this is a *You Say Which Way* adventure and you can go back and make different choices.

It is time to make a decision. You have three choices. Do you:

Go back, choose differently, and decide to help Rooth fight off the zegar? **P140**

Or

Go to the big list of choices and read a different part of the story? **P365**

Or

Go back to the beginning of the story and start over? **P98**

Agree to travel home with the girl

Agreeing to trek back to the stronghold with the girl seems your best option. Who knows what dangers you'll face if you live amongst these strangers during the migration. From what you've heard, they're always moving from place to place. Besides, imagine the look on everyone's face when you arrive home riding a zeebok!

You also wonder what's happened to Zenan. Was he captured or did he die in the fighting? Maybe news of another tribe nearby will ease the tension between the hunters and the water guardians.

Your agreement to go with Lona has everyone in the settlement excited. This nomadic band hasn't had contact with another tribe for many seasons. Drought has made traveling hard, and grazing for their herd of zeeboks is scarce.

"I've never heard of the name Lona," you say to the girl. "What does it mean?"

She points to the pale pink moon hanging in the sky. "It means light in the sky. What do they call you?"

"Apprentice. It means one who studies to do something. But when I become an adult, and have done something worthy, the elders will give me a new name."

"Maybe they'll call you Zeebok Rider?"

You smile. "It's possible. I'll be the first rider in my tribe. When will we leave for my home?"

"We can spend tomorrow getting ready and then leave at first light the day after. I'll need to teach you how to ride first. Lucky for you, it's not very hard." She grins. "Unless you'd prefer to walk?"

"No, no. Riding looks like fun. As long as I can sit upright."

"Of course!" She laughs. "I'll gather some items to trade while you practice. No point in turning up empty-handed."

"Good idea."

"But now it's nearly dark. We should sleep." Lona points to a narrow opening in the cliff face. "Sleep in that cave. It's small, but it'll protect you during the night. Just pull up the ladder once you're inside and the zegar won't be able to sneak up on you."

The next morning, your aches and pains are almost gone. You look forward to your first riding lesson. You lower the ladder, climb down, and walk over to where skewers of havera roast over a bed of coals. The cook tosses handfuls of yonobo leaves on the fire to give the meat a smoky flavor.

Lona sees that you're up and grabs some meat for the two of you.

You sit on a rock and admire the zeeboks in their pen. "So tell me, Lona, how do you capture these zeeboks?"

She swallows a piece of meat. "Sometimes we ride out and encircle them with rope, other times they are drawn to the spring late in the dry season. It's one of the few places where they can be sure of a drink."

"Does it ever run dry?"

Lona shakes her head. "Not that I remember. Sometimes, before we go travelling, our trappers build temporary walls of branches that funnel the zeeboks into the valley but make it hard for them to get out. We caught many zeeboks last season. There was much singing and feasting."

"So where do you go when your tribe isn't catching zeeboks?"

"There is a high valley on the escarpment with a lake and a wonderful waterfall. There are many crackleberries and a cave where we can live in safety. The shredders never fly that high and the path into the valley is easily defended."

"I've heard stories told about crackleberries, but have never tasted one. I was beginning to think they were just a myth."

Lona smiles and reaches into her robe. She pulls out a small slice of something deep purple in color. "Taste this," she says.

You take the slice and pop it into your mouth. For a moment, there is not much flavor. But as it softens, a burst of sweetness explodes in your mouth. "Oh yum!"

Lona's eyes sparkle. "Is that a myth?"

The intense flavor of the crackleberry is like nothing you've ever experienced. Your eyes close and you feel like you're about to float off the ground. Finally, after the last of the fruit has dissolved, you open your eyes and look at Lona. "I don't suppose you have any of those to trade, do you?"

"Maybe," Lona says with a grin. "Do you think your people might like some?"

"Would they ever!" you say. "They would insist you become prime guardian if you had enough of these."

"Guardian?" Lona asks. "What is a guardian?"

"The guardians are the ones who look after the *Well of Tears*. They say how much water everyone can have and make most of the rules."

Lona looks confused. "Like tribal leaders, you mean?"

This makes you think for a moment. "I—I suppose so."

"And that is why you ran away, because of these guardians?"

"There was a conflict with some of the hunters who wanted more water. The prime guardian got angry and ordered them killed."

Lona frowns. "Doesn't everyone get an equal say in what happens?"

"That's what Zenan, one of our hunt masters, was saying. That the guardians should be servants of the tribe, not its rulers."

"Well," Lona says, "it sounds like our trip is going to be an interesting one. I hope the guardians will forgive you. I'd hate for you to be killed."

"How could they kill a rider of zeeboks and a bearer of crackleberries?" you say, trying to sound confident. "Returning with such treasures, I am hoping to be awarded many bloodstone beads."

"Bloodstone?" Lona says. "What is bloodstone?"

You pull the thin leather thong from around your neck and show her the polished red stone in the shape of a teardrop. "This is bloodstone. The more beads you have, the higher your status. I only have one bead at the moment, but I plan on earning many more."

"Status?" she asks. "You mean some people are worth more than others?"

"Well, not worth more, it's—it's more like you're given a little more food and water. And you get to sleep further down in the stronghold where the air is less smoky."

"And the tribe allows this?" Lona asks. "Isn't everyone worthy of clean air?"

Lona is asking you things you've never really considered.

"The stronghold has always been this way," you say. "Everyone wants more beads. Some get them and others don't. The stories tell us that is the way. It has always been so."

Lona's questions have made you a little uncomfortable. You need to think.

"Hey, when am I going to get this riding lesson?" you ask, changing the subject.

"If you're ready, we can start now. But first, we should weave you some protection for your head. If you have another fall so soon, you might not get up."

Lona takes you to a pile of vines, grabs a long length and measures around your head. "I will make you a head protector out of this vine so you don't get hurt. It will only take a few moments."

But you are really keen to get riding. "I didn't see the others using head protectors."

"No, but they're experienced riders."

"How hard can sitting on the back of a zeebok be?"

Lona shrugs. "Well, I can't force you to wear one. It's up to you."

It is time to make a decision. You really want to get riding. You only have one day to get good enough to impress your tribespeople. But then you did take quite a fall from the cliff. Maybe Lona is right.

It is time to make a decision. Do you:

Wait and let Lona make you a head protector? **P165**

Or

Forget about the head protector and go riding right now? **P178**

Stay with the strangers until after the migration

You think for a moment. "I'd like to stay with you. You have so much to teach me, and this knowledge would be of great help to my tribe."

Lona smiles. "Maybe you could capture and train your own zeebok while you're here."

"Could I?"

Lona nods. "We are going on a zeebok hunt tomorrow. Everyone who participates gets a share of the animals we catch. You, being the least experienced, will have last choice, and there's a chance we won't catch enough for you to have one at all, but if we do …"

Any chance of having your own zeebok is one worth taking. Imagine the look on everyone's face when you arrive back at the stronghold riding your own zeebok!

The next morning, the strangers gather around the pen where the zeeboks are held. Each member of the hunting party grabs an armful of vootgrass and hand feeds their animal.

"Feeding the animals creates a bond," Lona explains. "My zeebok especially likes crackleberries."

She pulls a few dried slices of the fruit from a pocket in her robe and holds it out for her zeebok. The animal snorts and eagerly slurps the purple slices off her hand.

Once the feeding is done, those participating in the hunt climb aboard their zeeboks and prepare to move out. Those staying behind begin collecting vootgrass and making repairs to the pen.

Lona signals her zeebok to kneel. "Get on," she says. "You don't have a zeebok yet, so you'll have to ride with me."

Sitting upright on a zeebok is much more comfortable than lying on your belly.

"Hold on to me until you get the hang of it," Lona tells you. "When the zeebok steps with its right legs, lean in the opposite direction so you don't slide off."

One of the youngsters opens a gate in the zeebok pen, and the caravan of fifteen riders takes off. You and Lona are at the back of the group.

It only takes a few moments for you to settle into a rhythm. Lean left, then right, left, right, left, right.

"I think I'm getting the hang of it," you say over Lona's shoulder. "This is fun."

Lona laughs. "Wait till we start running before you get overconfident."

Zeeboks cover the ground much faster than walking, so it isn't long before a herd of wild zeeboks is spotted in the distance. Their dusty coats have turned from white to a light reddish-brown that almost blends with the ground beneath them. It's only the dust cloud they leave in their wake that gives them away.

The hunter in charge brings his zeebok to a stop and issues instructions. Another member of the group brings out a long white rope made from braided zeebok hair. Each rider in turn grabs onto the rope at regular intervals. This keeps the rope off the ground as the riders move around the wild herd. The wild zeebok don't seem to notice that the zeeboks joining them have riders on their backs.

"Because zeeboks run by moving both legs on the same side at the same time, they can't jump much," Lona says. "If we don't spook them, they'll stay inside the rope."

"Wow, that's clever," you say.

Lona grabs hold of the rope as you pass. The makeshift pen is long enough to surround all of the zeeboks.

"Once we surround the zeeboks," Lona says, "we'll slowly move them in the direction of the canyon. Then we'll open one end of our rope and funnel them into the pen."

It all sounds so simple. But what of the other dangers on the grassland? "What about shredders and zegar?" you ask. "What happens if they attack?"

Lona chuckles. "Then you'd better hold on tight because a frightened zeebok can run like the wind!"

For most of the day, the group of wild zeeboks is gently guided towards the canyon. Meanwhile, you start making calculations. There are fifteen hunters but only fourteen zeeboks. That means you're going to miss out. You mention your disappointment to Lona.

Lona does a quick headcount. "Don't worry, you'll have other chances."

The escarpment fills more and more of the horizon as you near the canyon. It's only when out on the grassland that you get a real feeling for how high this natural boundary is. Far to the south is the stronghold. Further north, the escarpment disappears into a shimmering heat haze.

The transfer into the pen at the head of the canyon goes without incident. After eating some food, and as the light is fading, you climb into your little cave and pull the ladder up.

The next morning, as you walk towards the zeebok pen to watch the training begin, you get a surprise. Wobbling on its long slender legs next to its mother is a baby zeebok. Its skin glows pink through its sparse white fuzz.

Lona is feeding her zeebok. She waves you over. "Looks like you've got yourself a zeebok after all."

Your mouth drops. "You—you mean …?"

"Yes. The baby. The others have already chosen. That means the baby is yours."

You can't believe your luck. "Can I feed it now?"

Lona laughs. "No. Its mother will do that for the next moon. But soon."

You know zeeboks are quick growers, but how fast, you're not quite sure. "How long before I can ride it?"

Lona explains that by the end of the migration your zeebok will be big enough to ride.

"Then I can ride it home?"

"Yes."

The strangers don't give their zeeboks names. Maybe it's because they don't want to become too attached. When times are hard, these animals are also food, so you guess it makes sense. But you swear you'll never eat your zeebok and, in secret, you name him Cloud Runner for his fluffy white hair and endless energy.

As the migration progresses, between long days hunting vootbeest and havera, Lona teaches you everything you need to know about caring for Cloud Runner.

Before long, the baby zeebok shuns its mother's milk, preferring the vootgrass you hand feed it each morning. Occasionally you slip it a slice of crackleberry.

It's quite a thrill to have Cloud Runner rush over when he sees you. His rubbery lips tickle as he takes the vootgrass gently from your hands.

By the end of the migration, Cloud Runner is large enough for you to ride. He's not fully grown yet. But then neither are you, so it's a good match. You've been putting the strap around Cloud Runner's snout for quite some time and you've taught him to kneel on command.

"Today's the day," Lona says with a grin. "You ready?"

You've been riding other zeeboks for a while now. What could go wrong?

Cloud Runner kneels on command and allows you to climb onto his back. Once he's back on his feet, you take him for a quick circuit of the pen.

Lona seems pleased with your technique.

"Hey, Lona. How about a ride to the end of the canyon?"

She grins. "Okay. If you think you can stay on his back that far."

Cloud Runner may be smaller than Lona's zeebok, but he makes up for his size with his speed and stamina. You've become expert at swaying from side to side while gripping the zeebok with your knees.

It isn't until the two of you reach the mouth of the canyon that you see a dark cloud in the distance.

"Shredders!" Lona yells.

"Geebus! Let's get out of here."

The two of you whirl your zeeboks around and give them sharp taps with your heels. The animals sense the danger and accelerate to top speed in a matter of strides.

"The camp is too far," you yell. "We'll never make it!"

"I know a place!" she yells back. "Follow me!"

Lona rides low on the zeebok's back, her head almost lying on the beast's neck. You do the same, as Cloud Runner flies after the older zeebok.

Every once in a while, you glance over your shoulder at the approaching swarm.

Not far into the canyon, Lona pulls her zeebok to the right and has it running alongside the cliff. Then you see where she's going. There is an opening not far ahead.

The sound of flapping wings and high-pitched screeches fills the canyon behind you as Lona and her zeebok swerve into the cave's opening, followed closely by you and Cloud Runner.

Lona doesn't stop until the light from the cave's opening is a distant pinpoint.

Shredders can't see in the dark. And rarely do they enter caves. From the sounds of it, though, a couple have followed. Your blood runs cold as you hear their leathery wings scrape against the cave roof and a sound of screeching and snapping as they strike out blindly.

The zeeboks keep moving further into the cave system. Beneath you, Cloud Runner trembles as she follows Lona. Soon the sound of the shredders fades. They've given up the chase and rejoined their swarm.

Bringing Cloud Runner to a halt, you leap off his back and rush to where Lona is cowering under a low ledge along the cave's wall. She trembles like a yonobo leaf in a strong wind.

"We're safe," you say. "They've gone on towards the settlement." And then you understand why Lona is shaking. It's not fear for her life, but fear for the others.

"They'll see them coming and take shelter," you say. "I'm sure of it."

"But the zeeboks can't run. They're trapped in the pen." A tear runs down Lona's face.

Your heart goes out to the thirty or so zeeboks in the pen at the head of the valley. Then you turn and look at Cloud Runner, thankful he's safe at least.

As the two of you sit in the cave, the dot of light in the distance goes dark, and then some time later, as a new day is born, returns. The cave is quiet. Thankfully, you've managed to get some sleep.

Cloud Runner and Lona's zeebok are resting on their knees. Cloud Runner snorts and wobbles his lips. A sign he is hungry.

Lona's eyes are still closed, so you sit for a while, not wanting to disturb her. It is then that you hear what sounds like drumming coming from within the cave.

Boom, ba-boom, ba-boom.

It's very faint, but the more you listen, the more certain you are.

You shake Lona's shoulder. "Hey, wake up."

"Wa—what?"

"Can you hear drumming?"

She sits up straight and cups a hand around one ear. "No, silly, that's not drumming. That's the ancestors telling us trouble is coming."

"The ancestors? How do you know that?"

Lona shrugs. "Pappie told me. He says that thunder coming from inside the earth is a sign."

You think about this for a moment. "Do you know how far this cave goes?"

She shakes her head. "We've been told the cave is home to the ancestors, and not to go past the first narrows. Others tried but never returned."

"How long ago?"

"Many, many generations ago."

"Hmmm …" you say, sounding a bit like your friend Thamus.

"We should go and see how many of the others survived," Lona says. "The shredders will be gone by now."

"Okay." You go over and climb on Cloud Runner's back. "Up you get, boy."

When you reach the settlement, all is normal. Zeeboks munch vootgrass, while others cook and dry meat for the winter. Children run around pretending to hunt each other.

When Lona's pappie sees her, he comes running over. "You're safe! I thought you must have been taken by the swarm."

"How did you survive?" she asks.

Her father smiles. "We saw them way down the canyon, but as we ran for the caves, they veered off and went south. They must have smelled blood."

Two days later, you revisit the cave where you heard the drumming. This time it's just you and Cloud Runner. It's early in the morning, about the time the water ceremony would be starting in the stronghold. You ride into the cave until the entrance is a pinpoint of light and dismount. You tie Cloud Runner's strap to a rock, and walk further into the cave.

Before long, you are in complete darkness. You take your sparker stones and light the torch you brought, and then walk some more.

The 'narrows' are two massive stalactites that hang from the roof of the cave like the teeth of some massive beast. The tunnel beyond looks like the monster's throat.

Boom, ba-boom, ba-boom.

There it is again.

Ahoooooooooooo!

Longhorns! Now you know this cave links with the stronghold! You can't wait to tell Lona.

Back at the settlement, you take Lona aside and tell her of your discovery. She is skeptical, yet excited at the prospect of a possible link between your home and her canyon. After a long discussion, the elders agree to let the two of you go exploring and see where the cave goes.

Lona fills a bag with torches, food and water, and the two of you climb onto Cloud Runner's back and head towards the cave. Your zeebok grows stronger every day and carrying the two of you is no problem. Lona's zeebok is left behind because it is so much taller and you're afraid its head will hit the roof in some areas.

Apart from having to dismount to get through the narrows, the two of you are able to ride most of the way. With torches to light your way, finding a clear passage is easy and you make good progress.

At one point, you stop to collect a pocketful of bloodstone pebbles that have washed down an old watercourse.

After a long ride, the cave finally ends in a passage too narrow to ride through. But you are so close now you can hear noises coming from the stronghold.

After a brief search, you find another passage that exits onto the escarpment. It's been overgrown by a huge patch of mintwort, so it's no wonder nobody's spotted it before.

The two of you ride the last bit to the stronghold's entrance.

To say the guards at the gate are surprised to see you would be an understatement.

"By the waters!" one of them says. "It's the apprentice riding a zeebok!"

Congratulations, you have reached the end of this part of the story.

You have survived the migration with the strangers, tamed your own zeebok, and most importantly found a safe route for your tribe to trade with the strangers from the canyon. You take the bloodstone pebbles you found and make yourself and Lona a necklace to rival those of the hunt masters, and even the water guardians are pleased to have you back.

The newly gained knowledge of how to capture and train zeeboks will increase your tribe's ability to hunt. This means more tender marrow for the guardians and more meat for the tribe. Oh, and everyone loves the crackleberries you've brought them. But still the choices go on.

158

It is time to make a decision. Do you:

Go back to the beginning and read a different track? **P98**

Or

Go to the big list of choices? **P365**

Stay seated and allow Zenan to be caged

Although a dozen hunters rush to Zenan's defense, the citadel guards have spears and outnumber the rebels two to one. Any sort of fight and the hunters will lose.

Thamus grabs your arm and whispers. "Did you know this was going to happen?"

You shake your head. "How would I know? I'm only an apprentice."

After a brief scuffle, the citadel guards force Zenan, and those that leapt to his defense, to drop their weapons. The guards secure the rebels' hands behind their backs and lead them out of the citadel.

The rest of the tribe sits in stunned silence. Most have friends or family amongst the rebels.

You lean towards Thamus. "What do you think will happen to them?"

His eyes narrow and he rubs his chin. "Hmmm … it won't be good. Did you see the prime guardian's face? It was so red I could almost feel the heat coming off him."

You can't stop thinking about your fellow hunters. "But isn't the punishment for rebellion starvation?" you ask. "Who will supply us with food if half the hunters are out of action? We'll all starve if nobody hunts during the migration."

Thamus nods. "Exactly. Nor can the guardians survive if they allow themselves to be challenged. The stories tell of many rebellions put down by the citadel guards. All I know is I wouldn't want to be Zenan right now."

Now the rebels are gone from the citadel, the prime guardian motions for the other guardians to sit. He then lifts his bloodstone crown and raises it high above his head. After a moment, he lowers the crown to his lips and kisses each piece of bloodstone in turn, rotating the crown as he does so, before replacing it on his head.

"This crown, given to me by the council of water guardians, signifies my right to make the final decisions on behalf of the tribe in all matters to do with water and its distribution. Without this rule, disputes over water would tear our settlement apart."

The other guardians nod in unison.

"Now that we have a dozen fewer tribespeople to water, today's ration will be a full skin."

A few halfhearted cheers run through the crowd, but many must be wondering how the tribe will gather enough meat to feed itself. The citadel guards may be big and strong, but hunters they are not. Most couldn't kill a vootbeest if it was tied to a yonobo tree.

There is a murmur of voices as people discuss what's just happened.

"This is crazy," you whisper. "What does the prime guardian think he's doing?"

Thamus shrugs. "Don't ask me, I'm just a storyteller."

"But don't the old stories tell of revolts? Is there nothing to be learned from the past?"

"Hmmm ..." Thamus looks up as if he's searching his memory. "There is a story about a hunter who wanted more water. He made a fuss during a water ceremony, and was caged for three sleeps. He was so dry by the end of it, he promised never to doubt the guardians again."

"And that was it?"

Thamus chuckles. "No, just the opposite. The hunter waited until he was strong again, then in the middle of the night, he snuck down to the lower levels of the pit, overpowered the guards, and killed the prime guardian as he slept, before fleeing the stronghold. The stories say he has been seen riding a zeebok, and still hunts on the grassland when both moons are full."

"Ha!" you laugh. "Riding a zeebok? Now there's a strange tale if ever I heard one."

"Who's to know? Some historians believe it. Stories say the hunter will return one day with an army of warriors, all riding zeeboks."

You can't help smiling. "Wouldn't that be a sight?"

Ba-boom! Ba-boom!

"Silence!" the prime guardian yells. "That's assuming you want your water rations today!"

Thamus turns to you just as the citadel goes silent and says, "What a dorf!"

His words ring out across the citadel. Everyone turns and stares at Thamus.

"I didn't mean …"

You glance towards the prime guardian, who stands red-faced and pointing directly at Thamus. "Seize him!"

Thankfully, all the citadel guards are escorting the rebels up to the great chamber where the cages are kept.

You grab Thamus' arm. "Run. Quick, before the guards return."

Thamus' run is more of a skip. But with you to support him, the two of you are out of the citadel before anyone has time to react.

As you scurry down the tunnel towards the pit, you hear a commotion behind you. A glance over your shoulder shows fighting in the citadel. Is someone aiding your escape?

"Where to?" you ask Thamus. "We can't go up to the great chamber, the guards will be there."

When you reach the pit, the two of you pause briefly. Then Thamus pulls you up the steps. "One level up is the chamber where we learn the stories. There's an unexplored passage running off it. We can hide in there."

You've nothing better to suggest. "Okay, let's go."

Thamus uses your shoulder for support. "Down here," he says, pulling you into a narrow tunnel. "The story room is at the end."

The tunnel is dark once you get away from the scant light filtering down the pit from above. You and Thamus navigate your way by touch.

"Here," Thamus says, grabbing your arm, and pulling you towards the back of the chamber. "Get on your belly, the opening is low and steep."

You feel for the opening. Thamus wasn't wrong about the entrance being low.

"Are you sure this is safe, Thamus?" you say, reaching in and feeling around.

"I never said it was safe, I just said it was unexplored."

"Geebus! Thamus, it's damp. Must be water seeping into it from somewhere. The rock is slicker than vootbeest snot."

Before you can discuss an alternative plan, the sound of heavy footsteps echo down the tunnel. And they're getting closer. You smell the smoke of torches.

"We have to go," Thamus says. "Either that or be caged."

Dare you risk entering this slippery passage? Maybe being locked in a cage for a few days is a better idea. At least you'll have the company of Zenan and his hunters. Surely, the hunt master will be able to figure a way out of this dilemma.

Quick, you are out of time. Do you:

Enter the slippery passage with Thamus? **P181**

Or

Don't risk the slippery passage? **P190**

Support Zenan

Having made your decision, you rush to stand with the other hunters who have come to Zenan's aid.

The guards, their spears leveled at Zenan, circle the group of hunters nervously. They weren't counting on Zenan having such support.

You draw your knife but don't think you could actually use it against one of your own tribe.

"Hold, hunters!" Zenan roars. "Guardians, if you want to turn this sacred place into a slaughterhouse, be my guest. I'd rather die right here than be dictated to by old men who've not seen the light of day since they were children—men who have their every need catered to by the tribe. Kill us, and who will bring you sweet marrow?"

There's doubt in the guards' eyes. Would they be capable of killing Zenan? And what about the vootbeest migration? The guards have families that need feeding too.

Ba-boom!

"You are not the only hunt master, Zenan," says the prime guardian. "Who are you to challenge the traditions?"

"Old does not mean true!" Zenan says. "Times change, old man. We too must change or we'll all perish."

Despite the cool of the citadel, your skin is covered in sweat. You shuffle from foot to foot awaiting Zenan's orders.

Zenan glares at the guardians. "You have not advanced the tribe. When was the last time our population grew? When was the last time we had enough spear bearers to travel and trade with other tribes? How many here have tasted the sweetness of a crackleberry? The stronghold grows stagnant. A couple of seasons without rain and we are finished! Time moves on, yet you remain the same."

The prime guardian's face changes from a pale alabaster to bright red in a flash. His eyes widen.

You expect smoke to burst from his ears at any moment. He raises a gnarled finger and points at Zenan. "Kill him! Kill them all!"

The citadel erupts with a clash of weapons.

"Fight!" Zenan yells.

The guards and hunters are unevenly matched. The guards have spears and the hunters only have knives. One after another the hunters fall. Zenan fights like a wild man.

"To the tunnel!" Zenan yells to his remaining forces.

You see an opportunity to dive between two combatants and make a break towards the pit. A spear flashes past and clangs against the wall. You snatch it up and run towards the staircase.

Three levels up you chance a glance behind you. Fighting echoes from below, but no other hunters have made it out of the citadel.

What now? Should you leave the stronghold? Would you even survive outside on your own? Perhaps you could hide somewhere inside the stronghold. Surely, Thamus would help you.

Whatever you decide, you'd better do it quickly because the guards will be after you soon.

There is no time to waste.

You must make a decision. Do you:

Run up the stairs and exit the stronghold? **P205**

Or

Duck into one of the many tunnels and hide in the stronghold? **P191**

Wait for head protection

It doesn't take long for Lona to weave you a solid basket. She places it on your head and secures it under your chin.

"Now if you fall off you won't get hurt so bad," Lona says. "We always wear these when we first learn to ride. Zeeboks can be skittish if they don't know you."

She leads the way to the zeebok pen, pulls a slice of something out of a pocket in her robe, and whistles sharply. A beautiful white zeebok comes rushing over.

"This is my zeebok. She loves the taste of crackleberry."

The zeebok nuzzles the girl's hand, finds the treat, and starts making funny sucking sounds.

Slurrrrp! Slurrrrp!

As the zeebok finishes its treat, Lona slips a loop over its snout and hands you the other end. "Hold this."

The zeebok kneels at Lona's signal. "Climb on, but be careful not to jerk the strap too hard. Zeeboks are happy to go where you lead them, as long as you do it gently."

As soon as you're on the zeebok's back, it stands up.

"Look, I'm riding!" you say.

Lona chuckles. "No, you're sitting. The riding part happens once the zeebok starts moving. Tap your heels lightly against the zeebok's rump and she'll start walking. Then, to turn, pull the strap gently in the direction you want to go. Another tap on her rump will make her speed up. Two soft tugs straight back to bring her to a halt."

"Okay," you say. "I think I've got it."

"Now remember, zeeboks step with both legs on the same side at the same time, so what you're going to feel is a side to side rocking motion. Just lean in the opposite direction so you don't fall off."

"Right." You give the zeebok a light tap with your heels and the animal lurches off. The sudden drop to your right almost has you slipping, but you counter the lean just in time and hang on with your knees.

"Now get ready to lean the other way!" Lona says.

This time you're ready for it. As the zeebok's right legs step forward, you lean left. Then as its left legs move forward, you lean right. Once you get the hang of the rhythm, it's easy.

"Now faster," Lona says.

Tap, tap.

After riding around in circles for a while, Lona climbs on behind you and really puts the animal through its paces.

She gets one of the children to open the gate and points the zeebok out of the enclosure.

"You ready?" she whispers into your ear.

Before you have a chance to say anything, she taps the zeebok's rump and the animal springs forward, increasing its pace.

As you ride towards the canyon's exit, you concentrate on shifting your weight at the right time. "Whoooooo hoooooo! This is fun!"

"See that big cave up there?" Lona says, pointing over your shoulder. "Guide the zeebok into there."

The cave is not far from the entrance to the narrow canyon. You gently pull the zeebok left, and get a surprise when the animal shows no hesitation going in.

"She knows this place," Lona says, anticipating your surprise.

"Where does it lead?"

"South, deep under the escarpment. It's my tribe's special place. I think you'll like it."

The floor of the tunnel slopes down slightly and goes on and on. The darkness doesn't worry Lona's zeebok.

Occasionally you feel your leg brush against the smooth walls of the tunnel, and give the strap the lightest of pulls, but for the most part the zeebok finds its way without help, despite the darkness.

When you're about to think this tunnel goes on forever, a speck of green light appears in the distance.

A short while later, one spot of light turns into four and an intricate wall of vootbeest horns comes into view. The hairy man with the bone belt you saw yesterday stands by the wall holding a spear. The green light is four glowing stalactites hanging from the ceiling.

"Amazing," you say. "What's causing the rock to glow?"

"I'll show you." Lona orders her zeebok to kneel, and the two of you climb off. She leads the animal into a small pen built along one side of the tunnel and slips another slice of crackleberry between its rubbery lips. Then she's back by your side. "Right, follow me."

The hairy man swings back a gate built into the wall of horns without saying a word, and the two of you walk through.

The tunnel continues in the same direction, but before Lona goes any further, she bends down and removes the lid of an ornate stone bowl sitting on the floor in the centre of the tunnel.

As Lona lifts the bowl's lid, the cave is bathed in green light.

"Wow," you say, looking at the contents of the bowl. "What is that stuff?"

"Liquid light."

"Amazing. Why didn't you use it around the camp last night?"

Lona shakes her head. "It can only be used down here where it's colder. Any closer to the surface, its power fades and dies. Grab a stick from that pile and dip it in," Lona says, nodding towards a stack lying next to the bowl. "No need for fire to see our way from now on."

You dip a stick into the bowl, and when you pull it out, it glows as brightly as any torch. "By the waters! This is a miracle!"

"No, not a miracle. If you look really closely, you'll see it's caused by a whole lot of tiny animals. The only place we've ever seen them is down here in this part of the cave. There are stories that they grow larger, but nobody's seen any recently."

"Won't the creatures run away?" you ask as you marvel at the glowing stick in your hand.

"After a while they will climb off the stick to search for food, but as long as we return them to the bowl or some other stone surface, they are quite happy to stay put."

You can see Lona smiling in the light.

"Follow me," she says. "It gets more difficult from here."

The tunnel narrows and turns. Patches of green light begin to appear on the ceiling of the tunnel. Then after working your way past a couple of minor rock falls, the tunnel opens out into a cavern filled with light.

Every surface—the roof, the hanging stalactites and stalagmites rising from the floor—all glow green. Even the floor glows.

Lona spins around. "So, what do you think?"

"I think it's amazing." Then you notice seating along one wall. "Do you hold ceremonies here?"

"Yes, this is where we sing to our ancestors."

"You sing? Your whole tribe?"

Lona nods. "Sometimes. We do it to ensure a good hunt."

Your mind is whirling. Is it possible that the singing your tribe hears is Lona's tribe singing? You do some calculations. You've come a long way into a cave that runs south under the escarpment. It's quite possible the sound of a large group singing would carry far enough for your tribe to hear it.

You start singing the song you've known all your life despite not knowing what the words mean. Three long low notes followed by a series of higher notes.

Lona is so startled you can see white all the way around her diluted pupils. "How—how is it possible that you know our sacred song?"

It takes a lot of convincing, but Lona finally believes your explanation—how the water guardians say the singing your tribe hears in the stronghold is your ancestors telling the tribe that the hunt will be good.

"My tribe is nomadic," Lona says. "We only travel this far south when the zeeboks are plentiful."

"And at other times?" you ask.

"We stay in a valley to the north and live on havera and dried food."

It all makes sense. During good seasons, Lona's tribe comes south and sings. And your tribe has a good hunt. It's no wonder the water guardians believe the singing is a portent to good hunting. It is! Just not for the reason they think.

Then you have a thought. "Hey, Lona, I have an idea that will ensure our trading mission is successful."

"What is that?"

"Do you think you could convince your people to sing a special song?"

Lona looks confused. "Special? How?"

The two of you sit on one of the stone benches in the green glow as you lay out your plan.

Later that day, after a long conversation with the settlement's elders, most of the tribe mount their zeeboks and ride back to the cave. After passing the wall of horns and walking to the glowing chamber, they take their seats along the stone benches.

After singing to their ancestors for a while, they start to sing a new song. One you wrote and taught them earlier. It's a simple tune, with a melody similar to their own, only this time they sing words you can understand.

It is a song that tells of the return of a young apprentice riding a zeebok, and how this young hunter is to be given much bloodstone, put in charge of all trade negotiations, and given the title of hunt master.

Congratulations, you have finished this part of the story. You've discovered one of the secrets of the singing cave, and used it to your advantage. But have you read all the other paths the story can take? The cave has many secrets. Maybe it's time to check the big list of choices for any paths you may have missed.

It is time to make a decision. Do you:

Go back to the beginning of the story and try a different path? **P98**

Or

Go to the big list of choices? **P365**

Flee the stronghold to find a new tribe

"I have to get out of here," you say. "Manaria is power mad. If she's still angry in the morning, who knows what she'll do to me. For all I know, she's planning to kill me during the night."

Thamus looks at you for a moment, then nods. "I hate to say it, but I think you're right."

Rooth hands you a bundle of dried vootbeest. "For your journey."

On tiptoes, the three of you approach the guards. Thamus and Rooth hold sleepwort flowers under their noses to keep them from waking up.

"Thanks for the help," you say as you pull the gate open. "Maybe I'll come back one day."

Both moons are high in the sky, and a pale pink light filters through the upper branches of the trees growing along the hillside.

You take a familiar path down a short distance, and then turn onto a well-worn track that sidles along under the towering cliffs.

The path leads to a riverbed that tumbles down to the grassland. It's dry at the moment, but many havera dig burrows there. Maybe there's one you can hide in until you decide what to do.

You've just started down the riverbed when a familiar sound in the distance sends shivers down your spine.

Yip, yip.

The zegar must be hunting havera in the moonlight. You stand still and listen. Their calls are getting closer. Thankfully, the wind is blowing across the slope and they haven't caught your scent. Otherwise, you'd be in real danger.

Time for a change of plans. There are caves in the cliffs. Maybe you can find one to shelter in before the zegar notice you.

The riverbed has many loose rocks to negotiate. You pick your way carefully up the steepening slope so as not to send any tumbling down and alert the zegar to your location.

Higher and higher, you climb. You scan the towering cliffs for a place to shelter.

Yip, yip, yip.

The zegar are closer, but their calls are not ones of excitement.

You're still safe.

The only problem is, you're running out of time. You're nearly at the base of the cliffs and you've not spotted somewhere to hide.

You're busy looking up, when you dislodge a rock.

Clack, clatter, clack, it tumbles down the hillside.

You freeze.

Yip! Yip! Yip!

Time is up. You have to move, and quickly!

Clambering up the riverbed, you no longer worry about how much noise you make. If you don't scale the cliff, the zegar will get you.

Then you see it. The spot where the water cascades down the cliff in the rains. The power of the water has worn away the rock and created a narrow slash that angles back into the rock.

You just hope you can climb it.

Yip! Yip! Yip! Yip!

The zegar smell you now. The sound of them scrambling up the riverbank is louder.

At first, the climb is easy with plenty of handholds. But the rock is worn smooth, and you're forced to spread your legs and place a foot either side of the gap to support yourself. With hands and feet pressing hard, you clamber up the narrow slot in the cliff.

Yip! Yip! Snarl! A zegar rushes at you, its paws scrabbling at the rock as it lunges for your legs.

You kick out, then scramble higher.

Another zegar has a run at you, but it too slides back.

You shimmy higher, jamming whatever body part into the gap that it takes to keep you from falling.

The pack waits eagerly for you to fall. Their yellow eyes glow in the dark.

You reach a point where you've climbed higher than the highest yonobo tree.

Beyond the canopy, the moonlit grassland stretches to the horizon.

Far to the north, a wisp of cloud hangs low in the sky, a sign of the coming rains.

A little higher, you reach a narrow ledge. Exhausted, you sit—arm and leg muscles burning, the skin on your knees and elbows grazed and sore.

The pack is far below now. With a final *yip,* the pack leader admits defeat, turns and heads back down in search of havera.

You watch the sunrise before climbing again. Seeing where you're going makes a big difference. At the top of the escarpment, you survey your world and wonder if you are the first to climb to such heights.

In the distance, a massive herd of vootbeests kicks up a cloud of dust. Further down the riverbed, the pack of zegar lie in the shade of a thorn bush, munching on havera. Zeeboks and other pastoral animals graze on vootgrass as they plod endlessly north.

174

But what now for you? There are so many choices. Maybe you should explore the lands beyond the escarpment. There looks to be rich grazing there.

Far to the north, a mountain range glistens in the morning sun. Towering peaks of napstone, shiny, black and formidable, make you wonder what tribes might live on those heights.

To the south, near the horizon, a moon hangs over a body of water that looks too large to be real. It is time to make a decision.

Which way do you go? There are so many places to visit. So many choices to make.

May you never thirst.

Congratulations, this part of your story is over. What would you like to do now? Have you read all the possible tracks? Have you solved the secret of the singing cave, or found the chamber of light? Have you ridden a zeebok, or met the strangers?

It's time to make another decision. Do you:

Go to the beginning of the story and read a different path? **P98**

Or

Go to the big list of choices to find parts of the story you've missed? **P365**

Go tell the prime guardian your side of the story

Having decided to tell the prime guardian what Manaria has done, you and Rooth leave Thamus and head deeper into the pit.

Only a few torches burn outside the stink holes so people can find their way in the night if they need to relieve themselves. Otherwise, the place is dark and quiet, except for the citadel, where two guards stand at either side of the entrance to the guardians' chambers.

"What do you two apprentices want?" one guard says. "It is past fires out. You should be sleeping."

You step forward. "We need to speak to the prime guardian about an urgent matter."

The guards exchange glances, and then burst into laughter.

"You expect to see the prime guardian now?"

They laugh again.

"Get back to your chambers or we'll lock you up. You know the rules."

You grit your teeth and clench your fists. "We need to see the prime—"

Rooth grabs your arm and pulls you away. "Shut up before you get us locked up. We'll see the prime guardian in the morning." She pulls you into the tunnel leading back to the pit. "And keep quiet. You'll wake up the whole stronghold."

"But this isn't fair!" you say. "I demand justice!"

You glare into Rooth's face, your hands defiantly on your waist.

But Rooth isn't looking back at you. She's looking over your shoulder towards the pit.

"I thought I heard you whining, apprentice," Manaria says. "Up so late for one so young."

176

"You're evil," you yell at the hunt master.

Manaria throws her head back and snorts. "I didn't become a hunt master by playing nice." She grabs your arm and drags you towards the pit. "I'll teach you to abuse me in the great chamber!"

"Run, Rooth!"

But it's too late. Two of Manaria's spear bearers have entered the tunnel. Rooth is trapped.

"Right," says Manaria, "to the stink holes with these apprentices. Throw them in."

Oh no, not the stink holes! Gross!

As Manaria and her spear bearers drag you and Rooth towards a very nasty end, you fight, scratch, and yell at the top of your voices.

The nearest stink hole is only a few steps away.

"What do you think you're doing, Manaria?" shouts Zenan. "Take your hands off those apprentices!"

Then you see Thamus. He must have followed you to the citadel and heard the commotion when Manaria arrived, and gone to fetch Zenan from the level above.

"By the waters," Rooth says. "I thought we were in the poo for sure."

But Manaria isn't one to back down. She pulls her knife out of its sheath and steps towards Zenan.

Zenan smiles and pulls a knife of his own. "If that's the way you want it, Manaria, I'm happy to have your bloodstone."

You've reached the end of this part of the story. In case you hadn't guessed, Zenan won the fight with Manaria. She lives, but is too injured to hunt again. Instead, she spends most of her time in an alcove on level four begging for food and water. Despite what she put you through, you often pass her a piece of vootbeest after a successful hunt.

177

So what now? Have you read all the different story tracks? Have you solved the mystery of the singing cave or ridden a zeebok?

Time to make another decision. Do you:

Go to the beginning of the story and read a different track? **P98**

Or

Go to the big list of choices and find parts of the story you've missed? **P365**

Go riding right now

"Okay," Lona says, shaking her head. "It's your choice."

"I'll be fine," you say. "I've been training to be a hunter. My balance is good."

You hear Lona mumble something as she walks towards the zeebok pen.

Behind the barricade, one of the strangers has a youngish-looking zeebok tied to the end of a long tether. He runs the zeebok around and around in a circle, speaking gently to it as he does so.

"Once you feed a zeebok, and they know you mean them no harm, they are quite friendly. The trick is giving them food and water for a few days before you attempt to ride them."

"And that's all?"

"You still have to get used to the way that they run. Both legs on the same side at the same time. It makes the rider sway from side to side, so you have to learn to lean in the opposite direction. If you get your timing wrong, you'll go flying."

"Yeah, I noticed that on the trip here. It made me feel queasy."

"Some people get so sick from the rocking that they can't ride for more than a few moments without ralphing."

"Ralphing?"

"You know." Lona pretends to stick her finger down her throat. "Raaaaalllllph!"

The two of you burst into laughter.

"Just remember to grip the zeebok's back with your knees, and gently tug the strap in the direction you want to go. Careful; if you tug too hard, the zeebok will buck you off."

Lona whistles sharply, and a pure white zeebok comes running over. She takes a thin slice of crackleberry and holds it up to the zeebok's snout.

The zeebok snorts as rubbery lips gently take the crackleberry out of her hand.

You chuckle as the zeebok makes funny sucking noises. "Oh, he likes that."

While the zeebok enjoys its treat, Lona takes a leather strap with a loop on one end and slips it over the zeebok's snout.

"Right," she says. "Are you ready for your first ride?"

"I—I think so."

"Okay," she says. "Get ready to jump on his back."

Lona pulls down on the leather strap, and the zeebok kneels. "Now."

You hop onto the zeebok's back and wait.

"Up!" commands Lona.

The zeebok rises.

"I'm doing it!" you say. "I'm riding!"

Lona chuckles. "No, you're just sitting. Here, take the strap. And remember gent—ly."

You grip the zeebok's back with your knees and pull the strap softly to the right.

As the zeebok starts walking, you start rocking. Walking, rocking, walking, and rocking. This is easy.

But a momentary lack of concentration has you leaning the wrong way. The zeebok takes another step and you're sliding off. "Whoooooaaaa!" you say, giving the strap a sharp jolt.

Before you know it, you're flying through the air. You throw out an arm as the ground rushes towards you, but your head hits a rock.

180

Oops! You might have survived the fall if you'd been wearing head protection. But because you were too eager to go riding, you didn't wait for Lona to make you some. Not the best decision you've made so far. Luckily, you're reading a *You Say Which Way* adventure, which gives you choices.

What do you want to do now? Do you:

Go back to your last decision and choose to have Lona make you some head protection? **P165**

Or

Go back to the beginning of the story and read a different track? **P98**

Or

Go to the big list of choices and pick another section to read? **P365**

Enter the slippery passage with Thamus

"Geebus!" you yell, sliding feet first into the darkness. "This passage is slicker than I thought."

It doesn't take long before you're gaining speed.

"Wheeeeeeeeeeeeeeeee …" Thamus yells behind you.

You relax your knees. Nothing worse than coming to a sudden stop with locked knees—sure-fire way to break something. Then you think of poor Thamus behind you, his damaged knee locked permanently in place. Oh well, at least he'll have you to cushion his stop.

It's easy to tell you're sliding down a natural watercourse because the stone is so smooth. You just hope it doesn't end badly.

Sliding in the dark is nerve-wracking, but before long, you feel the slope flattening out and your speed decreasing.

Sploosh. You skid to a stop in a puddle of water.

Sploosh. Thamus skids into the back of you. "Hmmm … that was fun," he says.

"Are you crazy?" you laugh, happy to be alive. "So what now?"

The darkness is total. You find Thamus' arm and help him to his feet. Then you squeeze some of the water from your robe. "Brrrrr …"

"Where do you reckon we are?" Thamus asks.

You make a mental map of the stronghold and try to imagine where the slide has taken you. "We were on level seven when we started. We've dropped another three levels at least."

"Hmmm … so that puts us on the same level as the *Well of Tears,* then."

"It's possible," you say. "Now we just need to find a way out."

Exploring blind isn't much fun. For one thing, it's easy to crack your head on stalactites hanging from the roof. Or, if you're really unlucky, step into a sinkhole like Thamus did when he injured his knee.

In these situations, you've found it's best to hold one arm up in front of your face, while feeling around with the other. Saves a lot of headaches and broken noses that way.

"There's no echo," Thamus says. "This chamber must be pretty small. Let's hope it goes somewhere."

Thamus is right. The chamber is small. It only takes you a short time to find a narrow passage running off it. Thankfully, it doesn't take you further underground.

Progress is slow in the dark. Every step must be tested. In some places, the passage narrows so much it's an effort to squeeze through. At other times, you're on your belly wriggling along the ground using elbows and toes.

You've been at it a while when the two of you decide to have a break. You sit with backs against the wall and munch on some dried vootbeest Thamus had in the pocket of his robe.

"Did you hear that?" Thamus says.

"Singing?"

"No. I think it's a bucket boy."

You stop chewing and listen. Then you hear it too. First, a distant splash—then the sound of water dripping followed by the faint grunt of someone straining at the ropes.

Your mood lifts. "I hear it. It's a bucket boy, all right."

But then Thamus brings the mood down again. "Hmmm … but bucket boys work for the guardians. If they know we're down here, won't they blab?"

Thamus has a point. The bucket boys are novice water guardians, after all. Each hopes to sit on the council one day. Some of them would give you away in a heartbeat if they thought it would advance their prospects.

"Let's wait until they stop drawing water," you say. "The ropes are tied to a log at the top so they don't fall in the well. We can climb up unseen once they've gone."

"What if they leave the buckets up top when they go?"

You hadn't thought of that, but you don't want Thamus to worry. "Then we'll figure something out. Don't worry, we'll be fine."

A bit further on, you find the *Well of Tears*. Light flickers down a long shaft from a chamber above, illuminating a rocky ledge around a deep pool of inky-black water.

Splash. A bucket lands in the pool and sinks. Water drips as slack in the rope is taken up and the bucket begins its rise to the chamber above.

"Hmmm … so what now?" Thamus asks.

"Shhh … They might hear us."

After a dozen or more buckets are drawn from the *Well of Tears*, the bucket plops down one last time, but this time nobody pulls it up.

"Phew!" you say. "I was worried we'd be stuck down here."

"I thought you said we'd be fine?"

Instead of commenting further, you lie on your belly and reach for the rope. Once you have a grip of it you give it a tug to test how strong it is. "Should be okay."

"Are you going to climb up?" Thamus asks.

"Let's wait a while longer to make sure they've gone."

The two of you sit by the well and listen for sounds from above.

Thamus stares at the water, his fingers making ripples in its reflective surface. "Does this well seem full to you?"

You study the water level. "It certainly looks full."

"Do you see any watermarks higher up the wall?"

Then you understand what he's saying. The well is as full as it can be, because any excess water would run down the passage you've just come through.

You scan Thamus' face as the horrible truth dawns on you. "So what you're saying is the water guardians are only saying the well is low?"

Thamus nods. "You have another explanation?"

"So they're telling us water is short, so that when they give us just enough, we're grateful and see them as good guardians of the well?"

"Hmmm … and to keep us under their control."

"Plonkers!" you say. "And this has been going on …"

"… forever?" says Thamus with a shrug.

You let it sink in. "Wait till the others hear about this."

"Let's get out of here first," Thamus cautions. "We can exact our revenge later."

When neither of you have heard any movements in the chamber above for a while, you stand up.

"Time to make a move. I'll climb up first," you say. "When it's your turn, I'll help pull you up. If you get tired, you can sit on the bucket and rest your leg."

"Good idea," Thamus says.

The well's shaft is narrow. But in one way, that makes it easier. When your arms get tired climbing, you rest by bracing your legs on one side of the shaft, and your back against the other.

It isn't long before you're at the top looking down. "You ready, Thamus?"

As Thamus climbs, you keep the rope tight by looping it around the log. That way when he gets tired, he can sit on the bucket and rest.

Thamus is about half way up the well shaft when you hear footsteps behind you.

"What are you doing?"

You spin around and see Breven, one of the bucket boys. He's about your age and wearing a white robe. You've know him since you were young.

"I'm trying to get my friend up the well," you say, hoping that by acting casually the boy won't wonder why.

Breven walks over to the well and peers down. "That's Thamus, isn't it? He's the one who called the prime guardian names."

"He didn't mean it," you say. "He wasn't thinking."

"Don't worry," Breven says. "I won't blab. I like Thamus. He tells the best stories."

"I don't suppose you could help me pull him up?" you ask.

Without another word, Breven grabs the rope. With the two of you working together, Thamus rises to the top of the well quickly.

"Thanks," Thamus says. "I'm pooped. I don't think I would have made it."

"That's okay," Breven says. "Would you like me to show you a way to the pit without being seen by the citadel guards?"

"Sure," you say. "But why would you put yourself at such risk?"

Breven looks like he's about to cry. "The water guardians treat us badly—like slaves. And then there's the matter of the well. I'm guessing you saw that it was full."

You and Thamus nod.

"Why do the guardians lie to us?" you ask.

"They're afraid that if everyone knew there is plenty of water in the well, they would serve no purpose, and their privileged lives would end. They have lived deep in the stronghold so long, change scares them."

"But aren't you a novice training to be one of them?" Thamus asks.

A tear runs down Breven's cheek. "Yes, but I hate it here and it's against the rules to leave. If we try, they'll order the guards to put us in a cage and leave us to rot."

"Geebus," you say. "That's terrible."

Breven sniffs a couple of times, then looks a little embarrassed and faces away. "Come this way," he says. "We don't have much time. The others will be back soon. The prime guardian wants us to draw him a bath."

"A bath?" you ask as you follow him up a sloping tunnel leading to the next level. "What is that?"

When the boy tells you how the guardians soak in precious water to clean themselves and then throw the water away afterwards, you're shocked. "Geebus! We don't even get enough to drink. Wait until everyone hears about this."

At the top of the tunnel, Breven escorts you to a set of steps cut into the rock. The steps are narrow and steep. They lead up to the citadel, entering the large chamber behind the platform where the guardians normally sit during the water ceremonies.

"Quiet," the boy says, ducking behind a stalagmite. "There are two guards on duty by the entrance to the guardians' chambers. They're usually half asleep, so if we walk quietly, we can sneak out without them noticing."

The three of you cross the floor of the citadel as quietly as a breeze and make your way into the tunnel that leads back to the pit's staircase.

"I'll leave you here," Breven whispers.

"Don't you want to come?" you ask. "You're a part of this too."

He shakes his head. "Go and tell the others about the well. In the meantime, if the guardians discover I'm missing, they'll call out the guard, and you'll be caught. Besides, the other boys will be afraid if I leave them too long. I'm the oldest and try to look after them."

You and Thamus thank Breven once more before climbing the steps to level four, where most of the hunters have their chambers. There are two tunnels leading off level four.

Thamus points down one of them. "Let's split up so we can tell as many hunters as possible what the guardians are doing. I'll go this way. Afterward, we can meet in the great chamber and overpower the citadel guards who are watching Zenan and the others."

Hunter after hunter is roused from their quarters and told the disturbing news.

The citadel guards watching Zenan are not hunters. Because of this, they never suspect the ambush that is about to befall them. Hunters have been setting ambushes for as long as your tribe has existed. And with practice comes perfection.

Filtering into the great chamber in ones and twos, the hunters blend with the others going about their normal business. By the time the ambush is sprung, the guards have no chance.

Zenan and his fellow rebels are released without the need for bloodshed, and the surprised guards are put into the cages in their place.

"Well done for spreading the word," Zenan says. "The story you tell is a shock, but if we don't change things now, our tribe will continue its decline."

There is much discussion before heading back down the pit to confront the water guardians. To your surprise, most of the citadel guards are just as shocked as you are by what's been discovered. They've been lied to as well. Only the guardians and the bucket boys know the truth.

"Remember, the bucket boys didn't have a choice," you say. "They want their freedom too."

The citadel guards plead to be included in the revolt.

Zenan takes a vote and the guards are finally released from the cages. After all, everyone is related here in the stronghold. And until now, being a citadel guard was considered an honorable profession.

Footsteps echo around the pit as Zenan and his supporters descend the staircase. News spreads fast and others join the hunters as they make their way to the citadel.

The two standing guard by the entrance to the guardians' chambers get quite a shock at the number of angry tribespeople.

"Halt," one guard says, lifting his spear to waist level and pointing it at the crowd. "Where do you think you're going?"

Zenan is a true leader. He sees that the situation calls for calm, not violence. Rather than barge through the guards with his superior forces, he explains to the citadel guards why everyone is here. As Zenan talks, the spears gradually lower. By the time Zenan has finished his explanation, tears of anger and betrayal run down the guards' faces.

Zenan and six of his trusted spear bearers enter the tunnel leading to the guardians' chamber. A short while later, they return leading the thirteen water guardians and a dozen or so bucket boys back into the citadel.

Breven leads the bucket boys to the benches where many others have been waiting. The guardians are told to sit at their regular places.

The citadel guards now have their spears pointed towards the guardians.

"I never thought I'd see this," says Thamus.

Zenan stands at the front of the crowd, while everyone else takes a seat. He turns to face his people. "We have recently been told a disturbing story. One that most of you have heard second hand. Now I'd like you to hear it directly from those who were instrumental in bringing this important information to our attention. Come forward, please."

You, Thamus, and Breven walk to the front of the chamber. The crowd stomps their feet in appreciation.

"Who would like to speak on your behalf?" Zenan asks.

You look at Breven and then at Thamus. "Thamus, you're the storyteller. Why don't you do the honors?"

A smile creeps onto Thamus' face. This is his biggest audience yet.

A hush fills the citadel.

Then Thamus starts weaving a story that has everyone perched forward on the edge of their seats. They hang on his every word. He tells a tale of adventure, danger, and deception. A story that will be repeated over and over in the seasons to come. It is not a story that the tribe will be proud of, but it's one that needs telling, if only to make sure something similar never happens again.

Congratulations, this part of your story is over. The rule of the water guardians is over, and the residents of the stronghold look forward to a future where resources are shared equally. A future where the saying, "May you never thirst," really means something.

However, there are still decisions to make. Have you discovered the secret of the singing cave? Have you found the underground river? Ridden a zeebok?

What would you like to do now? Do you:

Go to the beginning and read a different path? **P98**

Or

Go to the big list of choices and check for parts of the story you've missed? **P365**

Don't risk the slippery passage, get captured instead

"It's too dangerous, Thamus."

"I'm sorry," Thamus says. "This is my fault."

You feel Thamus squeeze your arm, and then hear him crawl towards the passage.

"What are you doing?"

"I'm not going to surrender. This can't be the end of the story."

Stomp, stomp, stomp.

When you see the look on Thamus' face, you know you have to take a chance, if not for your own sake, but for his.

"Okay," you say. "Let's do it! I'll go first."

Enter the passage before the guards arrive. **P181**

Hide in the stronghold

Much of your childhood was spent exploring the stronghold's labyrinth of tunnels, hiding from friends, and playing games in the dark. Together, you and your friend Thamus found many passages that you never had a chance to explore. It was on one of these adventures that Thamus fell into a sinkhole and injured his knee.

Maybe one of those unexplored tunnels will provide a hiding place. Who knows where they might go? Surely, the citadel guards would never find you there.

But what will you do for food and water? A quarter-skin of water and a pocket full of dried vootbeest won't last long.

At pit level three, you duck down the tunnel towards your sleeping chamber. You don't have much time before the guards come searching for you. You grab a torch and sparker stones for making fire. These are wrapped in a spare robe, tied into a bundle and slung over your shoulder.

The sound of footsteps echo in the stairs of the pit, and they're getting louder. The guards are coming.

Outside your chamber, you turn left, away from the staircase. It is too dark to see, but your fingers slide along the wall and read the symbols as you pass other chambers. When you feel three dots, you enter a short tunnel. This passage leads to a small natural cavern, one that has formed by groundwater seeping through the stronghold during the rains, season after season. You know there are unexplored passages running off this chamber from when you played here as a child. Hopefully, one of them will provide you with a hiding place. Then, once the citadel guards stop searching, you can explore further and see if you can find an alternative exit to the outside world.

192

You can't afford to light a torch. The guards will smell smoke or see the light, so you try to picture the cavern from memory. A vague image pops into your mind.

Using your left hand as a guide, you move along the wall to where you recall there being an old watercourse sloping away from the floor of the chamber. It looked promising back when you and Thamus first saw it. Tunnels formed by water often are. Water has to go somewhere, and with the local rock being porous, over time the stone leeches away leaving pipes, passageways, and even large chambers like this one where once there was only stone.

You and Thamus always planned to explore it further, but then Thamus injured his knee and that was the end of that.

Clomp, clomp, clomp.

The guard's footsteps are close. You need cover … and soon. Where is that tunnel? Your hand flies over the wall, feeling for an opening.

Then you find it. The opening is only waist high and just wide enough for you and your bundle to squeeze through. The walls are smooth. An old watercourse for sure. More importantly, smooth walls means you don't need to worry about snags.

On hands and knees, you crawl along, one hand sliding the spear as you go.

The tunnel slopes down for a while, veers left, then right. Water always finds the easiest track, the softest stone to wear away.

You hope the tunnel will open out into another chamber and not narrow further so you have to crawl back up backwards.

After crawling for a while, you stop and cup a hand around one ear.

Voices echo from above, but the words are muffled. As you listen, the footsteps get louder. The guards have entered the chamber.

You freeze.

"Look!" a guard yells. "Footsteps in the dust!"

Of course, the cavern hasn't been entered for ages. And the guards will be carrying torches. That's why it's got three dots carved by its entrance. They mean danger, no entry.

"Here," the guard says. "Down here."

More footsteps. A murmur of voices.

"It's too small for me," another voice says.

Maybe you'll be okay after all. If the guards can't fit in the tunnel, they can't come after you.

You wait in silence. Then you hear grunts and a hollow scraping sound. What are the guards up to? A thud reverberates down the tunnel and then silence. What's going on? Then you realize what you've heard. They've heaved a big rock over the entrance! You're trapped.

Or are you?

It is time to make a decision.

What do you do? Do you:

Crawl back up the tunnel and try to move the rock? **P204**

Or

Keep going and hope you find another way out? **P207**

Go hunting with Zenan

As the drums sound for the morning's water ceremony, Zenan and his group of twelve spear bearers march up the stairs from their sleeping quarters on level five. It's an impressive sight. Many of the stronghold's residents have friends or family members amongst the group.

You've been up since first light making a leather pouch and sling for your thorn thrower. After its success against the slavers, you're eager to try it out in the field. A weapon that gives hunters extra time to reach cover during a shredder attack will save many lives. And, it is sure to earn you many bloodstone beads.

"Welcome, apprentice," Zenan says. "I hope we won't need your new contraption today, but if we do, I hope it works."

A few of the spear bearers chuckle nervously. Leaving the stronghold is always a risky business regardless of how strong your numbers. And with the increased numbers of shredders around, even the bravest hunter has good cause for concern.

The guards swing open the gate and a spear bearer steps outside to check the vicinity for danger.

"*Toooo-wit. Toooo-wit.*"

All clear.

"We head north today," Zenan says, "along the escarpment before going down onto the grassland. With shredders so plentiful this season, the longer we can stay under the canopy, the better."

Trekking the tracks of the escarpment is more difficult than walking on the grassland because of the slope of the ground and the many rocky outcrops to negotiate, but what Zenan says makes sense. There is no point exposing the group to a swarm if it can be avoided. You like going this way. The towering cliffs are beautiful and cast a cooling shade.

After descending briefly, Zenan turns north and leads the group along a narrow path. Views over the grassland are spectacular. It's a path you know well, one often used by collectors of mintwort and other herbs that grow under the canopy of the broad-leafed yanobo trees.

You pick a mintwort leaf as you pass, crush it in your hand, and lift it to your nose to inhale its fresh scent before popping it into your water skin to add flavor.

The escarpment stretches for as far as the eye can see in either direction and forms a startling contrast to the flatness of the grasslands. Occasionally dark eyes look down on you—cave openings in the cliff. You catch glimpses of dust clouds on the grassland, churned up by the herds as they march north towards better feed. Vootbeests on the move.

"Right, it's time to descend," says Zenan. "We'll follow this watercourse to the grassland, then head inland towards the herd. Keep a sharp lookout. Those slavers might still be lurking."

You'd almost forgotten about the slavers.

On the grassland, the sun beats down. It feels as if the ground has absorbed the heat just so it can throw it back up as you pass.

Zenan pauses. "We'll stick to the bank of the riverbed. It may be dry now, but thorn bushes are more plentiful along its course. Better for us if shredders are about."

Knowing the location of the nearest thorn bush is one of the first lessons an apprentice hunter learns. Today you are especially vigilant. Part of you would be happy if you never saw another shredder as long as you live. But the inventor in you wants to try out your newly constructed thrower.

"*Tweet to to. Tweet to to.*" One of the spear bearers has spotted something.

Havera. Big fat ones.

Although a medium-sized vootbeest is twenty times the weight of a fully grown havera, there are six of them digging for water in the riverbed, and none so far have spotted your group.

Zenan directs his spear bearers with a series of hand signals. Your job is to stay on the riverbank and keep an eye out for predators while he and the spear bearers do the stalking.

Stalking havera isn't that difficult when they are otherwise occupied. With their broad rumps in the air, powerful forelegs fling dirt and gravel behind them at a furious rate.

Zenan and the spear bearers creep slowly towards the unsuspecting havera until they are within throwing range.

As one, they draw back their arms and, on Zenan's signal, let fly. Four of the havera are killed instantly, while the other two spin around in fright and hurtle themselves into the brush on the opposite bank.

"Voot! Voot!" shout the spear bearers.

In their elation, none of the hunters sees the swarm of low-flying shredders coming up the riverbed.

"Shredders!" You scream at the top of your voice.

Zenan and his spear bearers glance up, see the rapidly approaching threat, and run for their lives.

The nearest thorn bush is just behind you on the riverbank. But you're not sure all the hunters will make it in time. Zenan is fast, as are some of the others. But three of the spear bearers have been eating too much dried vootbeest and not doing enough exercise over the winter.

You pull your thorn thrower from its protective pouch and walk towards the approaching swarm. Half the swarm swerves towards the slain havera. The rest fly straight towards the running hunters. Yikes! There must be two or three hundred of them!

You'll have to time your throw perfectly. Too early and you'll hit the hunters, too late and you'll be shredded.

You take a wide stance in the gravel of the riverbed and take aim at the approaching swarm. "Get ready to duck!" You yell at the fast approaching hunters. Then you cock your arm and bring the palm of your other hand up level with your shoulder.

Zenan rushes past. Then a few others. Time has run out, and there are three hunters left. You bring your arm forward as hard as you can and *smack* your fist into your palm.

Thorns jolt from the handle and fly towards the swarm, just missing the slowest of the hunters. Twenty or more shredders nosedive into the streambed, killed by flying thorns. The others whirl around to devour their fallen comrades, the smell of blood too strong to resist.

You turn and run for your life up the riverbank and dive under the thorn bush, where your comrades are panting and puffing and shaking at their narrow escape.

It's a tight squeeze with all of you under the same thorn bush, but nobody's complaining. In a flash, the swarm has eaten the havera and the fallen shredders. Nothing but bones remains.

Then, as if called by some silent signal, the swarm streaks off to the north.

Zenan is first to crawl out from under the thorn bush. He scans the area. "*Toooo-wit. Toooo-wit.*"

The others soon follow.

As you brush the dirt off your robe, Zenan approaches. "That is the first time I've seen someone walking towards a swarm of shredders," he says. "Well done. That thrower of yours is quite the weapon."

198

Praise coming from a hunt master of Zenan's status is rare indeed. The spear bearers whose lives you saved pass you their water skins in turn, inviting you to drink deeply.

"Right, before we move out, let's pick some thorns and get the thrower reloaded. Never know when those horrible things might return."

Later that day, your group brings down two vootbeests and returns to the stronghold safely loaded with meat and horns. At the feast that night, every hunter tells the story of your bravery. You are awarded three bloodstone beads. One for each life you saved. Then you are given a new name, an adult name. A name that lets the entire tribe know that you are no longer an apprentice. A name suitable for a fearless hunter.

Congratulations, you have reached the end of this part of the story. But have you discovered the secret of the singing cave yet? Have you ridden a zeebok? Sung with the strangers? Have you found a secret lake or the chamber of light?
It is time to make another decision. Do you:

Go back to the beginning of the story and take a different path? **P98**

Or

Go to the big list of choices and choose another place to start reading? **P365**

Go with Thamus to the chamber of interesting things

"Follow me, Thamus. The chamber of interesting things is on pit level five."

Thamus grins. "Thanks. I can't wait."

Down the circular staircase, past numerous corridors and alcoves, level five is cool and less smoky than the great chamber. You head down a long dark corridor—your hand running along the wall feeling the carved markings.

"You sure this is the right way?" Thamus asks.

"Just a little further."

"Hmmm … I hope so, my knee is killing me."

You feel a symbol shaped like an eye. "Here we are."

With sparker stones, you light a torch and hold it up to admire the chamber. "So, what do you think?"

The walls are covered in holes of different sizes. Some are only big enough to fit your hand in, while others are much larger.

Thamus gawks. "Wow, so many."

"Yeah," you say. "I don't know where to start looking."

Apart from holes full of interesting things, the roof is interesting too. It's covered with tiny stalactites that sparkle in the torchlight, making the roof of the chamber resemble the night sky.

As you are about to start your search, you hear it. "Shhh … Is that singing?"

You hold your breath. Then you hear it again. The song is all around you. A series of low notes, followed by a run of notes going higher and higher up the scale before starting over again. So familiar, but with words you can't quite make out.

"Do you think it's coming from the citadel?" Thamus asks. "It's only three levels below us."

You shake your head. "The water guardians swear that the singing doesn't come from them. They say it's our ancestors, but I'm not so sure."

"Not sure? Why?"

"Well, firstly, the words sound familiar, but nobody understands them. Secondly, it's the same song every time." You hum a bit to Thamus. It's a song everyone's heard hundreds of times. "Besides, if our ancestors were singing to us, wouldn't they sing in a language we'd understand?"

Thamus shrugs. "But what else could it be?"

"I don't know. But just because the guardians want it to be our ancestors doesn't make it so. Maybe there's a clue in one of these holes. Zenan told me people have been preserving stuff in this chamber for generations."

"Hmmm …" Thamus says. "We'd better get looking, then."

During your search, the two of you come across all manner of interesting things. Quills, oddly shaped bones frozen in rocks, dried leaves, unusual markings and drawings on clay tablets, primitive spearheads, rocks with paintings of animals on them, and the skulls of creatures you don't recognize. But nothing that solves the mystery of the singing. The day goes by quickly as you check hole after hole for clues.

"Hey," Thamus says. "Look at this."

Thamus stands over a large skin he's unrolled. On it is a diagram instantly recognizable as the stronghold. Drawn on it are tunnels, chambers, and the pit itself, all in great detail. Most of the passages and chambers on the map are familiar, but some are only partially drawn.

"I've seen something similar once before," Thamus says, running his finger over the drawing. "These are all the known tunnels throughout the stronghold. Most have been explored. The others could go anywhere."

"I wonder if the stronghold links up with another cave system."

Thamus glances over at you. "And you think that's the source of the singing?"

You shrug. "It's possible. We know there are other tribes living on the escarpment to the north."

"Remember the cave where I hurt my leg?" Thamus asks. "That had unexplored passages running off it."

"They're all over the stronghold," you say. "Most are too dangerous to enter. They marked that chamber with three dots after you got hurt."

"Hmmm … do not enter," Thamus says, absentmindedly rubbing his knee. "Yeah, I remember."

The longhorn sounds for the evening meal. Your torch is nearly out anyway.

You help Thamus roll up the map and slide it back into its hole. "We'd better mark this. We might want to take another look tomorrow."

After a night dreaming of maps and singing, the next morning you return to the chamber of interesting things. There are still hundreds of holes to check.

One hole contains a collection of round stones, each rounder than the next. "Hey, Thamus, what do you think these round stones are for?"

Thamus' eyebrows knit together as he studies the jet-black rocks. "No idea. A game, perhaps?"

You roll one across the chamber floor. But as you bend down to retrieve it, you hear something familiar. "Shhh …" you whisper. "Hear that?"

You sit on the floor and listen. "Sounds like it's coming from somewhere nearby."

Thamus cups a hand around one ear. "One of these holes, maybe?"

"Is that possible?" you say, pulling Thamus to his feet. "If that's the case, we'd better find out which one before it stops."

You and Thamus listen to as many holes as you can. But every time you press your ear against one, the volume of the singing decreases. You drop to your knees to check the bottom rows.

Then, with one hole you try, the singing gets louder. "Here, Thamus! It's this one!"

Thamus limps over and listens. "You're right."

You hold the torch up and peer inside. "It's smooth in there, like an old watercourse. Not like the others that have been cut by hand."

As the singing continues, you listen carefully. If the sound is coming through an old watercourse, it could originate anywhere. Sound can travel a long way underground, especially when the air is cold.

After listening a while, you stand up. "It's like someone's singing. A real person, not ancestors."

Thamus nods. "It does a bit. But then I've got no idea what an ancestor would sound like."

You pull out your knife and scratch a mark on the wall over the hole. "There, we'll be able to find it again now."

"We should tell Zenan," Thamus says.

"Can't. He's hunting today."

"Who, then? The prime guardian?"

The singing stops.

"Tempting," you say. "But I'm not sure that's the way to go."

"Why's that?" Thamus asks.

"Well … The guardians say the singing is our ancestors informing us the hunt will go well. I'm not sure they'll want to hear a theory that contradicts them—that suggest it might be coming through an old watercourse from another cave system."

Thamus mulls it over. "Wouldn't they want to know the truth?"

"But what if the truth weakens their power?"

Thamus rubs his chin. "Hmmm … I see what you mean. What should we do, then?"

You give Thamus a big smile. "Let's go exploring."

"But my knee …"

"Oh, right," you say. "What if I go exploring while you stay here and search for clues. At regular intervals, shout into the hole that the singing was coming from. If I'm heading in the right direction, I should hear you shout. Sound travels in both directions, you know."

Thamus looks unsure. "Going into unexplored tunnels is risky. Are you positive you don't want to tell the guardians first? Maybe they're right and it is ancestors singing."

It is time to make a decision. Do you:

Go searching some unexplored tunnels in the hope of finding a link to a new cave system? **P210**

Or

Go tell the prime guardian about your theory? **P220**

Try to move the rock

There is no light, no sound, and no draft. All you can hear is the thumping of your heart as it tries to beat its way out of your chest. Despite the cool temperature, a film of sweat covers your neck.

The long crawl back up the narrow passage is a matter of moving one leg at a time followed by its opposite arm. It didn't feel this steep crawling down. But now that you're doing it in reverse, you have to take frequent breaks to rest.

All you can think about is whether you'll have the strength to shift the rock blocking the entrance. Judging by the struggle the citadel guards had maneuvering it into place, it was a heavy one.

By the time you reach the top, your forearms ache. You set the spear aside, slip the bundle off your back, and roll over. The cool stone feels wonderful on your sweaty back. After a few moments, your strength returns.

But now what? Do you try to turn around in the narrow tunnel and use your shoulder to push the rock, or do you stay on your back and use your legs?

It is time to make a decision. Do you:

Use your legs? **P247**

Or

Use your shoulder? **P252**

Exit the stronghold

With spear in hand, you sprint up the spiral stairs of the pit. As you reach the great chamber, you slow down and try to act normally. If you seem in a rush, the gate guards might be suspicious and prevent you from exiting.

As you walk across the great chamber, you pass hunters making spears, trimming leather hides and carrying out all the other tasks of daily life. A deep breath helps steady your nerves.

There are two guards on duty at the main gate. You've known them all your life.

You smile as you approach. "I've been instructed by the guardians to collect some mintwort."

"What? On your own?" one of the guards asks.

You nod. "I saw a patch not far down the hill as we left for hunting the other day. I wish I hadn't mentioned it now."

"Better you than me."

"At least it's not too hot yet," you say as casually as possible. "Best I get it over with."

The guards exchange glances and then open the gate.

"May you never thirst," they say as you slip through.

It's time to get far away, and quickly! You head across the slope rather than going down towards the grassland.

You feel safer up here on the escarpment. And while zegar and slavers sometime visit these upper slopes, shredders tend to stick to lower altitudes where there are fewer trees. It's cooler up here under the canopy too, and there are caves. The cliffs are full of them. You might need to hunt on the grassland if you're to survive, but right now, all you want to do is find a safe place to hunker down and think.

206

Dry leaves crackle underfoot as you walk. What grasses remain are brown and shriveled, but will bounce back once the rains arrive in another moon or so. To the north, the rains have started already. Hence the migration of vootbeest, zeeboks, and other pastoral animals.

Occasionally the trees thin out a little and give you a view over the grasslands below. There are clouds of dust, way off towards the horizon. A sure sign of vootbeests.

The heat is intense, even here in the dappled shade. Thankfully, you find a narrow track that makes the going easier and enables you to keep up a good pace. When the sun is directly overhead, you spot a small cave in the cliff. It's on the shady side of the hill, so even the afternoon sun shouldn't penetrate its cool depths. A good place to hole up while you decide what to do.

But what if the cave is being used by slavers or some other animal?

You make your way to the base of the cliff for a closer look. It'll be a tricky climb, but you've seen worse. There are sufficient handholds, but, in parts, the cliff is near vertical. You throw a few rocks into the cave's opening from below, and watch for a reaction. Nothing.

Have you come far enough from the stronghold to be safe from the guardians and their elite guards? Should you rest during the heat of the day or put more distance between yourself and the stronghold?

It is time to make a decision. Do you:

Take a chance and climb up to the cave? **P223**

Or

Keep moving and look for somewhere else to hole up? **P235**

Keep going down the passage

You can't see much point in crawling back up the passage only to find out that it's impossible to move the rock the citadel guards have placed over its exit. You may as well save energy and explore further. You can always come back later if this passage turns into a dead end.

This certainly isn't the outcome you expected when you went to the water ceremony this morning. But there's no point regretting your decisions—you're here now.

The floor of the passage gets cooler the further down you go. Thankfully, it isn't getting any narrower. If this doesn't go somewhere, you doubt you'll have the energy to crawl back up to the top, especially backwards.

There is the steady *clack* … *clack* … *clack,* as your spearhead hits the ground as you crawl through the winding tunnel. After a while, you stop to rub your knees and take a drink from your water skin. How much further can this tunnel go?

A bit further along, even though it is pitch black and your eyes are useless, you sense a slight steepening of the grade. A short while later, there is the sound of water dripping.

"May you never thirst," you mumble as you crawl a little faster.

It isn't long before you see a point of light in the distance. It's not bright, but after so much darkness, your eyes have adjusted and your pupils have grown large in their search for it. Is the light coming from the outside? Or have you circled around to another part of the stronghold where a fire is burning?

There is no smell of smoke, so it must be coming from outside.

208

As you crawl, the point of light grows and the tunnel widens. You can even stand up, providing you duck your head. Then, as you walk around a slight bend, it's as if the mountain itself has spread its arms in welcome.

Huge glowing stalactites hang from the ceiling of an enormous cave at least three times the size of the great chamber. The glow from the stalactites light up the space better than a dozen torches.

You take a few steps and run your hand over one of the hanging monsters. Despite the light coming from the stalactite, it feels cool to your touch. And when you remove your hand, it takes with it a slimy substance that makes your fingers glow.

Liquid light. How is it possible? You raise your hand to your nose and smell this strange substance. It's earthy, but not unpleasant.

As you walk around the chamber, your eyes devour the strange and magnificent sights before you. Even the floor has a coating of light.

The further you go into the chamber, the louder the sound of water gets.

As you step around a stalactite that has grown so long that it has merged with the floor and formed a column, you see the most wonderful sight ever.

A glistening pool of water, so still it reflects the multitude of glowing formations hanging above it. The pool stretches off into the distance and disappears around a corner. Endless water. More than your tribe could drink in ten generations.

You kneel by the pool, cup your hands, and drink. "Ahhh…"

But what do you do now? The guardians are still after you. Will they forgive you if you go back and share this wonderful discovery? Or do you carry on and see how far this new part of the cave system goes?

209

It is time to make a decision. Do you:
Go back and try to move the rock? **P204**
Or
Try to find another way out of this chamber of light? **P239**

Go check out some unexplored tunnels

The singing must be coming from another part of the cave system. It makes sense. There are plenty of holes and tunnels that could carry the sound from one place to another.

You've also seen signs of other hunters past the dry riverbed to the north while out on the grassland with Zenan.

Why else would the skeleton of a vootbeest have its horns missing? Zegar and shredders don't eat horns.

You head up the pit towards the chamber where Thamus injured his knee a few seasons back. There are two unexplored passages that run off it. Following one of them might lead you to the singing.

Thamus said he'd yell into the hole at regular intervals. As sound travels in both directions, you figure that if you can hear him, then maybe the singers can too.

If that's true, you have a chance to find the path that leads to them.

Before you enter either of the passages, you wait to see if you can hear Thamus' voice.

"Poooooooooooo."

You chuckle. Thamus has been spending too much time with the children. Only the young ones find such a topic funny.

Still, the sound of Thamus' voice is clear. So far so good. You hold up a torch to light the way and head down the unexplored passage on the right hand side of the chamber. "Here goes."

"Poooooooooooo," Thamus yells.

In the beginning, the tunnel goes down steeply before leveling out.

But that's the last of the easy stuff.

The next part is a jumble of broken rock that nearly blocks your path. Over one boulder, under the next. Hard work. A couple of times you drop your torch and it goes out. When that happens, it feels like the earth is closing in on you.

"Poooooooooooo." At least you're still on track.

The next section narrows, then dips again. Unusual swirls appear in the glint of your torch. Some of them remind you of the drawings you saw in the chamber of interesting things. You keep expecting to come across another chamber, but so far, this tunnel's been a mess.

"Poooooooooooo." Thamus must be laughing his head off up in the chamber of interesting things.

You're wondering who else can hear him when a strange light appears up ahead.

"What's that?" you mumble.

It's no torch, that's for sure. The light glows green and pulses bright, then faint, then bright again. Very strange indeed.

When you round the corner, you stop dead. You've finally reached another chamber, but what's in this chamber is like nothing you've ever seen. A huge blob of pulsing green light lies pressed in up against one wall. A faint scratching sound comes from it. And there are more swirls on the wall.

But this thing, whatever it is, is not all that's glowing. The stalactites and walls of the chamber glow green as well. In fact, everything in the chamber is covered in glowing green slime.

You reach out and touch the nearest wall. Now your finger glows green too. Then there's a horrible squirting sound and a rush of green slime shoots out of the big green blob.

Is the blob is some sort of creature? It must be. And it sounds like it's eating the rock. "Ewwwwww."

"Poooooooooooo."

"You've got that right, Thamus."

Whatever the blob is, it doesn't react to you being in its chamber. But where is the exit?

Then you spot what looks like a passage between a pair of dripping stalactites. A hole as high as your waist but quite wide. Unsurprisingly, it is covered in green slime.

You wade through the mess to get to the hole and climb in, pleased to be away from the squirting green blob.

You wonder how Thamus is going with his search for clues.

"Poooooooooooo." Much fainter now.

As you carry on down this new tunnel, your glowing green legs light the way. At least the slime doesn't smell, and you have to admit it makes seeing where you're going a lot easier.

You're thinking about how this slimy new discovery could help light the stronghold when you hear singing. This time it's close.

A little further along the passage, you come to a narrow crack. On the other side of this crack is a well-lit chamber filled with singing strangers. The strangers sing the song you've heard all your life.

After their song finishes, they turn and file out of the chamber.

If only the crack were wider, you could squeeze through and make contact. You think about shouting, but then stop. What would the strangers make of you? Would they see you as a threat? Do you want to give yourself away before you know more about this new tribe?

One girl, about your age, lingers behind the rest. She cups a hand around her ear and listens.

"Poooooooooooo." Thamus' call is barely audible now, but by the look on the girl's face, you're pretty sure she heard it.

You turn and are about to head back the way you've come when you hear the girl chuckle. "Poo?" she says softly, before shaking her head and walking from the chamber.

Congratulations, you've discovered one of the secrets of the singing cave and you can't wait to tell Thamus about the strangers you've discovered. Between the two of you, you're sure to work out the best way to make contact with them. But the cave has many more secrets. Have you found them all? Have you ridden a zeebok? Been awarded bloodstone? Fought off the shredders?

It is time to make another decision. Do you:

Go back to the beginning of the story and try a different track? **P98**

Or

Go to the big list of choices and check for parts of the story you've missed? **P365**

Go hunting on your own

Hunting on your own might be risky, but great risk can bring great reward. Showing the others that you're no coward is important if you're ever to become a respected hunt master like Zenan.

The next morning, after gathering enough supplies for a couple of days and topping up your water skin, you head up the pit stairs and across the great chamber towards the main gate.

"Let me out, I'm going hunting," you tell the guards.

The guards give each other a sideways glance and then break out laughing.

"By the waters, we've got a crazy one here," the larger of the two says.

The smaller guard steps forward and looks you in the eye. "Is this about Manaria?"

It seems word travels fast in the stronghold. "Yes. Now open the gate."

The big guard swings the gate open. "Good luck, apprentice. You'll need it."

"Be careful," says the other guard. "May you never thirst."

You're careful as you follow the well-worn path down to the grassland, stopping regularly to listen for the yip of zegar and to scan for shredders. Once there, you follow a zigzag path from thorn bush to thorn bush, ready to hide at the first sign of danger.

As the sun climbs in the sky, all you see migrating north are a few zeeboks and a family of havera. Not what you're after. Only a pair of vootbeest horns will prove you've faced death head on and triumphed.

But it's hot. Too hot. You need to hole up somewhere or this heat will be what gets you, not the shredders. And you've seen plenty of evidence of them, having just passed a dozen small piles of zegar bones. An unlucky pack caught in the open, by the looks of it.

You spot a large thorn bush ahead and decide to shelter under it for a while. When it cools off later in the afternoon, you'll search some more.

But under the thorn bush, you get the surprise of your life. A baby zegar, not more than a couple of moons old, is lying in the dirt looking thirsty, hungry, and a little frightened.

Where is its mother? Was she one of those piles of bones you just passed?

Yip, goes the baby zegar. It sounds more like a squeak than the call of an adult. He's a brave little fellow, and presses his wee nose against your skin and sniffs. His big brown eyes are as cute as any baby's.

You pull out your water skin and pour some into your hand. The baby zegar laps it up with a squeak of delight. After six handfuls, you feed it a piece of dried vootbeest. This is gobbled up in a flash and the baby starts nosing inside your robes looking for more.

"Stop it," you chuckle, "your little whiskers tickle."

You give the zegar another piece of meat, and then have one yourself. The baby licks your face.

You wonder if this zegar could become a hunting companion. A friend out here would be a big help. There are stories of people training zegar, but you've always thought they were myths.

"Would you like to come hunting with me, little zegar?" you say, giving the baby a scratch under his chin.

Yip, squeaks the zegar.

Rather than resting, you and the baby zegar play under the thorn bush. You even teach him to lie quietly and to yip on command. He's a quick learner, and will do almost anything when there is a bit of dried vootbeest as a reward.

But then your mission comes back into focus. You need to find some vootbeest horns, and to do that, you need to find a vootbeest. Rather than go hunting that afternoon, you decide to give yourself and the baby zegar a little more time together. Maybe that way he'll follow you when you leave the thorn bush to go hunting.

The next morning, as you are feeding a few treats to the baby zegar, you hear the distant snort of vootbeests. You crawl out from under the thorn bush and look across the grassland. A herd of vootbeests is close. This is your chance.

You can't hunt in a conventional manner with chasers and ambushers, so you'll have to be creative. But how?

To the north, you spot a really big thorn bush. If you could crawl under that without being spotted by the herd, a vootbeest might come close enough to give you a chance to throw your spear.

"Come on, zegar. Follow me."

You stalk the herd, keeping as low as you can. Often, you're on hands and knees. The baby zegar creeps behind you, thinking this is just another of your games.

With patience, you make it to the big thorn bush without being detected.

You give the baby zegar a treat for being quiet and signal him to lie quietly. Now it's a matter of picking the right animal and the right time.

Animals stream by for most of the morning before one wanders close enough to your hiding place for you to have a chance of killing it. Without wasting any time, you grab your spear, crawl out from under the thorn bush and sprint into position.

The baby zegar follows you into the vootbeest's path. *Yip, yip, yip, yip, yip, yip, yip!*

The vootbeest is startled. Not only by you, but also by the baby zegar's constant yipping. It swings its glistening horn up in a scything arc, bellows and flails its front hooves in your direction.

It's now or never.

You throw your spear with all your strength and then dive back under the thorn bush.

Whump! The vootbeest hits the ground.

You've done it!

The excited zegar runs around the fallen vootbeest. *Yip, yip, yip, yip.*

It's a long walk back to the stronghold. The horns are heavy and the day is hot. Despite the heat, the little zegar is playful, rushing ahead, then running back. You rest often and share pieces of fresh vootbeest.

When you arrive at the stronghold, the gate guards are surprised to see you. They're even more surprised by your companion. The friendly little zegar gets plenty of attention. People offer him pieces of meat from their own supplies. The zegar is an instant hit with the children, who argue about who gets to rub his belly and scratch behind his ears.

But no matter who tries to tempt the zegar away, he always stays nearby and comes running when you call.

The water guardians give you two bloodstone beads for the vootbeest horns, a rare occurrence. And Zenan's offered to take you hunting and to train you to become a hunt master.

Bringing back the horns entitles you to speak in the great chamber, and after hearing your story about Rooth's near miss, few are willing to hunt with Manaria. There is even talk she may leave the stronghold altogether.

Oh, and the children name the little zegar Squeak. You have them look after Squeak when you go on big hunts. Every three or four days you take Squeak out to scout the area and then you tell Zenan which way the herd is going.

As he gets older, you take him hunting, and together you earn many bloodstone beads. But one day Squeak trots off. He looks back a few times as you call him, but he stubbornly keeps going. He is a wild creature, after all. You shed a tear, but count yourself fortunate to have had his company for so long.

On your first hunt the next season, you're leading a group of apprentices so young you're worried they'll be injured. Were you this young and vulnerable? Your group comes around a bend in a canyon while following a trail and you spot a pair of zegar with their new baby feasting on a carcass. The male, a huge specimen with familiar markings, looks up. Everyone freezes.

Yip, yip, yip.

Is the male calling to you?

The big zegar picks up the baby by the scruff of its neck and trots towards you. Incredulous, you scratch at the baby's fur as Squeak licks your face. After a time, his mate cautiously approaches and is fed some dried vootbeest. The rest of the day, the zegar hunt with your young team. They make great chasers. Together you bring down a vootbeest and all share in the meat.

That night, back at the stronghold, as you feast and receive a bloodstone bead from the guardians, the zegar family settles down under a rocky overhang just outside the cave.

There is debate in the tribe about whether the three zegar are a good or a bad thing. But the next day, when the zegar give early warning that a band of slavers is nearby, everyone agrees they are an asset to the tribe.

But when the herds move on, the zegar go too.
The next year they are back with two new babies.
Yip, yip, squeak, squeak.

Congratulations, this part of your story is over. You have become a hunt master and proved your bravery. But have you read all the possible tracks? Have you solved the mystery of the singing cave, met the strangers, ridden a zeebok, and found the chamber of light?

It is time to make another decision. Do you"

Go back to the beginning and read a different track? **P98**

Or

Go to the big list of choices and find tracks you might have missed? **P365**

Go tell the prime guardian what you've discovered

"Okay, Thamus," you say. "You're right. We should tell the guardians we think the singing is coming down this watercourse."

Thamus nods. "They might even know about it already."

"I hadn't thought of that."

"Hmmm …" Thamus says. "The guardians have had plenty of time to do their own investigating, you know."

You and Thamus trudge down to the citadel. The sacred chamber is empty except for two guards beside the entrance to the guardians' private chambers.

"Can we speak to the prime guardian?" you ask.

One of the guards signals you to wait and disappears down the tunnel.

As you wait, you look around the citadel. You don't often see it from this angle. Normally you're sitting at the back of the chamber with the others. There are quite a few holes in the citadel's roof. Some have fine stalactites hanging from them.

There is a *chuff, chuff, chuff* of feet as the prime guardian shuffles into the citadel. "You wish to speak with me?"

You glance at Thamus and swallow the lump in your throat.

Then Thamus blurts it out. "We think the singing is coming from another cave system, not our ancestors."

You notice a hardening of the prime guardian's face, a squinting of his eyes, and a clenching of his jaw. His normally pale skin turns a pale shade of pink.

"And you believe this because …?"

"We were in the chamber of interesting things and heard singing coming from one of the holes," Thamus says. "To us it sounded close, not like it does when we hear it in the citadel or the great chamber. Clearer, somehow, like it wasn't that far away."

The prime guardian stiffens. You notice the pulse in his neck. His face reddens further.

He raises his bony finger and says to the guards. "Seize them!"

"What?" you cry, struggling with the guard. "What did we do?"

The guards drag you and Thamus down a tunnel towards the guardians' private chambers. They turn into a smaller offshoot. This leads to another chamber with small cubicles cut into its back wall. Each cubicle has bars made from vootbeest horns.

"Cage them," the prime guardian says.

"Why?" you say. "Don't you want to know where the singing comes from?"

The guards throw you and Thamus into a cage and then brace its door shut with more horns. Once you're secured, the guards march back out to take up their post in the citadel once more.

"Why are you doing this?" you ask. "We're just trying to discover the truth."

"We have our truth," the prime guardian says. "A truth that has lasted for thousands of years. Why would we want a new one?"

Unfortunately, this part of your story is over. The guardians have power, and they don't want some young upstart like you putting it at risk. Even if you are right. You and Thamus are doomed to rot away in this dungeon for the rest of your lives. Often you'll hear singing.

It is time to make another decision. Or maybe you'd like to change your mind, go back, and make that last decision over again.

222

What would you like to do? You have three choices. Do you:

Go back and explore some new tunnels rather than talk to the prime guardian? **P210**

Or

Go to the big list of choices and find a different chapter to read? **P365**

Or

Go back to the beginning of the story and take a different path? **P98**

Climb up to the cave in the cliff

The first part of the climb is easy and footholds are plentiful. But that doesn't last long. Before you know it, the rock face steepens and footholds crumble away when you put weight on them. This is too dangerous without a rope. It's time to go back down and find somewhere else to hole up.

But spotting footholds as you climb down is even more difficult than going up.

Suddenly the cliff crumbles underfoot and you are falling.

D

O

W

N

You have no idea how long you've been unconscious. Your head throbs like there's a drummer inside your skull.

Ba-boom! *Ba-boom*!

When you open your eyes, light stabs your brain, forcing you to close them again.

Then, as you lie there quietly wishing the pain away, you realize that whatever you're lying on is moving!

You open your eyes—only slower this time—and see that someone has tied your wrists together and placed you, belly down, over the back of a zeebok! By the waters! Zeeboks are wild animals! What is going on?

The zeebok's gait is faster than you could jog, and the ground below moves by quickly.

The rope securing your wrists runs under the animal's belly and is tied around your ankles, holding you securely in place. Every step the zeebok takes rocks you back and forth. Drops of sweat drip from your head and are lost in the dust below.

Klopp klopp, klopp klopp, klopp klopp, klopp klopp, go the zeebok's hooves. It sounds like there are quite a few of them.

You shift your eyes left.

Behind you, a stranger sits atop another zeebok. A leather strap runs from the stranger's hand to a loop around the zeebok's snout. Behind him, two more zeeboks follow, both with riders.

Are they slavers? You pretend to be asleep in the hope of hearing something useful, and try not to throw up from the rocking motion.

How long have you been out to it?

The sun is low on the horizon, so it's been a fair portion of the afternoon. Where are they taking you?

But before you have time to consider the question, you drift off to sleep once more.

As the sun dips below the horizon, you're roused from your sleep. The terrain is changing. Thankfully, the throbbing in your head has subsided and your memory is returning.

You remember falling. These strangers must have found you. But until you discover more about them, you remain still. The more you learn about them, the more chance you'll have to escape should the need arise.

The travelers enter a narrow canyon that cuts back into the escarpment. High cliffs on either side shade the canyon from the burning sun. Zeeboks graze at the head of the canyon, penned in by a barricade of stout branches. As you near a modest settlement, you pass piles of vootgrass stacked in bundles beneath a stone overhang to keep it dry from the seasonal rains.

What is this place? Who are these people? And how did they capture and train zeeboks?

Calls of welcome ring around the canyon. Faces appear from cave mouths. Near the zeeboks pen, water seeps down the side of the cliff to form a shallow pond at its base. Permanent water, a resource worth defending.

Scrawny children swarm down a rickety ladder and scurry over to get a closer look at you. Adults stop what they're doing and edge nearer too. The strangers look similar to your own tribespeople except for the red patterns decorating their white zeebok-skin robes. Most are family groups that look too friendly to be slavers.

You know a few of their words. Their language is similar to your own, but with a sing-song quality that rises at the end of each phrase.

After untying you from the zeebok, the hunters carefully lower you to the ground. One gives you a drink from his water skin, while the others lead the zeeboks away towards their enclosure.

Thankful for his kindness, you smile and sit quietly with hands in your lap, watching the crowd and trying to understand what they're saying. Another hunter hands you a damp piece of soft leather to clean the cuts you received during your fall.

As you listen to the strangers' chatter, you wipe the blood from the side of your head and wriggle your fingers to get the circulation moving again. From the words you understand, the ones who found you were hunting havera up on the escarpment and found you lying injured beneath a cave they sometimes use as temporary shelter.

The more you listen to them, the more words you recognize. One word is repeated many times, but you've no idea what it means.

Tiver. What is a tiver?

At least you've not heard the words 'slave' or 'kill'.

A woman approaches. She lifts your chin and looks into your eyes. Her stare makes you uncomfortable.

Then she speaks softly. "Est dat you, Tiver?"

Ah … Tiver. It's someone's name! You're getting the hang of this accent.

But how are you supposed to reply? Your name isn't Tiver.

In the stronghold, adults always told you that if you don't have something important to say, say nothing and listen. So that's what you do. You try to smile but your body aches all over and you're afraid the smile is more like a grimace. More sleep is what you need.

The woman inspects you a moment longer, and then shakes her head, turns, and walks off.

One of the hunters shrugs to the others. "I would have sworn this was Tiver. The eyes are so similar."

"It's been many seasons since Tiver was taken," a villager says. "Children change."

"True, but a mother never forgets her child," the hunter says. "What do we do now? We already have enough mouths to feed."

A hairy, well-muscled man, wearing an ornate belt of bone and leather over his robe, steps forward. "We could make a sacrifice. Then maybe the rains will come early."

Is he talking about sacrificing you or one of their captured zeeboks? By the waters! You'd better think of something important to say, and fast just in case!

"Um—er—maybe we could trade, my people and yours?" you say, doing your best to imitate the musical lilt of the stranger's speech. "I'm sure it would be good for us all."

Your eyes search their faces. Have they understood?

One of the hunters steps towards you and tilts his head as if trying to decipher your words.

"Tr—ade," you say. "My people … can give … you things … like spears and bloodstone." You point towards your spear that one of the strangers has dumped on the ground nearby. "Spear."

"Spar," the hunter says.

You lift the single bead hanging around your neck. "Bloodstone."

A girl about your age steps forward and smiles. "He wants to trade, Pappie."

She understands! You nod vigorously. "Yes … Trade."

After more discussion, the elders, with help from the girl, finally understand what you're proposing. One of the hunters is impressed with the sharpness of your spear and wants to know more.

"Vat stone est dis?" he asks, running his finger down the narrow edge of your spearhead. "Sharpa dan mi spar."

"We call it napstone. We dig it from the ground near my home. There is much to share."

"Gud," the hunter says, handing the spear back to you. "Like spar."

You turn to the girl. "How do you capture zeeboks? It must be good to ride on their backs sitting up rather than lying on your belly."

The girl chuckles. "Yes, much better. Here, you must be hungry." She hands you a chunk of meat.

This is going better than you expected. It doesn't take long before you and the strangers agree both tribes have much to gain by cooperating.

An elder turns to the girl. "Lona, would you be willing to go and negotiate? Your ability to understand his language is of great benefit."

So her name is Lona. But is he suggesting the two of you make the journey back to the stronghold on your own?

"But—but won't that be dangerous?" you ask. "We are not experienced hunters."

The elder shrugs. "The migration has started. All our people are busy hunting and trapping."

You glance over at the girl. "What do you think, Lona? Could we make it?"

"They say it's only half a day to the cave where you were found. Is your home far from there?"

"Not far." You don't want to tell more than you need to, just in case.

"Or," the elder says, "stay here until after the migration. Then we could send a larger group to ensure your safety."

Lona shrugs. "What do you think? I'm willing to take the risk if you are."

What should you do? Do you stay with these strangers and wait until after the migration? Imagine what your tribe will think if you return riding a zeebok! Will discovering new trading partners and the benefit that brings make the guardians forgive you for standing with Zenan against them? Or perhaps it is better to let the guardians cool off for a while before returning home.

It is time to make an important decision. Do you:

Agree to travel home with the girl? **P144**

Or

Stay with the strangers until after the migration? **P149**

Complain about the hunt master

You thump your spear handle on the stone floor. "Stop! All of you!"

A few in the crowd cease their hollering and turn to stare at you.

"You shouldn't be cheering!" You point at Manaria. "Sh—she left Rooth to the zegars!"

Rooth's face goes bright red. She looks down at the floor.

You take a deep breath. "Isn't it the job of the hunt master to keep everyone safe?"

More tribespeople stop their celebrations to listen.

"When Rooth tripped and nearly got taken by a pack of zegar, Manaria ran off with her spear bearers. She didn't even try to help. Said there would be one less mouth to feed. Manaria should be stripped of her beads for such actions!"

A rumbling of voices echo around the great chamber. There are even a few nods of agreement.

Maybe complaining was a good idea after all.

But when Manaria leaps off her rock and storms over to you with her skinning knife out, you know you're in trouble.

Manaria grabs your arm, nearly pulling you off your feet, and drags you towards a row of cages along the far wall of the great chamber.

"Time to teach you a lesson, you sniveling little apprentice! How dare you challenge my authority! Have you seen my beads? Did I not kill the vootbeest? You're not a hunter. You're just a useless child who deserves to be caged for such disrespect!"

Before you have a chance to react, Manaria and three of her spear bearers toss you in a cage, and drag a huge rock over to block the door. She laughs as they return to their adoring crowd.

"Help me!" you scream. "That monster is the one who deserves to be caged! Didn't you hear what I said? She just left Rooth for dead! Please, listen to me!"

Rooth slinks off into the crowd.

Thamus catches your eye and shakes his head. Then he ducks behind the crowd and disappears as well.

"Manaria, let me out!"

But the crowd is back cheering for the hunt master. You're young. Why should they listen to you?

"Fools, don't you see what a monster she is? Let me out!"

You keep yelling in the hope that someone will listen. Meanwhile everyone else is eating roast vootbeest and listening to stories of the hunt.

"Psssst …"

You peer through the bars and spot Thamus crouching beside a nearby cage.

"Stop yelling," he says

"Why?" you say. "I don't deserve this."

Thamus tries to smile, but his heart really isn't in it. "I'll come back after the feast and get you out. Just promise to stop yelling at Manaria. Okay? You're making things worse."

"St—stop yelling?" you splutter.

It is time to make a decision. Do you:

Agree to keep quiet and hope Thamus can set you free later? **P231**

Or

Keep shouting to be released? **P237**

Agree to keep quiet

"Give Manaria a chance to cool off," Thamus pleads. "If you yell abuse at her in front of the whole tribe, she's likely to do something drastic."

"But—but—"

"Trust me," Thamus says. "I'll come back and let you out once the feast is over and everyone's in their sleeping chambers."

Thamus' words have a calming effect on you. They always have, ever since you were kids.

"If you say so."

Thamus pulls a chunk of meat from his robe and tosses it through the bars of your cage. "Chew on this and don't go anywhere."

Don't go anywhere? What the—?

You're about to snap when you see the smirk on his face. After that, it's an effort to stop yourself from smiling. When he sticks out his tongue, you both snort with laughter.

The feast goes on for ages. Then it's story time. Every spear bearer has his or her own version of events to tell. Usually it mentions their bravery in facing down the mighty vootbeest, how much meat they carried home, or how deserving they are of recognition and bloodstone. Not one mentions Manaria's disregard for Rooth's safety. If only apprentices could speak. You and Rooth would certainly have a different story to tell.

When the spear bearers are finished, Manaria is last to speak. She describes the rage in the charging vootbeest's eyes before throwing her spear and the accuracy of her aim. In her version, the pack of zegar comes across as far less dangerous, and she tells of how she and her spear bearers were ready to rush back at a moment's notice to help Rooth if she thought it was necessary. Your part in the hunt barely gets a mention, apart from a sarcastic comment about you panicking and giving your meat up too readily.

There are numerous times you're tempted to shout out and call her a liar, but you've promised Thamus to be quiet. Instead, you sit and seethe in anger and plan your revenge.

When the stories are over, the guardians award the lead chaser and Manaria a bloodstone bead each, and the horns sound for fires out. Before long, the great chamber is quiet. All you hear are snores as the gate guards nod off.

You wonder if the ancestors will sing tonight. As you're drifting off into an uneasy sleep, it starts. Low notes at first, followed by a melody rising higher and higher before looping back to the beginning. The sound is hypnotic, and it's hard to tell where it's coming from—everywhere, yet nowhere. A spirit that drifts through the cave at different times from different places. You've heard singing in the pit when it's quiet and in the citadel of course, but never in your sleeping chamber. You wonder why the ancestors never sing you to sleep.

The voices sing words you feel you should know, but as the words float and echo, their meaning is always just beyond reach. The familiar sound is comforting, and you find your eyelids getting heavy.

Thamus prods you through the bars. "Wake up."

You sit up and see that he's brought Rooth with him.

"I needed help to move the rock," he whispers.

You glance over towards the main gate where two burning torches illuminate the sleeping guards.

Thamus puts a finger to his lips, and then gives Rooth the signal to start dragging the rock away from the cage door. This must be done carefully if they're not to wake the guards. The scraping seems incredibly loud from inside the cage. Thankfully, most of it is disguised by the guards' snoring.

Once the rock has been moved far enough, you squeeze out and the three of you creep across the chamber towards the stairs of the pit.

Thamus pulls you into an alcove. "What now?" he whispers.

You shrug. "I don't know. If I go to my sleeping chamber and pretend nothing's happened, Manaria might get angry and put me back in the cage, or worse."

"Would she do that?" Rooth says. "She must realize what she did was wrong. I nearly died."

You shake your head. "She'll never admit it."

"Hmmm … what do we do, then?" asks Thamus.

You look at Rooth. "Maybe we should speak to the prime guardian. If Rooth and I tell him our side of the story, maybe he'll protect me."

"I'm willing," Rooth says. "You saved my life, after all."

"Or you could escape the stronghold," says Thamus. "Find another tribe to join. Manaria is going to make life impossible for you from now on. She's known to hold grudges."

Leaving the stronghold is risky. "How will I get past the guards?"

Thamus pulls a bundle from his robe and lays it out on the ground. He unwraps a bunch of bright red flowers. "Sleepwort," he says. "Rooth and I will hold a sprig under each guard's nose while you open the gate. Assuming that is what you want. The guards will never hear those creaky hinges."

If you're to escape, night is a good time to do it. Shredders don't fly once the sun has set, leaving only zegar to worry about. If you keep to the upper slopes of the escarpment, and can find a cave to hide in before sunrise, you might just make it. But that means leaving your friends and home. It means Manaria gets away with her bad behavior. But it also means you can get stronger, return once you're older, and challenge Manaria on your own terms.

It is time to make a decision before one of the gate guards wakes up. Do you:

Flee the stronghold to find a new tribe? **P171**

Or

Go with Rooth to the prime guardian and tell your side of the story? **P175**

Keep moving and look for somewhere else to hole up

Upon closer inspection, the climb up to the cave looks a little too dangerous. Instead, you decide to keep going.

You continue along the escarpment until you find another cave. This one doesn't involve much of a climb. Instead, there is a ramp of rock that leads to its entrance. Someone has cut ridges in the ramp for extra grip, and a length of rope hangs down from the mouth for you to grab for support.

Is this cave already occupied? Or has someone just left the rope in place for next time?

The ground is littered with rocks, so you pick one up and throw it into the cave's opening. Nothing.

You throw another. This time you hear a grunt and a hairy man runs to the cave mouth carrying a club. He is followed by five more.

Slavers!

You take off along the escarpment through a glade of yonobo trees, and dive into a clump of mintwort. You dig and burrow your way deep into the thicket.

Heavy footsteps pound along the path past you. Then stop.

"No more tracks," one of the slavers says.

You freeze.

More footsteps. Then there's the sound of mintwort branches being pushed aside.

Oh no, they've found you.

A rough hand grabs your arm and twists it behind your back. A loop of leather secures your wrists. The slaver pulls you out of the thicket with a jerk.

"Ouch!" you yell. "Let me go!"

The slaver ignores you and drags you back towards the cave. "If you fight, we will kill you," he says as he pushes you up the ramp into the cave. "You can be slave, or you can be food."

Sorry, but this part of your story is over. You've been captured by a band of hairy men and are destined to become a slave. Lucky for you, this is a *You Say Which Way* adventure and you can go back and make that last decision differently.

It is time to make a decision. Do you:

Go back and try to climb into that last cave you saw? **P223**

Or

Go to the big list of choices and pick another section to read? **P365**

Keep shouting to be released

You don't care what Thamus says. It's unfair that you've been caged when Manaria is the one who's done wrong.

"Let me out!" you scream. "Why won't you fools listen to me?"

Thamus shakes his head as he slinks off.

"Thamus, wait," you say.

But he's gone.

You yell once more.

Manaria catches your eye and bares her teeth in a silent snarl.

You can tell she is growing impatient with your constant insults.

She leans towards one of her spear bearers and whispers into his ear.

The spear bearer glances in your direction.

What are they saying? Is she telling him to come and release you?

"Let me out! This is unfair!" Your throat is sore from yelling.

The spear bearer puts down his chunk of vootbeest, gets up, and disappears into the crowd.

"Let me out!"

Then you see the spear bearer again. He's with one of his friends, and they are walking in your direction. Both have knives in their hand and a murderous look on their faces.

Unfortunately, this part of your story is over. Sometimes it's better to be silent and live to fight another day, especially when outnumbered. Lucky for you, this is a *You Say Which Way* adventure and you can go back and make different choices.

238

So, what's it to be? You have three choices. Do you:

Go back, make that last decision differently, and stop yelling? **P231**

Or

Go to the big list of choices and read a different chapter? **P365**

Or

Go back to the beginning and read a different track? **P98**

Try to find another way out of the chamber of light

There must be another way out of this chamber. You just need to find it. You walk around the edge of the pond, hoping to find another passage, but soon there's no dry path left. The water is icy cold and about waist deep. You walk on, as the tunnel narrows further.

You stop and listen. Is that a trickle up ahead? Maybe it's a way out. Water is soon up to your chest, and the walls are squeezing in too.

Ahead, the roof is covered in lightcicles. Their reflections in the water reveal small ripples, and it isn't long before the water has a gentle current and flows into another passage.

You once saw a flowing river during the brief rains last season, but that was on the grassland. You never expected to come across a river down here.

As the water gets deeper, your near-empty water skin floats up in your face. Maybe if you emptied the skin completely you could use it to float down this underground river. You'll have to do something. If you can't keep your head above water, you'll have to turn back.

You remove the wooden stopper and empty the water skin. After tucking your spear under your arm, you grab the bobbing skin tightly with both arms and pull it to your chest. Now, if you lean forward, your head and chest float clear of the water.

By kicking your feet, you move along the surface. As the tunnel narrows further, you feel a current pull you and your water skin along.

There are still some isolated patches of green slime on the ceiling, so most of the time you can see where you're going. But seeing isn't your worst concern. There's a noise coming from further down the tunnel, and it's getting louder. Like water running, only much deeper.

The tunnel keeps narrowing, the current gaining speed. It doesn't take long before you're doing well just to hold on to the water skin as you rocket down the narrow flume. Around the next corner, a circle of light appears in the distance. And you're racing right towards it!

You're about to exit the cave in a rush. But what then? You've seen waterfalls plummeting off the escarpment. Most end up on rocks at the bottom. Not a comforting thought.

White water rages around you. You're nearly there.

Like a spear, you shoot through the circle of light. You only have a second to survey your surroundings before you start falling. You clutch your water skin for dear life.

Splash! You hit water, barely managing to hang on to your water skin. For a moment, your head goes under. Then you bob back to the surface, gulp for air, and realize your spear is gone.

You kick towards a flat rock protruding from the water and pull yourself out. The rock is warm from the sun and feels wonderful against your shivering skin.

After a moment's rest, you sit up and survey your surroundings. This lake is even larger than the one underground. High cliffs rise all around it. The waterfall is about twenty feet high. Mist from its veil drifts in the breeze. Caves dot the cliffs.

Plants grow all around the lake. Some you've never seen before. One of the bushes has bunches of bright red fruit hanging from its branches. You've heard about the crackleberries traders used to bring to the stronghold. These look exactly like the fruit in the stories.

But where are you?

You need to get to the top of the canyon wall to get your bearings. But how?

You search the steep walls for a way up. A few caves show signs of habitation, but not a way up.

Then you see a narrow ledge on the other side of the lake. It runs at a steep angle, up the cliff from the canyon floor, to its rim. Could that be the path out of here?

You fill your pockets with crackleberries as you walk around the lake towards the ledge, eating as you go. Then you refill your water skin.

As you approach the ledge, you see that it is a path. It's a natural formation for the most part, but someone has cut steps on some of the steeper sections. You wonder about the people who made them and what hard work that would have been.

In places, the ledge is less than a foot wide. "Please don't let the shredders find me now," you mumble as you climb.

You're going to be out in the open, without shelter, all the way to the canyon rim. You move slowly and carefully. Now would not be a good time to get a cut. Shredders can smell blood from a long way away.

By the time you get to the top, sweat pours from your forehead. But the view is worth the climb.

Below, the grassland stretches all the way to the horizon. The escarpment curves in a gentle arc for as far as you can see in both directions. Its cliffs glisten in the setting sun.

To the south is a narrow strip of bare earth. That must be the riverbed north of the stronghold. You remember crossing its rocky bottom on a few of your hunting trips.

How did your tribe not know about this place? And now that you've found it, what do you do? Do others still come here, or has the secret valley been abandoned?

You sit for a while overlooking the vast expanse before you, thinking about all you've discovered. Imagine what your people could do with the light-emitting slime you found in the chamber of light. And most importantly, imagine what they can do with all the water you've discovered. Not to mention finding crackleberries! You'll be a hero for sure.

The old saying, 'May you never thirst,' could become reality. And it will all be because of you.

You pull a crackleberry from your robe and take a bite. Juice runs down your chin as sweetness explodes in your mouth.

It's been a long day, but with the taste of crackleberry in your mouth, you're absolutely sure it's been worth it.

Under the shelter of a slight overhang, you watch the sun disappear and the stars rise in the sky. The two moons hang low in the sky like a pair of eyes. You eat one last crackleberry, and pull your robes tight and lie down to sleep. You've a dangerous walk back to the stronghold tomorrow. But if you follow the escarpment, and stay under the shelter of the trees, you should be okay.

You can't wait to tell Thamus about what you've found. The underground lake and the liquid light will make life in the stronghold so much easier.

That night you dream of crackleberries.

The next day, as you make the long hot trek back to the stronghold, you keep an eye out for danger. It's a tense time. More than once you shimmy up a yanobo tree when you think you hear zegar approaching.

Finally, you breathe a sigh of relief when you see the path leading to the main gate.

"Apprentice!" a large guard says. "Where have you been?" He's an old family friend and seems pleased to see you.

The smaller guard swings back the gate. "Welcome back."

In the back of the great chamber, you spot Zenan and his spear bearers sitting in cages. They all look dejected and thirsty.

The guards are curious how you escaped the stronghold, but soon stop their questioning when you give each of them a crackleberry to eat.

"This is so good," the big guard says as juice runs down his chin.

As the guards eagerly devour the fruit, you explain what has happened and what you've discovered.

"Really? Liquid light? And an underground lake? That's amazing."

Then you tell them how you're afraid the guardians will cage you.

"But that means no more crackleberries," the big guard says. "Me like crackleberries."

"That's right," you say. "No more crackleberries. But if you help me free Zenan and his spear bearers, we can spread the word of my discoveries, and everyone can share in our new riches."

The guards are a little unsure.

"Look," you say, "the water guardians will have no choice but to give up control now that there is another source of water accessible to everyone. Don't you want the words, 'May you never thirst,' to mean something?"

"Yeah, but …" the big guard says.

You hold up some more crackleberries and dangle them in front of his face.

He stares at the berries with open desire.

You smile, knowing you've won. "Let's get these cages open first."

Congratulations, this part of your adventure is over. You've managed to free Zenan, discovered plenty of water, a new source of light, and a secret canyon where the crackleberries grow. Your place in the history of the stronghold is guaranteed. Stories will be told about your discoveries for generations.

But have you followed all the different paths the story takes? Have you ridden a zeebok or fought off the shredders? It's also a good idea to check the big list of choices for parts of the story you might have missed.

It's time to make a decision. Do you:

Go back to the beginning of the story and try reading a different track? **P98**

Or

Go to the big list of choices and check for parts of the story you've missed? **P365**

Enjoy the feast

Manaria is too powerful to challenge. When you're older, things might be different. In the meantime, you're hungry and tired after the long walk back to the stronghold.

The aroma of massive chunks of vootbeest roasting over a bed of glowing embers makes you drool. Fat pops and sizzles as it drips onto the coals. From time to time, the cooks throw handfuls of herbs onto the fire, releasing a cloud of sweet-scented smoke that swirls towards the roof of the cave.

You find a seat on one of the benches away from the heat of the fire and watch as more and more tribespeople stream up from the pit below. Many have lost weight over the long dry. Chewing tough strips of dried vootbeest takes almost as much energy as it provides. But now that the herds have arrived, there will be fresh food aplenty.

Thamus makes his way over. He walks with a strange gait, his bad leg swinging in an arc with every step. "A successful hunt, I see," he says as he sits down beside you.

"Apart from nearly getting eaten by zegar and having to drop two loads," you reply.

Thamus raises an eyebrow. "Really?"

"Yeah, really. Manaria and her spear bearers acted like Rooth and I becoming the pack's lunch was some sort of joke. Said there'd be two fewer mouths to feed."

"Hmmm… That's nasty. Are you going to say something?"

"Who to? I'm an apprentice. Who's going to listen to me?"

Thamus shrugs. "I hear hunt master Zenan's got a friendly ear. Surely others will listen too."

246

What do you do? Maybe you should complain while everyone is gathered for the feast. What happens when the next apprentice is left behind? But is it worth provoking Manaria?

It is time to make a decision. Do you:

Complain about the hunt master? **P229**

Or

Find Zenan and tell him your problem? **P250**

Use your legs to move the rock

Good choice! The thigh muscles are the largest in the body. If you're going to shift that rock, you'll need all the power you can manage. But first, you need to get in position.

The bundle containing the torch and tinder will make a good pillow to support your head and neck as you push. With that in place, you scoot forward and place the soles of your feet on the rock. A couple of deep breaths and you push with all your might. The rock blocking the tunnel rocks just a little. Then it rolls back into place.

"This is hopeless!"

Still, you've never been one to give up. You scoot towards the rock until your knees are resting on your chest. A few deep breaths and you push.

"Arrrrgggggggh!"

Once again, the rock rolls a little. And once again, it rolls back as soon as you stop pushing.

You lay back, exhausted, and think. What can you use to wedge the rock in place once you've moved it?

"Of course! The spearhead!"

The spear's point is made of stone and shaped like a large teardrop. It's sharp at the point but thicker in the middle. The only problem, the shaft is too long to turn around in the narrow tunnel and the point is facing down, not up where you need it.

You'll have to weaken the spear's shaft with your knife, and then break it in half if you're going to get the tip pointing in the right direction.

It takes a while, but eventually you break the spear into two pieces and turn the point towards the rock. After a brief rest, you slide the tip of the spear into position and once again scoot up to the rock. With a big grunt, you push as hard as you can.

Phhaaaaarrrrrt!

"Ewwwwwww." You wave your arms frantically, trying to disperse the stench. This is what happens when you eat too much dried vootbeest.

When the smell clears, you wriggle up to the rock again and push. This time, as you run out of steam, you slide the point of the spear under the rock. The rock begins to roll back, but then as it encounters the bulge of the spearhead, it skids a little sideways as it rolls off.

You pull the spear back and use it to investigate the gap between the rock and the left hand wall. There's a tiny gap.

Again, you wriggle into position.

"Arrrrgggggggh!" you scream as you push as hard as you can.

And again, you jam the spearhead under the rock. You test the gap. It's bigger! This is going to work!

By the time you've shifted the rock enough to squeeze through a narrow gap, your legs are weak and your back is drenched. But at least you've made it out. You collapse on the floor, exhausted.

Too exhausted to fight off the citadel guard who stayed behind.

The guard is twice your weight and it only takes him a few moments to subdue you and tie your wrists behind your back.

"Well, that wasn't very smart," the guard says. "You should have kept going. You might have found a way out. Now all you have to look forward to is the inside of a cage."

Sorry, but this part of your adventure is over. Lucky for you, this is a *You Say Which Way* story and you can start over and make different choices.

249

What would you like to do now? You have three choices. Do you:

Go back to the beginning and try a different path? **P98**

Or

Go to the big list of choices and start reading from another part of the story? **P365**

Or

Go back to your last decision and choose to carry on down the passage instead? **P207**

Find Zenan and tell him your problem

Zenan is the tribe's most decorated hunt master. Unlike Manaria, he looks after his apprentices.

You find him sitting with some of his spear bearers, a huge chunk of meat in one hand and a full water skin in the other.

"Excuse me," you say. "I need to talk to you about today's hunt."

"Talk to Manaria. Wasn't she the hunt master?"

"That's the problem," you say, feeling your face beginning to redden. "She's a danger to her apprentices."

Without saying a word, the spear bearers around Zenan rise and move to other seats. It's as if they don't want to hear anything bad about another hunt master.

Zenan gives you a stern look. "You'd better not be whining, apprentice. Manaria is an accomplished hunter. Wasn't it her spear that killed the vootbeest?"

Maybe this wasn't such a good idea.

"Spit it out, apprentice. I've got feasting to do."

So you tell him the story. No frills, just the facts.

"Look, apprentice, I can't fight your battles for you."

"So you can't …"

"No. But what I can do is offer you a word of advice. Either say what's on your mind to Manaria—you never know, she might listen—or go out on the grassland and kill your own vootbeest. Actions speak louder than words. You bring the water guardians a pair of horns, and people will listen to you. Prove you're not the coward Manaria makes you out to be. Who knows, you might even end up a hunt master yourself one day."

What Zenan says makes a lot of sense. But to go out on the grassland by yourself? That's so dangerous. Maybe it would be safer to complain. You have friends. Surely, someone will listen.

It is time to make a decision. Do you:

Complain about Manaria? **P229**

Or

Go hunting on your own? **P214**

252

Use your shoulder to move the rock

Your arms and shoulders are never going to be strong enough to move that big rock! Leg muscles are much stronger than arms and shoulders.

It is time to make a decision. Do you:

Try using your legs to move the rock? **P247**

Or

Go back and carry on down the passage? **P207**

MOVIE MYSTERY MADNESS

Movie crew at the manor

You're rolling through the wealthy part of town on your scooter. It's early and you can race along the wide empty sidewalks as the high fences of the rich and famous flash by, their houses hidden from prying eyes.

Swerving around the next corner, you glide to a halt. Something's out of place here. A couple of large trailers, too wide to fit through the open gates, sit at the side of the road in front of a huge mansion. Three people stand there, clasping clipboards to their chests and looking around. Two of them are kids, and one, a teen girl with a long blonde ponytail, beckons you.

Curious, you scoot over to her.

"What's going on?" you ask.

"Glad you asked," she said, smiling. "It's the first day of shooting a movie here"—she jerks her head sideways to the house—"and lots of cast and crew have called in sick. We urgently need extra help. Are you interested?"

Are you interested in making a movie? What a question. Of course you are. Who wouldn't be? Trying not to salivate with your enthusiasm, you say as coolly as you can, "Yeah, I can fit that into my schedule."

"Awesome." She grins and holds out her hand. You go to shake it, then see she's handing you a pen. You take it and she holds the clipboard in front of you. Some sort of contract is clipped to it. She points at various places and says, "Sign here. And here. And lastly here."

"What am I signing?"

"It's a standard contract. Sign quickly so you can be inside for breakfast. Call Time is about now."

You'd like to read it first, but she's not giving you time. You scribble your signature.

The girl whips the clipboard away, tucks it under her arm, and then points through the gates with both hands. "In there. Hurry. Report to the second assistant director. Go, go, go!"

You scoot through the gates onto a wide, curved driveway lined by huge oak trees. Birds and squirrels are busy with their day as you race past. The landscaping is both professional and chaotic: gentle curves in the ground, subtle flowerbeds surrounding trees and shrubs dotted about randomly.

It's all rather fancy.

Further up the drive, there's a sign saying "Film Crew this way" pointing to a side pathway barely wide enough for a single car. It curves around a copse of trees and you abruptly find yourself at a meeting point. Dozens of people—men, women, boys, girls, and unknowns—mingle. Off to one side is a makeshift car park on the grass and several small enclosed trailers. From somewhere in that direction, the smell of frying bacon hits your nostrils, and you feel hungry.

Scooting on the grass is harder than scooting on the driveway, so you move slower, and that gives you more time to look around. Now, who's the second assistant director?

Near the director, you reason. Who will probably be at the center of things. You make your way through the outer fringe of people towards the middle.

Before you've got far, a short, bespectacled man in a yellow jacket climbs onto something so everyone can see him. A whistle blows. Everyone is silent.

"Listen up, everyone!" the man says. "I'm the director of this movie, and there's only one rule on the movie set: mine!

We have a tight deadline, an unfinished script, missing extras and PAs, the budget got cut last night, and the catering van has already run out of burritos!"

Gentle laughter comes from the crowd. The director frowns. "Listen, guys, that's all true. I wouldn't lie to you."

A somber silence replaces the good humor of a few moments ago. Probably because of the burritos, you think.

"But this is the movie business, and we're going to make the best kids' movie possible with what we've got! Now that we've all landed, for those of you who weren't here for rehearsals yesterday, I'll fill you in. The working title is *Murder Mystery Party*. It's a murder mystery themed birthday party. It's going to be awesome!"

Everyone cheers enthusiastically. You join in.

"And there's something 'extra' for the extras." The director chuckles at his wordplay. "The best-performing extra will be given a bigger role in the rest of the film. It'll be the start of a movie career for someone. Now, we're going to be rolling in one hour. Got it? Good! Let's go, people! Time to get ready!"

Most of the crowd moves off. As they part, you see a tall, bearded guy wearing a brown fedora with a flag stuck in the band. He's surrounded by kids about your age. You walk towards him until you can read the writing on the flag: 2AD. Ah, that must mean second assistant director.

He's giving people jobs. Nearby, a young woman wearing a similar hat has a flag saying 1AD. The first assistant director. She's chatting to the director. Now he's wearing a large yellow cap labeled 'DIRECTOR'. It doesn't make him any taller, but he's easy to spot.

You wait your turn to speak to the second AD. He smiles at you, though he looks stressed. "I'm George. You are?" he asks.

"A girl outside sent me in. She said you need help today."

"Ah, perfect. We need replacements. You look like a smart, cool kid. I'll put your name down. I'll call you Scooter."

"That's not my name," you say.

"It is today. It's a showbiz name. No one uses their real names in this business. Do you think my real name is George?"

"Um … well … I—"

"Decision time now, Scooter. Do you want to work as an extra in the movie itself or as a production assistant helping with the background tasks of making the movie?"

You think quickly. As an extra, you might be part of the film itself, though it could be anything from screen time with one of the stars to simply hanging around in the background of a scene. As a production assistant, you'll be helping with the organization of making the movie itself.

It's time to make a decision. Do you:

Choose to be an extra? **P311**

Or

Choose to be a production assistant? **P257**

Choose to be a production assistant

"I want to work as a production assistant, please," you say.

"Cool. Before you can do that, I need you to sign this one thing. Here. And here. And wear this hat." The 2AD gives you a green fedora. A flag labeled "4PA" sticks out of the band.

You don the hat and sign the form, not taking the time to even try to read it.

"Awesome. Naturally, you won't be paid for this—"

Of course not. You bet that was what you just signed.

"—because you have no experience. But you'll get some today, so that's your reward. All my PAs are kids, all unpaid. The director thought that because it's a kids' movie, the PAs should be kids too."

He's grumbling. You just nod.

"Anyway, I'll shuffle the jobs around. You can have a go at everything as long as you don't screw up. First, before filming starts, it's breakfast time."

"Great," you say. Your stomach is rumbling. That delicious smell of frying bacon is still wafting across from the catering trailer.

"Your first job is to get breakfast for the actors playing the parents. They're in compartments in a three-banger over there." He points at a long trailer. "Go ask them what they want. Once you've got them their food, you can get some for yourself if there's time. Then come back to me."

"Sure." You're eager to get started.

"If you need help, ask me or Goldilocks, the girl with the long bleached blonde hair. She's the first PA. Now go, go, go." He turns to another kid.

You scoot across the grass. Other kids and adults dash around you, scurrying to complete their assigned tasks or to get their own food. Some of the kids wear PA-labeled fedoras like yours, and they're all green. Some kind of color coding is in operation, you think.

The large trailer for the stars sits apart from the other trailers, which must have other purposes. Three labeled doors are on the side nearest you. You knock on the one labeled 'Conrad Pringle'.

"About time." A tall, chisel-jawed man opens the door. He sounds impatient. "Where's the PA who was here for rehearsals?"

"Ill, I think," you say. "I'm Scooter. Would you like me to get you some breakfast, Mr. Pringle?"

"Two poached eggs, bacon, hash browns, mushrooms on brown toast. Coffee. Got it?"

You nod, though you don't appreciate the guy's snappy attitude. He shuts the door in your face before you can say anything.

Grumpy. You head to the second door, the compartment for the actress who plays the mother in the movie. It's labeled 'Kathy Barnes'.

"Enter." That was much friendlier than the first one.

You go in, glad to have been invited as you are curious what a movie star's trailer might look like inside.

It's small but clean and tidy like a hotel room. A sofa bed sits on the opposite side of the compartment. On either side is a narrow wardrobe and a desk with a mirror. A flat screen TV is mounted high on the near wall. Next to the wardrobe is a doorway into what must be a small bathroom.

An elegant woman with hazel eyes and matching hair smiles at you.

"I'm Scooter. Would you like some breakfast, Ms. Barnes?" you ask.

"Yes, please. Porridge and English Breakfast tea."

"I'll be as quick as I can." You leave, grab your scooter from where you left it leaning against the trailer, and hurry towards the smell of frying bacon. It's easiest to find the catering trailer—it's the busiest.

A complete kitchen makes up half of the trailer. A man serves two kids in front of you while a woman monitors several frypans. Both are rotund and red-faced. Soon, it's your turn.

"I'm Pi, and this is my wife, R-Squared," the man says. "Who are you?"

"I'm Scooter. May I ask: why Pi?"

Pi grins. "I make the best apple pie in showbiz."

The woman grins. "And R-Squared goes nicely with Pi. The kitchen is open from before Call Time to wrap-up time each day. We've got most of what you'd want—except burritos, unfortunately. What can I get you?"

"I'm collecting breakfast for two actors. The first order is porridge and English Breakfast tea, please."

Pi ladles a bowl of porridge from a large steaming pot while R-Squared organizes a pot of tea. They put these onto a large tray, leaving plenty of room for the other meal.

"What's the other order?" Pi asks.

Yes, what was it? You are wondering that yourself. You say all that you can remember. "Two poached eggs, bacon, hash browns, brown toast, coffee. And one other thing." You strain your brain to remember. No doubt Mr. Pringle will be annoyed if you get the wrong thing. It was beans, wasn't it? Beans on the toast? Or was it mushrooms on the toast?

It's time to make a decision. Do you:

Order beans? **P260**

Or

Order mushrooms? **P263**

Order beans

"Baked beans on the toast, please," you say.

Pi and R-Squared swiftly assemble a plate of the fried treats you requested for the actor. You wonder how he is so thin if he eats this for breakfast every day.

The caterers cover the meals so they won't get cold and add some cutlery to the tray. You make your way back, carrying the tray on the handlebars of your scooter, wheeling it slowly so the tray won't fall off.

You knock on Ms. Barnes' door. "Here you are, madam," you say when she opens it. She thanks you, taking her bowl of porridge and the tea.

Now for the grumpy one.

He pulls the door open abruptly when you knock and glares at you. "You took your time."

"There was a queue, Mr. Pringle."

The actor lifts the cover off the plate and takes a sharp intake of breath.

"Beans!" His lips curl and vibrate with fury. "You got me beans instead of mushrooms. Beans! You want me to fart through every scene?"

You clear your throat so you don't laugh out loud. "No, sir. It was an honest mistake."

"I don't care. Now clear off. I'll make sure you don't work as a PA on this film again." He takes the plate and coffee anyway and slams the door behind him.

Shocked at his harsh behavior, you decide to get some breakfast yourself and return to the catering trailer, where Pi and R-Squared give you a tasty meal. As you're polishing off the last bite of sausage and hash brown, you realize you've been avoiding the issue you have to face.

You've got to report back to the second assistant director and hope there isn't trouble.

You scoot over to where you last saw George. He's there, dealing with another kid's question, and when he's finished, he turns to you.

"Scooter," he says, "Conrad Pringle called me. He said you messed up his breakfast order."

"I got one thing wrong," you say. "He was annoyed, and he didn't give me the chance to put it right."

George lowers his voice. "He's a difficult guy to work with. He wants you fired, but I told him 'no'. We need everyone we can get." He claps you on the shoulder. "The good news is that Kathy Barnes called to say you were prompt and polite."

You breathe a sigh of relief. That Pringle guy is trouble, all right. You'll stay clear of him if you can. "What's next?" you ask.

"Well …" George scratches his beard. "I want you to prove yourself this time. Take these." He hands you a large accordion file and a walkie-talkie radio. "The accordion file is a set box I prepared for you. It's got all the papers you'll need in it. Have a look."

You open the file. Inside, papers are neatly placed in their labeled compartments so everything is easy to find. It's way better organized than your homework.

"Can you see where copies of the scripts are?"

"Yes." You find one in the folder. It's remarkably thin—about four sheets of paper. "This is a movie, not a commercial, isn't it?"

"The scriptwriters were fired a couple of weeks ago due to budget cuts. The director wants to 'wing it'. Now, filming will start in about half an hour. I need PAs to deliver the sides and to do the flushing at the manor house. Your choice. What's it to be?"

262

Before you answer, two kids with '5PA' and '6PA' attached to their hats come running up to get the second assistant director's attention. You don't want to make him impatient with you by being indecisive, so you have to answer quickly.

But what are 'the sides'? Where do they have to be delivered? And what on earth is 'flushing' at the house? Surely, it's not toilet duty?

Maybe there will be some answers in the set box you're supposed to take with you.

It's time to make a decision. Do you:

Deliver the sides? **P281**

Or

Do the flushing? **P270**

Order mushrooms

"Mushrooms on the toast, please," you say. "I'm sure that's what Mr. Pringle asked for."

Pi and R-Squared swiftly assemble the combination of fried treats you requested for the actor. You wonder how he is so thin if he eats this for breakfast every day.

The caterers cover the meals so they won't get cold and add some cutlery to the tray. You set off, carrying the tray on the handlebars of your scooter, wheeling it slowly so the tray won't fall off.

You knock on Ms. Barnes' door. "Here you are, madam," you say when she opens it. She takes her bowl of porridge and the tea and thanks you.

Now for the grumpy one.

He pulls the door open abruptly when you knock and glares at you. "You took your time."

"There was a queue, Mr. Pringle."

The actor lifts up the cover, puts his rather big nose over the plate, closes his eyes, and inhales deeply of the breakfast smells.

You smell them too, and your tummy rumbles. Will you have time to get any breakfast yourself?

"Thanks," the actor says. "You got it right. At my last film, the PAs hardly ever got me the breakfast I ordered. I had five of them fired. But you seem to be okay."

"Thank you, Mr. Pringle," you say, itching to get back to the catering trailer before the bacon runs out. "Do you mind if I go and get myself some breakfast now?"

He ignores that. "I need a copy of the script. I left mine in the hotel. Fetch one for me, will you?"

You scurry off. If you hurry, perhaps you can still get something to eat. At the catering trailer, R-Squared is at the counter.

"What would you like, dear?"

"A bacon sandwich, please."

"Coming right up."

You race off on your scooter, taking a bite of the bacon-filled bread roll as you go. Who would have the scripts? The screenwriters? Where do they hang out? You decide to go back to the second assistant director, your boss, and scoot in the direction of where you last saw him. The crowd of people has thinned out a little now.

You swallow the last of the bacon sandwich while you wait to talk to George. Then he turns to you.

"Mr. Pringle would like a copy of the script, please. He left his in his hotel."

"Take these," George says, handing you a large accordion file and a walkie-talkie radio. "The accordion file is a set box I prepared for you. It's got all the papers you'll need in it. Have a look."

You open the file. Inside, papers are neatly placed in their labeled compartments so everything is easy to find.

"Can you see where copies of the scripts are?"

"Yes." You find one in the folder. It's very thin—about four sheets of paper. "This is a movie, not a web series, isn't it?"

"The scriptwriters were fired a couple of weeks ago due to budget cuts. The director wants to 'wing it', as he puts it. Now, do whatever Pringle wants, then come back to me. Go, go, go."

You scoot back to the actors' trailer, find a copy of the script in the set box and deliver it to Conrad Pringle. It seems like the work day of a PA is busy. And filming hasn't even started yet.

"I need a hot brick." He's not particularly polite. "Mine ran out after rehearsals yesterday, and I don't have a spare with me."

A hot brick? What on earth is that?

Whatever it is, he probably left the spare in his hotel room, you think. But before you can ask for details, the actor closes his door.

You scoot off a short distance, then open the set box and rifle through it, looking for anything mentioning a 'hot brick'.

Nothing.

Okay, you think. Maybe he wants an actual brick for some reason. Perhaps he needs it for some weird foot soothing treatment or something, like when people put their feet in a bowl of hot water. Maybe he has warts. You shiver at the thought.

Or it might be film industry slang for something. But what?

You look around for a trailer with props, set decoration, or anything similar, but in the expansive gardens of the manor house, your gaze catches sight of nearby flowerbeds.

They're bordered with loose bricks.

It's time to make a decision. Do you:

Fetch a brick from the garden? **P266**

Or

Ask someone what a 'hot brick' is? **P268**

Fetch a brick from the garden

What else could the actor mean but an actual brick? You lift one from the flowerbed border and brush the dirt off. Now, how to heat it up? The catering trailer, obviously.

You race over there and rush inside.

"Pi, could you do me a favor, please? I need this brick heated up in the oven."

He looks at you oddly but takes the brick and places it in one of the ovens. Several are operating at once, probably cooking foods at different temperatures. There are a lot of people to feed on the set.

"Snack while you wait, Scooter?" he asks.

"That'll be great." You choose a blueberry muffin and munch away on it. It's good, the sweet blueberries melting in your mouth. Delicious.

"Here's your brick," Pi says, handing you a wooden chopping board with the brick on it. "Careful, it's hot."

"Thanks, Pi."

You race off, balancing the board on your scooter handlebars. At the actors' trailer, you knock on the door of Mr. Pringle's compartment.

He jerks the door open. "Have you got it?"

You present the chopping board with the brick sitting atop it. "Your heated building material, Mr. Pringle."

"What the blazes is this?" he shouts. His face turns red as a beet. "Are you trying to make fun of me? Are you trying to sabotage this movie? Are you trying to ruin my career?"

Okay, so you made a mistake, but he's over-reacting. Paranoid, even. "No—"

He picks up the hot brick.

"Aargh!" He lets it go. It must be too hot to handle. Unfortunately, it falls on his foot. "Get away from me! I'll have you fired!" He hops on his other foot, shaking his burned hand.

I'm sorry, this part of your story is over. You've had a rather short time as a production assistant on the film set. After being recruited off the street for this unpaid position, you successfully fulfilled the actors' breakfast orders. After that, however, your mistake with the hot brick injured one of the stars of the film. You got yourself fired before filming had even started.

How might it go if you take that last decision again? Or perhaps you'd like to try a different pathway in the book and hope for better luck.

It's time to make a decision. You have three choices. Do you:

Change your decision about the hot brick and ask? **P268**

Or

Go to the big list of choices and start reading from another part of the story? **P366**

Or

Go back to the beginning of the story and try another path? **P253**

Ask someone what a 'hot brick' is

It must be movie slang for something, but what? You decide to ask someone for help.

A middle-aged woman is walking nearby carrying a large potted plant.

You scoot across the grass to her and introduce yourself as one of the new PAs.

"Hi Scooter, I'm Charlene the green," she says, chuckling. "Rhymes, I know. What do you want help with? I know most things and people around here."

"Um … I've been asked to get a 'hot brick' for one of the actors, but I don't know what he means."

She chuckles again. You think she must get a lot of enjoyment out of her job. "A new battery for one of these." She tapped the walkie-talkie hooked into her leggings. "They run out of juice real fast."

"Thanks," you say as she walks off. "Where do I get one?"

She glances back. "From the honeybadger. Have a look for the gator. It might be with that."

She's gone.

You scratch your head. Honeybadger? Gator? What are they? Some kind of creatures? Does the manor house have a menagerie? Is there an alligator on the set somewhere? You hope not. No, you decide that line of thought is clearly wrong. Why would spare walkie-talkie batteries be kept with a private zoo? No, honeybadger and gator must be slang words for film equipment. You look around, but you only see trailers: there's catering, wardrobe, lighting … nothing labeled honeybadger or gator.

Wait, next to the lighting trailer is a vehicle like an oversized golf cart. Could it be that? You scoot over. Yes, the vehicle is a John Deere Gator of some sort.

A little cart sits behind it. Inside, there's all kinds of batteries. You grab one labeled 'for walkie-talkies' and then a couple more in case anyone else asks you for a spare. Two minutes later you knock on Conrad Pringle's door.

"Good. Just what I need," he says when he answers. You notice he didn't say thanks before shutting the door in your face again.

You hurry back to the second assistant director, your set box balanced on the board of the scooter in front of your foot. He's walking across the lawn.

"What's next?" you ask him.

"Filming will start in about twenty minutes. I need PAs to deliver the sides and to do the flushing at the manor house. Your choice. What's it to be?"

You know you don't have much time to think about it. But what are 'the sides'? Where do they have to be delivered?

And what on earth is 'flushing' at the house? Surely, it's not toilet duty?

Maybe there will be some answers in the set box, or perhaps George will give you more details once you've chosen.

It's time to make a decision. Do you:

Deliver the sides? **P281**

Or

Do the flushing? **P270**

Do the flushing

"I'll do the flushing," you say. "I'm curious to know what that is."

George grins but doesn't break stride. "It's not what it sounds like. Flushing is simply directing the right people, or vehicles, to the right places. I'm posting you on the manor house main entrance. Your job is to only let in anyone who's required for the next scene to be filmed. People can leave, though. Clear?"

"Yes." Sounds like you won't see any of the filming at this time, though. That's a disappointment.

"Great. Check names against the sides to make sure they're allowed in. Now go, go, go!"

You scoot off, cradling your set box on the scooter handlebars, racing ahead of George to show your enthusiasm. A narrow path takes you out of the trees and shrubbery. Ahead of you stands the manor house: a magnificent three-story home complete with an enormous patio, multiple upper-story balconies, and pillars outside what must be the main entrance.

Wow, you think as you scoot toward it. Just wow. This is someone's home. It's like a modern-day castle.

At the front of the house, you lean your scooter behind one of the pillars and position yourself at the entrance. Time to search through your set box for anything that might help.

Vouchers for extras. Time cards. Crew list. Scripts. Schedules with today's date. Ah, those are what you need.

A minute later, George walks up, glances at you, smiles, and goes inside the house.

A moment later, he pops out again. "You didn't check if I'm required for the first scene today."

"But you're the second assistant director," you say. "I assumed that you are needed for every scene."

He chuckles. "Yes, I am. Just kidding you. But you need to check everyone else, apart from the director and the first assistant director."

"I will."

He goes inside again. Half a minute later, Conrad Pringle arrives. You'd seen him ambling towards you, a grim expression on his face. You check the schedule and skim the partial script for the first scene today. Yes, he's in it.

You smile at him and say nothing. He glares in return.

Next is a girl dressed as a policewoman, followed by Kathy Barnes. No problem with them being allowed to enter. As individual film crew members arrive, you check their names off a list.

This isn't a difficult task, you think.

Soon, people stop arriving. It's about time for filming to start for the first scene. Again, you feel disappointed that you're not involved inside. Maybe later in the day, if things go well.

The second assistant director comes out of the house. "Scooter, have you seen Alicia Tomova? She's missing." George looks serious.

You think fast. You'd recognize her if you saw her, as she's a well-known child star. But you haven't seen her this morning.

"She hasn't come this way," you say. "Maybe she came in through the back or side entrance?"

"She's not here." George sounds grumpy. "I need you to go over to her compartment and see if she's there. Bring her back with you if you find her." He gestures to your scooter. "You'll be faster than me."

"On my way," you say.

"Remember: the show must go on. Go, go, go!"

272

You've noticed that George loves to say 'Go' in triplicate, and it has an energizing effect. You're on your scooter and racing across the grass in a flash.

Shortly afterward, you reach the trailer where the actors have their compartments. Alicia Tomova's compartment is the third one.

A yellow star and a photograph of Alicia with a dressed-up poodle are pinned to the door under her name. The door is ajar.

You lean your scooter against the side of the trailer and step up to knock, but a sound from within makes you hesitate.

It's the sound of someone sobbing.

You feel guilty that you're eavesdropping on what must be a bad time for Alicia. But what do you do? You were told to fetch her.

Should you just leave and give her some privacy? Or bang on the door and demand she comes with you? Is she genuinely upset, or is she rehearsing for a scene?

It sounds genuine to you. She seems really upset.

It's time to make a decision. You have three choices. Do you:

Leave Alicia alone and tell George that she's upset? **P273**

Or

Tell George that you couldn't find Alicia? **P275**

Or

Knock on Alicia's door? **P277**

Leave Alicia alone and tell George that she's upset

Alicia does sound genuinely distressed, and you can't imagine how she could act her role in the film if she's so upset. You decide to leave her alone rather than intrude. She doesn't know you, and if you say that everyone is waiting for her and the filming can't start until she gets there, she might become even more upset. That won't help.

Silently, you get back on your scooter and retrace your steps to the manor house. George is standing waiting outside the front entrance.

"She's not there?" he asks.

"Oh, she is, but I heard her crying. I—I didn't want to disturb her."

"I told you to bring her back here if you found her, Scooter. The show must go on, I said."

"Yes, but—"

"No buts. She's a movie star, a professional. She might be upset this minute, and chirpy as a bird catching a worm in the next. I need her here. Now."

"I thought a few minutes' privacy would help—"

"No, it doesn't. The director's inside getting red in the face with impatience. We have a whole cast of actors and extras in there kicking their heels, a film crew with nothing to do except eat sandwiches and pick their noses."

Sounds like you've done the wrong thing. "I can go back and get her."

"Too late. I already gave you that task, and you didn't do it. I'll ask someone else. You're fired."

Unhappy, you leave, scooting down the long driveway and out onto the sidewalk. The girl with the blonde ponytail and the clipboard pays you no attention as you zoom away. You round the next corner and skid to a stop. There's another movie crew outside the next manor house! A convoy of movie trailers on the road are turning into a wide driveway, while another trailer is being unloaded outside. A young guy with a clipboard beckons you …

I'm sorry, this part of your story is over. You joined the film crew as a production assistant and met a couple of actors by getting them some breakfast. However, you didn't complete the task of fetching Alicia Tomova from her trailer, and that delayed filming. That got you fired. But five minutes later, another opportunity presented itself … but that is another story …

Fortunately, as this is a *You Say Which Way* book, you can change your previous decision to see if you can reach a better outcome and not get fired. Or maybe you'd like to try another pathway in the book? What would it be like to be an extra and be part of the film?

It's time to make a decision. Do you:

Go back and make that last choice differently? **P272**

Or

Go to the big list of choices? **P366**

Or

Go back to the beginning and try another path? **P253**

Tell George that you couldn't find Alicia

You decide that Alicia needs her privacy, at least for a while. After all, she must know that she should be at the manor house, but something has upset her and she can't go. Maybe if she's left alone for a few minutes she'll be all right.

But if you tell George that Alicia is in her compartment, he might be angry that you didn't bring her back.

So, you decide to lie.

Silently, you get back on your scooter and retrace your steps to the manor house. George is standing waiting outside the front entrance.

"She's not there?" he asks.

"No. Do you want me to look somewhere else?"

"Yes. We need to find her. Everyone's waiting on her. She's the child star. We can't go ahead without her for this scene, and it's all set up for filming. Go check the gardens, Scooter. I'll get one or two other PAs to help in the search."

Uh-oh. You hoped to give Alicia a few minutes to recover before "finding" her. Now you've been assigned to check the gardens.

"What are you waiting for? Go, go, go."

Never mind. You scoot off in the direction of the trees and shrubberies, thinking you'll give it ten minutes before returning to her trailer. Hopefully by then she'll feel better.

You pretend to search the gardens, but before you return to her trailer, your walkie-talkie comes to life, startling you.

"Goldilocks found her," George says. There's a chill to his voice.

"Great," you reply, but you don't feel great. A pit of despair is opening up in your stomach.

"The odd thing is that she said she was in her trailer the whole time."

"Um …"

"I don't want excuses, Scooter. I don't know what you think you were doing, but it wasn't your job. Get back here and leave your set box, walkie-talkie and hat with Goldilocks. You're fired."

I'm sorry, this part of your story is over. You joined the film crew as a production assistant and met a couple of actors by getting them some breakfast. However, you didn't complete the task of fetching Alicia Tomova from her trailer, and that delayed filming even more than it was already. That got you fired. Fortunately, this is a *You Say Which Way* book, and you can change your previous decision to see if you can reach a better outcome. Or maybe you'd like to try another pathway in the book? What would it be like to be an extra and be part of the film?

It's time to make a decision. You have three choices. Do you:

Go back and make that last choice differently? **P272**

Or

Go to the list of choices and start reading from another part of the story? **P366**

Or

Go to the beginning and try another path? **P253**

Knock on Alicia's door

You lightly knock on Alicia's door, wait a few seconds, then knock again more persistently. Nothing happens for a few moments, then the sobbing sounds stop. But the door does not open. Alicia either wants to be left alone or to pretend that she's not there.

You know she's there, so you knock gently once again.

Eventually, she pulls the door open. She's dressed in a pink ballerina outfit, including the shoes. A blue beanie sits atop her blonde hair, looking out of place with the rest of the costume. Her eyes are red-rimmed and her mouth is turned down. Even so, she's still pretty.

"What do you want?" she says in a manner that suggests she doesn't care.

"The second assistant director sent me. Filming is due to start, and they're waiting for you. I'm supposed to fetch you, but ..."

"But what?"

"Are you all right? I heard you crying before I knocked. Is there anything I can do or get for you that would help?"

"I haven't been crying. You're mistaken."

For an actress, she's not convincing. You can see from the state of her eyes that it's not true. But now you can deduce she wasn't practicing for a scene. There'd be no need to lie about that.

"I can see you're upset," you say softly. "Everyone's waiting for you, but why don't you tell me what the problem is while we walk to the house? Talking about it might help you feel better."

Alicia sighs. "Okay. I guess so." She steps out of her compartment and shuts the door behind her. "What's your name?" she asks.

"Everyone here just calls me Scooter."

"Why?" She gives you a blank look.

"Because I'm always riding that." You grab your scooter from where it's leaning against the side of the trailer.

Alicia stares at it like she's never seen a scooter before. "Oooh, cool."

"Do you have a scooter?" you ask.

"No, I have a Lambo."

"A Lambo?"

"A Lamborghini, I mean."

You frown. "But you're too young to drive that."

"My chauffeur drives me in it, silly."

"Oh, right." *Of course.*

She looks at you pleadingly. "May I ride your scooter, please?"

"Sure." *If I can have a ride in your Lambo*, you think, but you won't ask. You offer her the scooter, and she gets on it. You have to tell her how to use it. She catches on quickly, and you're soon trotting along beside her as she wobbles towards the house.

"So, what upset you?" you ask. "Do you want to talk about it?"

Alicia smiles at you. "Yes, I think I do. We've had two days of rehearsals, and now today, and barely anyone has spoken to me. They speak to my character, the girl in the ballerina outfit whose birthday it's supposed to be, but no one talks to me; the real me, I mean."

"I'm talking to you," you point out.

She considers this. "You are. And that helps. I've been so lonely, Scooter, with no one to talk to."

"What about the extras? There's lots of kids here."

"They're not allowed to talk to me. Director's orders."

"Oh."

"I don't have any friends."

She looks like she might start crying again. "I can be your friend," you say.

Alicia looks at you with narrowed eyes. "What will that cost?"

"It won't cost anything. You can't buy friendship." You shake your head. What kind of childhood has this girl had, if any?

"Will you let me ride your scooter again if we're friends?"

"Yes, of course. We can hang out together when you're not busy, play computer games, go for walks, maybe even go to a movie." Actually, that last one mightn't be a good suggestion for Alicia—too much like work, perhaps. "Scratch that last one."

She titters. "You're funny. I like you, Scooter."

You smile. At least she seems happier now.

You arrive at the house. George is waiting in the entrance hall, pacing up and down. He thanks you and gives you a thumbs-up when she steps inside onto the tiled floor. Two make-up artists rush to attend to Alicia immediately.

George takes you aside. "What happened?" he asks quietly.

You explain that you found Alicia upset, but don't go into details.

"She's done this on other films," George confides. "You did fine to get her here. Well done, Scooter. I'll keep you on. I need reliable, quick-thinking PAs like you."

Congratulations, this part of your story is over. You joined the film crew as a production assistant and met a couple of actors by getting them some breakfast. You also met a star and made her feel better when she was sad. Getting her to the set was an achievement. The second assistant director is pleased with your work. You don't get paid, but he lets you keep the fedora, and you had a day you won't forget. Even better, he invites you back tomorrow.

Maybe you'd like to try another pathway in the book? What would it be like to be an extra and be part of the film?

It's time to make a decision. Do you:

Go to the list of choices and start reading from another part of the story? **P366**

Or

Go back to the beginning of the story and try another path? **P253**

Deliver the sides

"I'll deliver the sides," you say. "I'll be real fast on my scooter."

"Cool," George says without breaking stride. "There are plenty of copies in your set box. Your job is to deliver three copies: to Jags, the gaffer; to Knuckles, the best boy grip; and to Mindy, the clapper. Got it?" He doesn't wait for you to answer. "Good. Go, go, go!"

The second assistant director turns away to deal with everyone else and, as yet another PA runs up to him, he starts walking away. Their voices fade as they turn behind a hedge.

Puzzled, you search your set box. The sides are there in their own subfolder. They appear to be a couple of pages from the script, probably for the scenes being shot today. But there's nothing in there telling you how to find the people to whom you need to deliver them.

The gaffer. What sort of job title is that? Did you mishear? Maybe the 2AD said 'grapher'. Someone who draws charts? Or is it short for 'photographer'?

And what about the best boy grip called Knuckles? Sounds like a wrestler.

And the clapper? Is that someone who is supposed to clap after a joke in the movie? Is the film's budget so low they can only employ one? Or maybe the jokes aren't much good and only one is needed.

You shake your head. This isn't helping. You'll have to ask someone or search for signs.

A short path takes you out of the trees and shrubbery you'd found yourself in when chasing after George for your next assignment. Ahead of you stands the manor house: a magnificent three-story home complete with an enormous patio, multiple upper-story balconies, and pillars outside what must be the main entrance.

It's like a modern-day castle.

There's hardly anyone around. They must all be either in the trailers or inside the house.

An unbidden thought comes to your mind. This is too hard. No one's watching. You could just stuff the set box into the bushes and scoot out of the place, leave this behind, get on with your day. It's not as if you're going to get paid for it anyway.

Or you could try to do the job you were given. You're on a film set for the first ever time. Who knows where this could end up?

It's time to make a decision. Do you:

Get rid of the set box and get out? **P283**

Or

Deliver the sides, seriously? **P285**

Get rid of the set box and get out

Yeah, you think, this is no fun. Not anymore, anyway. You've already had enough of actors slamming their doors in your face and being told what to do by a bearded guy with a funny hat.

This is a waste of your time.

You hide the set box and your '4PA' hat under a large shrub and scoot back to the driveway, taking one last look at the manor house before it's hidden from view.

Another world, you think.

You race at top speed towards the gate, which is half open, and go through it without a pause.

The girl with the long ponytail is talking to another kid and doesn't see you.

Moments later, you're half way down the street.

Good riddance, you think.

The rest of the day goes as you expect. You scoot around. Chat to a couple of friends. The usual day in the holidays.

In fact, it's just like almost every day in the holidays.

Maybe it is a bit boring, you think, but at least you're not doing unpaid work on a film set.

Though you can't help but wonder what's going on there.

I'm sorry, this part of your story is over. You joined the film crew as a production assistant and met a couple of actors by getting them some breakfast. But the next task you were given seemed to be too hard, and you gave up on the whole thing. That's a shame, but because this is a *You Say Which Way* book, you can change your mind or try a different pathway in the book. Maybe you'd like to be an extra instead, and be part of the film itself?

284

It's time to make a decision. You have three choices. Do you:

Change your decision about delivering the sides? **P285**

Or

Go to the list of choices and start reading from another part of the story? **P366**

Or

Go back to the beginning of the story and try another path? **P253**

Deliver the sides, seriously

You can figure this out. But where should you start? The trailers or the manor house? You have no idea who those people are, or where they might be.

So … who might know?

You spin your scooter around and head toward the catering trailer. Pi and R-Squared might know. Everyone gets food, after all.

You leave your scooter outside and go in. Pi and R-Squared are tidying up after serving who-knows-how-many breakfasts.

"Back for a snack?" R-Squared asks.

"I'd love a bottle of water. And can you help me, please? I have to find Jags, the gaffer, and Knuckles, the best boy grip, and Mindy, the clapper, but I don't know them or where they might be."

"Sure. Jags is the head of the electrical department. He could be in the electrical trailer, instructing his staff, or on the set. They'll be filming in the house any minute now, I think. Knuckles is a lighting technician, and Mindy is the second assistant cameraperson, who will hold the board with the scene details and clap it when they're about to roll. They're be in the house, I expect."

You take all this in. "Thanks."

"Hurry, though," Pi adds, handing you a bottle of water. "You'll have to get into the house before they lock it down."

"All right. Thanks. See you later."

You've no time to waste. You leave the catering trailer, grab your scooter, and head towards the trailers. It only takes a minute or two for you to find the one labeled 'Electrical'.

A red-bearded man steps out of the trailer as you come to a stop. Why are almost all the men on the film set bearded? Maybe their last movie was in Antarctica.

"Have you got the sides for me?" he asks.

"Are you Jags?" you ask, pulling the sides pages from your set box and handing them over.

"Yes. Thanks. Filming will start in a few minutes. I'm on my way to the house now."

"I have more to deliver," you say. "Can you tell me what Knuckles looks like, please?"

"Short girl, about twenty-five. Look for the people working on the lighting. Oh, and she has green hair."

Knuckles is a woman? You would never have guessed.

"Thanks. I'll hurry ahead," you say, and set off, wondering why Jags hadn't simply said to look for the woman with the green hair. Surely, she would stand out like a traffic light on a dark night.

You get back onto the driveway because you can scoot faster than on the grass, and you're at the manor house in a flash. How many miles are you going to cover on this job?

You lean the scooter up against one of the giant pillars outside the main entrance and head towards a set of double doors that open into a large tiled entrance hall.

"Wait. Do you need to be in there?" A tall boy with a fedora labeled '3PA' steps in front of you.

"Yes, I think so," you say.

"You *think* so? You don't know? Sorry, I can only let people inside who are needed for the first scene. They'll be rolling in a few minutes."

"Let me pass. I have to deliver some sides."

"Nah. They'll already have the sides. You'll have to wait out here."

You take a deep breath. This stubborn kid is blocking your way. The longer he delays you, the less time you'll have to deliver the sides. You're sure the people you need to get to are inside, but you're not involved with the first scene, so he won't let you in. What should you do?

It's time to make a decision. Do you:

Wait outside until scene one is filmed? **P288**

Or

Bluff your way inside? **P290**

Wait outside until scene one is filmed

You decide not to try to force your way in. After all, maybe Knuckles and Mindy aren't inside yet. They might arrive any minute, and you can give them the sides when they turn up.

Three minutes pass. The only other people to enter the house are not those you're looking for.

"Don't you have something else to do?" taunts the tall kid with the '3PA' hat. He sneers at you.

You have a sinking feeling in your stomach that maybe he deliberately did not let you inside. But how you could ever know that?

Another minute passes. You can hear sounds from inside the manor house. They're indistinct. Everyone must be behind a closed door somewhere.

You sit down on the house steps and wait. At least you have a bottle of water to drink.

After an hour, lots of people come out of the house. You gather it's some kind of break for the actors and film crew. George, your boss, strides over and looks down at you from his great height.

"Where were you? I told you to deliver the sides to Knuckles and Mindy."

"I was here, waiting," you say. "That dude wouldn't let me in." You indicate the tall kid who denied you entry.

The second assistant director glances at the other kid. You see the boy's face go white. "That's his mistake. Your mistake is not convincing him that you needed to get inside to deliver something important to the crew. I need people I can rely on. Unfortunately, that means you're both fired."

Unhappy, you leave, scooting down the long driveway and out onto the sidewalk. Four people are there, shouting and waving placards reading "We want more pay". It's the fired screenwriters, protesting the budget cuts that cost them their jobs. One of them calls out that he'll have to become a novelist for a few extra dollars each week. This movie is going to be a real mess. Lucky you're out of it.

I'm sorry, this part of your story is over. You joined the film crew as a production assistant and met a couple of actors by getting them some breakfast. However, you didn't complete your next task. That wasn't entirely your fault, but the second assistant director wasn't happy.

But what would have happened if you'd tried to bluff your way in? Or maybe you'd like to try another pathway in the book? What would it be like to be an extra and be part of the film?

It's time to make a decision. You have three choices. Do you:

Change your decision and bluff your way in? **P290**

Or

Go to the big list of choices and start reading from another part of the story? **P366**

Or

Go back to the beginning and try another path? **P253**

Bluff your way inside

You wave the bottle of water Pi gave you and speak with as much authority as you can muster. "I've got this for the second assistant director. You want him mad?"

The tall kid looks at the bottle of water like it's a hall pass. "Well, then, I guess you better go in. They're setting up in the dining hall. Go across the hall and turn left."

You make your way inside, following his directions, and emerge into a room dominated by a massive dining table covered in party food. You wonder if it's real or fake. A gigantic glittering chandelier dangles above it like a bejeweled octopus. Film crew and actors are everywhere. Conrad Pringle and Kathy Barnes are there, as are eight kids about your age in costumes you might wear for Halloween. You see a superhero, a ghost, a nurse, an alien and others. One is an actress you actually recognize, Alicia Tomova, dressed like a ballerina. The film crew are adjusting lighting or sound equipment. Two camera operators are on Segways.

Three women with green hair are in the room. Luckily, only one of them fits the full description Jags gave you. She's adjusting a light on a stand. You approach her, taking a copy of the sides out of your set box as you go.

"Knuckles?"

"That's me. Ah, you have the sides for me. Thanks." She beams at you.

"Can you point out Mindy for me?"

"Sure." She gestures towards a blue-haired woman standing a few feet away, holding a clapperboard.

You deliver the last set of sides and receive her thanks. Wow. You feel proud of yourself helping out on the film set. But what now?

"Well done, Scooter."

You spin. The second assistant director has come up behind you. "Thanks, George." You hope he doesn't mind you calling him 'George'.

"I'll need you to help with the lockdown when we have a break. For now, go and sit with Goldilocks over there and watch."

Great. That sounds like fun.

Goldilocks is sitting on a plastic chair in a corner, out of camera shot. You recognize her by the '1PA' label on her hat. Like the kid actors, she's also about your age.

You pull up a chair and introduce yourself. Goldilocks says 'hi' and smiles. There's a set box like yours sitting at her feet. You wonder why Goldilocks didn't give sides to Knuckles and Mindy, but then realize that she may have had other duties, and George probably wanted to see if you could carry out a task he gave you.

You're about to ask, but at that moment, the director stands and shouts. "Rolling in one minute! Everyone into position!"

There's a scramble as people take their places. The kids in costume sit at the table. Conrad and Kathy stand to one side. Conrad holds a booklet up as if he's about to read from it.

"Quiet on the set!" That was George.

Mindy claps the clapperboard.

"Rolling!"

The actors spring into motion. The costumed actors spring into activity at the table, eating food and jostling each other. Conrad and Kathy start talking about a murder mystery role play game they want the kids to play, where each one takes on a particular character in the plot. The kids all pick up envelopes beside their plates and look inside.

"Cut!" George calls.

"That's a take!" the director yells. "Let's do it all again, people!"

Does he ever speak without exclamation marks? You watch as the actors repeat the scene twice more until the director is happy. "Moving on!" he calls.

"Moving on?" you ask Goldilocks.

"He's happy with the takes for this setup. Now they're going to rearrange the equipment for another setup. It'll take a few minutes. Hey, watch my stuff. I need to go to the honeywagon."

"For a battery? I've got spares."

"No, silly. That's the honeybadger. I need a ten-O-one." She scuttles off.

Ten-O-one. That doesn't explain anything.

You watch as the camera crew and lighting technicians move their equipment. After a few minutes, Goldilocks returns.

"Did I miss anything important?"

"No, I don't think so." Though you can't be sure because this is the first time you've been on a film set.

"Quiet on the set!" George yells again.

The actors replay the scene, with the cameras shooting from a different angle. A couple of takes later, and the director is happy. You're never going to watch a movie again without thinking about how it's made.

"Break time!" he shouts. "Fifteen minutes, everyone. Food, water and coffee is in the entrance hall."

George beckons you. "You're on lockdown duty. Go to the side entrance and make sure no one leaves and no one comes in during the break. You can get a snack afterwards. Go, go, go!"

You hurry to the side entrance, grabbing a cheese and ham sandwich from the buffet in the hall as you pass, despite what George said. It only took a second. A sign directs people to port-a-potties immediately outside the back entrance. There's no need for anyone to leave the house except to attend to that personal business, and no doubt another PA is stationed there to make sure people don't wander off.

The cheese and ham sandwich is tasty. You should have grabbed two of them. Also, you're thirsty now and your bottle of water is in the dining room. You think about going to the entrance hall to get some water and more food, but that would mean leaving your post.

At that moment, the kid wearing the alien costume walks towards the door you're locking down.

"No one's allowed to leave," you say, trying to sound officious. "We're on a lockdown."

"It's really hot in this suit," the alien says. "I want to go out into the cool breeze."

You can understand that. It was distinctly warm in the dining hall with all the lighting and so many people. Would it matter if you let this poor over-heated alien outside for a while?

"Please. I'll only be a few minutes. Nobody will know."

It's time to make a decision. Do you:

Make the alien stay inside? **P294**

Or

Let the alien out? **P299**

Make the alien stay inside

"Sorry," you tell the alien. "The second assistant director gave clear instructions. No one's allowed to leave during the break."

"Okay, then." The alien nods, his antenna flopping back and forth. He turns and walks back toward the entrance hall.

The next couple of minutes pass uneventfully. Apart from your stomach rumbling, that is. The smell of food from the entrance hall is piquing your appetite. You saw cakes and cookies as well as sandwiches and hot snacks. What if they're all eaten before you have an opportunity to get a plateful or two? You don't want to miss out on those tasty treats.

You can nip back and get a drink and more food. It'll take two minutes. That shouldn't be a problem, should it?

But what if someone else tries to leave? You won't be there to stop them.

It's time to make a decision. Do you:

Leave your lockdown post and get some food? **P297**

Or

Stay in your lockdown post? **P295**

Stay in your lockdown post

You decide to follow George's instructions and stay put. It won't be for much longer anyway. There's a reason you (and presumably other PAs on the other exits) have been given lockdown duty. The director must want to be sure all the actors and film crew are present when he's ready to restart filming.

Hunger pangs claw at your stomach, but you wait patiently a few minutes longer.

"Break's over!" someone calls.

Great, you think, leaving your post and heading toward the entrance hall. The second assistant director meets up with you on the way.

"No one in or out, Scooter?"

"No, George."

He gives you a thumbs-up. "You've done a fantastic job. Just the PA I need—someone reliable. I'll keep you on. Now, go get some food. There's plenty left. The cheesecake is super yummy."

You grin. Sounds like you'll have more work coming your way. Though it's probably still going to be unpaid.

Congratulations, this part of your story is over. You joined the film crew as a production assistant and met a couple of actors by getting them some breakfast.

Then you successfully carried out a couple of other tasks the second assistant director gave you, and he's pleased. You don't get paid, but he lets you keep the fedora, and you had a day you won't forget. Even better, he invites you back tomorrow.

Maybe you'd like to try another pathway in the book? What would it be like to be an extra and be part of the film?

296

It's time to make a decision. Do you:

Go to the list of choices and start reading from another part of the story? **P366**

Or

Go back to the beginning of the story and try another path? **P253**

Leave your lockdown post and get some food

You decide it won't make any difference if you slip away and get more food. No one's around. It'll only take a couple of minutes.

You hurry to the entrance hall. Lots of actors and crew are still there. Including the 2AD, your boss, who spots you before you can grab a sandwich.

"What are you doing here, Scooter?" George says. "You're supposed to be on lockdown duty. Get back there."

Guiltily, you return to your post. Worse, no one tries to leave the house, so you're not even needed there.

"Break's over!" someone calls.

Now's your time to get food. You return to the entrance hall.

There's plenty left. You pile a paper plate with snacks of all kinds, take it into the dining room where filming will continue, and sit next to Goldilocks.

"Everyone: get ready for the next setup!" the director shouts.

The main actors and the extras take their places. It's the same scene as before, but again the cameras and lighting have been moved.

Unfortunately, one place at the table remains empty, and it's the spot next to Alicia Tomova, the star child actress.

"Who are we missing?" the director shouts. He doesn't seem to have a volume control.

A young woman with a clipboard steps forward. She has a yellow fedora with 'SS' on it, which contrasts powerfully with her striking red hair. "The alien's not here."

You groan. Goldilocks looks at you sharply.

298

George strides over, index finger jabbing inches in front of your face. "The alien snuck out because you didn't do your lockdown duty properly," he accuses.

Probably, you think. "Maybe," you say. "Am I fired?"

"Not yet. Find the alien. Go, go, go. Goldilocks, help look, please. We can't film with someone missing."

You get up, leaving your food behind. This is your fault, but maybe you can make amends. Outside the main entrance, you grab your scooter. Now, where should you look?

It's time to make a decision. Do you:

Search around the trailers? **P301**

Or

Search amongst the trees? **P307**

Let the alien out

You decide it won't matter if the alien actor goes outside to cool down for a short while.

"No problem," you say. "Just be sure you're gone no longer than a few minutes."

"Thanks." The alien clops past on rubber webbed feet. "I won't go far. I owe you one."

You feel good having helped someone out and maybe made a friend. However, that feeling lasts only five minutes. The alien hasn't returned.

Another five minutes pass, and you're getting worried.

"Break's over!" someone calls.

You look outside, but the alien is nowhere in sight.

Perhaps the alien came back in another way. Yes, that must be it. You've been worrying for nothing. Now's your time to get food, so you return to the entrance hall.

There's plenty left. You pile a paper plate with snacks of all kinds and take it into the dining room where the crew is about to continue filming and hope to see the alien in there.

Unfortunately, there's no sign of him there either. Nervously, you sit next to Goldilocks.

"Everyone: get ready for the next setup!" the director shouts.

The main actors and the extras take their places. It's the same scene as before, but again the cameras and lighting have been moved.

Unfortunately, one place at the table remains empty, and it's the spot next to Alicia Tomova, the star child actress.

"Who are we missing?" the director shouts. He doesn't seem to have a volume control.

300

A young woman with a clipboard steps forward. She has a yellow fedora with 'SS' on it, which contrasts powerfully with her striking red hair. "The alien's not here."

You facepalm. Why didn't the alien return when he said he would? Now you're going to be in trouble.

Goldilocks looks at you sharply.

George catches sight of that and comes over. "Do you know anything about this, Scooter?"

"Um … he wanted to go outside to cool down for five minutes. I thought he must have come back in a different way."

The second assistant director takes a deep breath. "I told you not to let anyone in or out during the lockdown."

"Yes, but—" You pause when you see your boss's stern expression. "Am I fired?"

"Not yet. Go find the alien. Goldilocks, please help. We can't film until he's found."

You get up, leaving your food behind. This is your fault, but maybe you can make amends. Outside the main entrance, you grab your scooter. Now, where should you look?

It's time to make a decision. Do you:

Search around the trailers? **P310**

Or

Search amongst the trees? **P307**

Search around the trailers

The alien character isn't in sight. You decide to go look over by the trailers. Perhaps he went back to wardrobe for something. Or to the catering trailer for a snack. He won't be in lighting or electrical or anything like that, and why would he have returned to the extras' holding room?

Wardrobe first, then.

You scoot across the grass towards the largest trailer parked in the manor gardens. This movie may have a low budget, but there weren't any cuts on the wardrobe department. It's the longest trailer you've seen. How it got in the gate you can't imagine.

Two people, a man and a woman, sit in deckchairs outside.

"Have you seen someone dressed in an alien costume?" you ask. It's hard to keep the desperation out of your voice.

The man responds. "Sorry, but we can't help you. We've been tidying up inside the trailer and only came outside three or four minutes ago. Haven't seen the alien."

"It's a great costume," the woman adds. "One of our best."

You agree. It's so realistic, the kid could almost be mistaken for a real alien if you didn't notice the plastic antenna flopping every which way.

Suddenly, you have an idea. Maybe there's another solution to this dilemma. If they have a *second* alien suit, then maybe someone else can take the place of the missing alien. Maybe you. After all, who would know?

"Do you have another alien suit, by any chance?"

"No. We only brought one with us."

"Thanks anyway." There goes that idea. You sigh and head over to the catering trailer, the second most likely place the alien might be.

As soon as you go inside, you see there's no alien.

"Hey, Scooter," Pi says. "You come back for a bacon sandwich?"

"No, thanks, I—" You pause. Why not? You left your snack uneaten. May as well have a bacon sandwich if it's offered. "Yes, please."

"Coming right up."

You leave the catering trailer with a double bacon thick cut sandwich. Hardly anyone is around, apart from the two people taking a break outside wardrobe and someone moving stuff outside the props trailer. No alien anywhere.

You take a huge bite of the sandwich while you think of where to look next. You've lost a bit of time. You'd better find him quickly.

But the bacon sandwich is so yummy. It would be impossible to scoot with the sandwich and your set box at the same time, so you decide to finish the sandwich before going any further. You take another enormous bite.

At that moment, your walkie-talkie crackles into life. "Scooter, are you there? Over." It's George.

"Mummmph," you reply, your mouth full.

"Are you eating? Over."

"Um, hum."

"You're supposed to be looking for the alien. Over."

You finally swallow the mouthful of buttered bread and bacon. "I am looking. I'm at the catering trailer in case he was here. Stop." Do you say 'stop' when you're finished speaking, or it that for telegrams?

"Goldilocks has found the alien. Get back here. And don't say 'stop'. It's 'over'. Over."

"What's over? Are you firing me? Please don't. Stop."

"I'm not firing you yet. I'm telling you not to say 'stop' when you finish talking. Say 'over'. Over."

"Okay. Over, over."

"Just one 'over'. Over."

"I said only one over, over. Over, over."

"Look, just get back here. Now. Over."

You're totally over this conversation and clip the walkie-talkie back onto your clothes.

After finishing the bacon sandwich, you pick up the set box and head back to the manor house. Goldilocks and the alien arrive just as you do. George is at the main entrance, waiting.

"Well done, Goldilocks," he says, then turns to you. "Scooter, I don't think you're taking your job seriously. You're fired. Hand over your set box, walkie-talkie, and fedora, and get out of here."

Wait, there's more: As you scoot slowly away from the big house and all the activity inside, you see a smaller truck has cut across a lawn on one side and parked up under some trees.

That's kind of odd. Why is it so far away from everything else? On a hunch, and also because you've got nothing else to do with your day, you scoot closer, trying to see why it's there.

The sign on the side says *Kooky Kostumes* and one of the back doors is slightly open. The first thing you see when you open it a little more is an alien costume. It's exactly the same as the alien that got you fired. Why did those people back at the big costume trailer say there was only one?

The second thing you see answers your question.

The truck is full of art and antiques. Those people in deck chairs are thieves!

While the film crew is in lockdown they are ransacking the rest of the house and filling up this truck. You need to tell George. You reach for your walkie-talkie, but of course it isn't there. You'd better scoot back.

But what if George doesn't believe you? What if the person on the door won't let you in? Your eye travels to the alien costume. Of course!

It's a struggle, but you eventually squeeze in. Then you scoot back to the house. The guard on the door is the same kid you had to bluff past before. At first you think he's going to try to stop you, but instead he looks amazed:

"How did you get outside again? Get inside before I get fired."

You sprint down the hall to the film set, where they're just finishing a take.

"That's a wrap!" someone yells, and then, "Hey, why are there two aliens?"

You wrestle off the alien head.

"George, I need to talk to you, urgently."

George looks bewildered but heads over to listen. "This had better be good, Scooter." He walks you off to one side of the set.

You quickly explain about the truck outside being filled with stuff from the house. George looks disbelieving, then angry, then worried, then excited. He should be an actor.

"If those thieves get away with stuff from this house, the film will be ruined. We don't have any insurance and the owners would kick us out before we finish. But maybe we can actually make this situation into movie gold." He snaps his fingers.

"Wendy! Paddy! Bring your hand-helds now. Everyone else stay here. Scooter—you're with me."

George directs the two camera folk to circle round the building under cover of the trees. "You head towards the truck, Scooter, and see what you can get them to say. Oh, and here's a mike." He pins a small device to the green material of your costume. "Now, action!"

You scoot quietly over the grass to the truck in time to meet the two people you'd talked to in deck chairs earlier just arriving there too. One holds two paintings and the other hefts a chandelier. They look at each other, at the things they are carrying and then the woman speaks up:

"We're just taking these things into storage."

"Yes, storage!" chimes in the man.

"You'd better head back to the film set. Someone was looking for you earlier."

The woman puts the chandelier on the grass and swings open the back doors of the truck. She looks inside and looks back at you, noticing you haven't gone.

"Can you just help me with this?" she asks you, beckoning you closer. You take a few steps closer, wondering when George and the camera crew are going to turn up. How long can you 'act natural' for?

Whump. Someone pushes you forward into the back of the truck. Slam. The doors shut and click. You fumble around in the alien costume, trying to wrestle the head off so you can try to get the doors open. There's the sound of the two thieves getting into the front cab and doors slamming.

They're kidnapping you!

"Go, go, go, Jake!" says the woman.

"The motor's not turning over!" the man replies.

"That's because we disconnected the battery." That's George's voice. "And smile, you two—you're on camera. How does it feel to be caught on camera stealing heirlooms and kidnapping an alien?"

The footage of the two thieves goes viral and everyone is talking about the alien kidnap. The studio brings in new writers and lots of money. The alien gets a bigger part and

306

you get to play part of the role. They also put vents in the costume and give you both plenty of breaks. Best of all, the studio keeps it a mystery as to who is inside the costume. You get to have a normal life without paparazzi following you everywhere.

Things can always go differently in the movies, though. Why not choose again and run another story?

It's time to make a decision. Do you:

Go to the list of choices and start reading from another part of the story? **P366**

Or

Go back to the beginning of the story and try another path? **P253**

Search amongst the trees

The alien said he wanted to cool down, so you reason that you're most likely to find him out of the sun and amongst the trees. The nearest clump of trees in the expansive gardens are not far away. You race over there.

Goldilocks must have had the same idea, because she's following, but on foot she is well behind you.

"Alien!" you call. "Are you here somewhere?"

No answer. You scoot around a few trees and a large shrubbery, and then you see him.

He's lying on the ground, fast asleep in the shade of a cedar tree. You're angry. The alien promised he'd be quick and got you into a lot of trouble when he didn't return. The entire film crew is waiting for him.

You shake him awake, none too gently.

"Wha—Whassat?" he says groggily.

"You're late!"

He sits up. "How long have I been asleep?"

"Half an hour. Get a move on. You've held up the filming, and they're blaming me."

"They should blame the costume designers. This suit needs vents. Vents and fans."

"Just get back there!" You're still angry.

"It'll be quicker on your scooter." He doesn't wait for your permission to take it but snatches it up from the grass where you'd left it, hops on, and scoots off in the direction of the manor house.

Dang. You jog after the alien, hoping he leaves your scooter somewhere you can find it.

You catch up with Goldilocks near the manor. She's walking back, and you slow to walk with her. "I see you found him," she says.

"Yeah. Hey, do you think George will fire me? I mean, it's only one mistake …"

"I don't know, but I'm sure he'll tell you soon enough." Goldilocks turns to you. "Let's get inside, see what's going on."

You look for your scooter, but it isn't outside. The 3PA waits at the front entrance and indicates that you can both enter the house. Inside the grand entrance hall, you see your scooter leaning against a wall, looking completely out of place under a portrait of a dour old man.

Goldilocks heads to the dining room. You follow, apprehensive about what George might say to you now that the immediate crisis is over. Will he still be angry, or will he be forgiving?

The director and the first assistant director are having an emphatic discussion about something. George sees you both and strides over.

"Well done for finding the alien," he says, "but it turns out to be of no use. Another child actor has just gone off sick."

"There's a lot of that going around on this set," Goldilocks says.

"Well, it's not something that an extra can fill in for. She sits opposite Alicia Tomova at the dining table and has a speaking role. No one's going to be able to take her place at this late stage."

"I can," Goldilocks says, beaming. "I've memorized the entire script."

"All eight pages of it. Well, that's some good luck at last. Get over to wardrobe, Goldilocks, find a superhero costume and get back here. We'll have to redo the first couple of setups but at least we won't waste the whole day."

Has he forgotten about you? "What do you want me to do?" you ask.

"You can leave, Scooter. I need my PAs to be reliable, like Goldilocks here. You let someone out during a lockdown. It's cost us money we can't afford. You're fired. Hand over your set box, walkie-talkie, and fedora, and get out of here."

Unhappy, you scoot off down the long driveway toward the road. Half way down, you see a silver saucer-like craft standing on five metal legs behind the trees, gleaming in the sunlight. Odd, you think as you skid to a stop, that wasn't there when you arrived earlier.

You decide to go closer. It's the size of one of the large trailers. Small windows line the top half, while a ladder extends to the ground from the bottom half. You reach up and touch the underside. It's metal. The budget certainly wasn't spared on this prop. But you can't imagine what it's got to do with the murder mystery party.

The alien descends the ladder and waves at you. You stare back. How on earth did he get here before you? Won't he be in even more trouble with George for skipping out again?

"Hey, alien," you say. "Get back to the house. They're all waiting for you."

The alien beckons you from the foot of the ladder.

You scoot over, about to give him a piece of your mind. He's cost you your (unpaid) job, and now he's AWOL again.

You reach the ladder. "Listen, alien, I don't know what you think you're doing, but—"

The alien gestures upwards. Does he want you to climb the ladder? Well, you're not doing that, but you look up to see what he's pointing at.

Staring down at you from inside the craft is another alien. What's going on?

The first alien grabs you, and, with unexpected strength, lifts you off the ground and shoves you up the ladder.

310

"Hey! Stop!" You turn and grab at the alien's plastic antennae. But they don't feel plastic. They feel real. This isn't a kid in an alien suit.

The alien's mouth opens in a wide 'O' and it emits an inhuman moan. You let go. He—or she, or it— shoves you further up the ladder. The alien above grabs you under the arms, and suddenly you're inside the craft.

Before you can look around much, one of them jabs you in the arm. A cold wooziness overcomes you. Your last thoughts before you pass out are that you're being kidnapped by real aliens. Why? Do they want to eat you for dinner? Conduct experiments on you? Exhibit you in an alien zoo?

I'm sorry, this part of your story is over. You joined the film crew as a production assistant and met a couple of actors by getting them some breakfast. You delivered sides to various crew members and watched a scene being filmed before you were asked to enforce a lockdown, which you utterly failed. That caused a delay in the filming and incurred the wrath of the director and the second assistant director, who fired you. Worse, you were then kidnapped by real aliens.

But, luckily, this is a *You Say Which Way* book, and you can make different choices or try different pathways, including trying out as an extra.

It's time to make a decision. Do you:

Go to the list of choices and start reading from another part of the story? **P366**

Or

Go back to the beginning of the story and try another path? **P253**

Choose to be an extra

"I want to work as an extra, please," you say.

"Cool. Before you can do that, Scooter, I need you to sign this simple contract. Here. And here. That ensures you'll be paid the proper day rate for an extra. Handy money for you."

You sign the document. "Do I have to learn any lines?"

The 2AD sighs. "Probably not. The scriptwriters were fired a couple of weeks ago due to budget cuts. The director says he wants to 'wing it'. Apart from some scripted lines at the start of the first scene, he wants to let the story unfold naturally. Just act in character for your small part. That's all you have to do."

"I can do that. What's my character?"

"*Murder Mystery Party* is a movie in which the main character, played by star Alicia Tomova, has a murder mystery game set up by her parents for her birthday party. And all the guests go in costume. You're a ninja."

This sounds weird, but it's the movies. Weird is just how they roll.

"So, get over to the wardrobe trailer, put on a ninja suit, and make sure you're inside the mansion in forty-five minutes. Oh, and help yourself to breakfast first if you want. Just follow the smell of bacon to the catering trailer."

"I will, thanks." You jump on your scooter and head off. You had breakfast at home, but why pass up the opportunity to eat movie food? It'll have to be quick, though, so you can get your costume and get to the house on time.

Five minutes later, you're tucking into a plateful of scrambled eggs, bacon, sausage, hash browns, fried mushrooms, beans, and toast. That ought to keep you going.

After that, you find the wardrobe trailer when you see a ghost and a superhero leaving it. It's the largest trailer on the set. You park your scooter outside and climb the steps.

A middle-aged woman greets you as you enter. "I'm Bonnie, and this is Clyde," she says, indicating a man searching amongst a rack of costumes. "What is it you need, dearie?"

Bonnie and Clyde? Are they really movie names? you wonder. "I'm supposed to be a ninja," you say. "Do you have anything for that?"

"Of course, dearie. It should be a perfect fit for you. Clyde, grab the ninja outfit, will you?"

"Right-o, Bonnie." He comes over with a completely black robe costume, hooded and long-sleeved, with a pair of matching soft shoes not unlike a pair of slippers. "Changing rooms are over there." He points to the far end of the trailer, where three small curtained cubicles are squeezed in.

Once you've changed, Clyde takes your street clothes and shoes from you. "We'll look after these," he says, and puts them in a large plastic bag he labels 'Ninja'.

"We'd give you some weapons to look the part," Bonnie says, "but you're out of luck. We had a plastic shuriken—a ninja throwing weapon—but we lost it somewhere on our last gig. And Clyde stepped on the katana this morning. Snapped it right in two."

"The sword was plastic too, then?"

"Yes. But the costume itself looks fab." She steps back. "Excellent. Isn't it, Clyde?"

"Well, blow me down if we don't have a real assassin of the night."

A floor-to-ceiling mirror reveals your transformation, and you startle yourself with your reflection. You look like a real ninja!

"Off to the manor house with you," Clyde says. "Filming will start in fifteen minutes."

"Thanks."

You leave with a smile and a parkour leap out of the trailer. On your scooter, you glide back to the driveway, then follow it up to the house. It's a magnificent three-story home complete with an enormous patio, multiple upper-story balconies, and pillars outside what must be the main entrance.

Who could live here?

You've often scooted through this part of town and wished you could look inside one of these houses, and now you will.

Wide stone steps and a zigzag wheelchair ramp lead up to the double-door main entrance. A tall boy wearing a green fedora with a label '3PA' sticking out of its band looks at you, glances at a sheet of paper in his hand, and indicates with a jerk of his head that you can enter.

Inside, the high entrance hall is square and tiled in a black and white check pattern like a supersized chessboard. A white staircase with a central red carpet runner stands directly in front of you. Portraits dot the walls.

A girl in a green fedora hat with the label '1PA' comes over. "We're using the front of the house only, and even that costs eight thousand dollars a day to rent, plus breakages, so try not to knock over anything priceless. I'll give you a quick tour."

"Great, thanks. Can I park my scooter here?" You motion to a spot beneath a portrait of a grumpy old man.

She shrugs. "Sure." Pointing in four directions one after the other, she rattles off, "Drawing room on your left. Ballroom on your right. Library to the right of the main staircase, next to the ballroom. Bathroom behind the main staircase and to the right, opposite the servants' staircase.

Dining room opposite the library, to the left of the main staircase, next to the drawing room. First scene is in the dining room. Got it?"

Your brain is whirling with her rapid directions, but you think you've understood where everything is. "I've got it."

"Good. Go through to the dining room, then."

You emerge into a room dominated by a massive dining table laden with party food. Is it real or fake, you wonder? A tremendous glittering chandelier dangles above the table. Film crew and actors are everywhere. Two of the actors are adults you don't recognize, and the others are young people in costumes, like you. One girl, dressed as a prima ballerina, is Alicia Tomova, a young actress you recognize from movies. Some of the film crew are adjusting lighting or sound equipment. Two camera operators are on Segways.

You chat with the superhero, a girl, for a few minutes. Then the director stands on a chair and calls out, "Attention, please, people!"

The room falls silent.

"As you know, the script is incomplete. The scriptwriters are no longer with us. We have extras performing the roles of the other kids in the movie rather than professional actors. We're going to ad lib, make it up as we go along, keep it natural. And we're going to make it one long, continuous shoot. That will give it the really authentic look I want."

You're not so sure about that. It sounds like madness to you.

"Everyone, take your places," the first assistant director says.

A young woman with red hair and a yellow fedora indicates where all the kids should sit at the table. You're sitting on the left-hand side of Alicia Tomova, and a kid in an alien suit sits on her other side. On your other side is someone dressed as a traditional cartoon white-sheeted ghost, a perfect contrast to your completely black outfit. On the opposite side of the table sit a girl knight, a boy wizard dressed in a full-length purple robe and tall hat decorated with stars, a girl dressed as a nurse, and the superhero.

The director tells you all about the first scene and what you should do when the cameras roll. Then he retreats to his director's chair.

Two adults, playing the parents of Alicia, stand at one end of the room. The man holds a booklet up as if he's about to read from it.

"Quiet on the set!" That was George.

A young woman with blue hair claps the clapperboard, signifying the start of shooting the setup for the scene. You try not to jump.

"Rolling!"

You chat to the ghost, discovering that under the white covering she is a girl, and reach for some fruit juice and a mini sandwich. It's real, and you take a bite. Around the table, the other kids animate, talk, pick up food.

The father character, a tall guy with a large nose, a chisel chin and a grumpy expression, says, "Welcome to the party, kids. This is a murder mystery party. One of the eight of you will play the role of the victim, another will be the killer, and the others will be ordinary guests who can try to solve the mystery."

"Sounds fun, doesn't it, kids?" the mother character says. She's elegant, poised, with hazel eyes and hair. "See the envelopes in the center of the table? Take one each, read it secretly, and be ready to follow the instructions when we start. Don't show anyone what's in your envelope."

Everyone scrambles to pick up an envelope. They're unlabeled; presumably, who gets which envelope is supposed to be random. Probably another element of the director's 'wing it' approach.

316

Out of the corner of your eye, you see one of the Segway-mounted cameras rolling toward you. You try not to look directly at it.

You open the envelope. Without taking the instructions out, you lift the edge of the paper and see the words:

YOU ARE AN ORDINARY GUEST.

"Dang," the ghost next to you says. "Hey, Ninja, want to swap?"

"What have you got?" you ask.

"Not saying," the ghost says.

The wizard speaks up. "Hey, Ninja, swap with me instead. And, no, I'm not telling you what I've got either."

You can't read anything from their expressions. Particularly the ghost's, as most of her face is hidden by the sheet.

It's time to make a decision. You have three choices. Do you:

Keep your original envelope? **P345**

Or

Swap envelopes with the ghost? **P321**

Or

Swap envelopes with the wizard? **P317**

Swap envelopes with the wizard

"I'll swap with you, Wizard," you say, handing your envelope across the table, and receiving the wizard's one in return.

"Hey, I asked first," the ghost moans.

"Sorry, Ghost," you say. "Nothing personal."

"I'll swap with someone else, then," she says.

All around the table, kids covertly check their envelopes. You check the page in your new envelope. At the top are the words:

YOU ARE THE VICTIM.

There are further instructions telling you where to go and what to do when the game begins. You skim through. They're rather short.

Well, this will be interesting, you think, and help yourself to another club sandwich and more fruit juice.

At one side of the room, the "parents" are talking together, a camera operator and a sound operator hovering nearby to catch their conversation. After a few moments, the father character turns to face the table and speaks with his formal, grating voice. "Kids, it's time to start the murder mystery game. You've all got your instructions … and … and … um …"

Has he forgotten his lines? Or is this where the script runs out?

The mother character jumps in. "So, let's have fun! Remember to follow the instructions in your envelopes."

The others leave the dining room. You follow, then slip along a short hallway behind the grand staircase. When you emerge on the other side, the library is to your right. That's your destination.

That's the room in which you're going to die.

For the movie, anyway.

The library is a beautiful room whether you love books or not. Wooden shelving fills three-quarters of the room from the polished wooden floor to the mural-covered ceiling. Fancy curtains filter the light through the room. Big leather sofas and comfortable chairs, desks and tables are dotted around the room. There's even a sliding stepladder to help readers reach books on the higher shelves.

You've got time, and when would you ever get the opportunity again? You stride over to the step ladder, step up and then gently push off in the direction that takes you the long way around to the windows. It's like a book scooter.

Quietly, the oiled wheels take you past shelf after shelf. There are so many books! Have they all been read over the course of time? Some of the volumes appear to be two hundred years old. Surely, someone read them, sometime. You reach the end of the shelving in three pushes. But could you do it in one? You set off again, leg outstretched like an ice skater, one arm extended and the other clutching the ladder. You look out across the room and spot the director, waving and smiling.

A camera operator and a sound person are there also. You don't know if they followed you into the room or were already there when you entered. It doesn't matter, though. The director waves, wanting you to do something. But what?

Ah, look at the books. That's right.

You walk around the bookshelves, pulling out the occasional volume to flick through. They don't seem to be sorted in any particular way. In fact, it's as if someone's deliberately set out to put them in as random an order as possible. An almanac of cricket matches in the 1800s is next to Jane Austin's *Emma*, which is next to a travel guide for Copenhagen, which is next to *Duel at Dawn* … hey, that one looks interesting.

You should keep moving, so you delve further. At some point soon, you're going to be murdered. Unfortunately, your instructions didn't specify exactly *how* the crime will be carried out. It's going to be a surprise, and you'll just have to die creatively.

The killer sneaks up on you like a ghost.

"I knew I'd find you here," she says ominously.

You jump and spin to face your murderer. It *is* the ghost. She has a pistol. It looks real, but it must be fake. What if it isn't? What if this whole thing has been some sort of elaborate—The ghost fires.

The gun makes a loud pop. Something wet and squelchy hits you in the chest, spilling onto the book you were holding. Luckily it was *Harry Potter* and not the old cricket almanac.

Now it's time for your big scene. Your death act. You groan and stagger backwards, clutching at your chest with one hand, sticky red goo spreading between your fingers. You keep a shocked and puzzled look on your face. The book topples from your other hand as you pretend to lose balance, partially falling onto a leather sofa with an airy oomph! and sliding onto the floor. After a last gasp, you lie still, listening as the ghost slips out of the room.

Bare feet. That's how she snuck up on you. Nice.

"Cut!" the director shouts. "Check the gate."

The camera operator checks something. "Yeah, we got it."

"That's a take, then. Ninja, remember your position. You're needed for the scene in which someone finds the body. Great work, by the way. Your death fall was so natural. You couldn't have done any better if you'd actually died."

"I think I twisted my ankle."

"Even more realistic. What was your name again? Scooter, wasn't it?"

320

"Yes," you grunt as you raise yourself painfully onto the sofa.

"You've got a future in the movies, Scooter. My PA will pass on your details to an agent friend of mine. You're going to be a star."

Congratulations, this part of your story is over. You joined the film crew as an extra, dressed as a ninja, and wound up performing a pivotal role in the murder mystery game of the movie—that of the victim. You died like a pro and pleased the director so much that he predicts you'll become a star … but that's another story. You had a day you'll never forget and loads of free food into the bargain.

What might have happened if you'd kept your original envelope or swapped with the ghost? As this is a *You Say Which Way* book, you can change your previous decision. Or maybe you'd like to try another pathway in the book? What would it be like to be a production assistant and help with the movie production?

It's time to make a decision. Do you:

Go to the list of choices and start reading from another part of the story? **P366**

Or

Go back to the beginning of the story and try another path? **P253**

Swap envelopes with the ghost

"I'll swap with you, Ghost," you say, handing over your envelope, and receiving the ghost's instructions in return.

"Hey, I asked too," the wizard whined.

"Sorry, Wizard," you say. "Nothing personal."

All around the table, kids covertly check their envelopes. You slip your replacement one out of its envelope. At the top are the words:

YOU ARE THE MURDERER.

There are further instructions telling you what to do when the game begins. Now you know why the ghost wanted to swap. You help yourself to more food.

The "parents" tell the rest of the party to follow the instructions in their envelope.

You mull over what you read: you have to execute your victim. Whoever that is. All you got were a few words in capital letters.

MURDER WEAPONS ARE IN THE CABINET TOP DRAWER. CHOOSE ONE.

YOUR VICTIM WILL BE IN THE LIBRARY.

So, you know where to find your victim at least. You wonder what they are thinking right now. Probably looking around the room for their murderer. You look around the room too, looking for a cabinet. Ah, there's one.

Everyone ambles out of the dining room. You hang back a little, checking your instructions and making sure no one sees them as they pass you. Once everyone has gone, and not before, you can make your move.

You edge over to the cabinet cautiously, being careful to keep your body between the drawer and the doorway so no one could see if they returned but giving the camera crew a good view of your exploration of the drawer. How realistic are these weapons going to be?

They're not realistic. It's not a real murder movie, it's a kid's party game in a movie. You have three options with which to carry out your deadly deed. You hold up each option so the camera can see it, and to give you time to think. First, there's a black plastic water pistol preloaded with some red gunge, next a novelty egg timer labeled 'BOMB', and lastly a yellow rubber chicken.

You scratch your head. It's obvious how the first two weapons work, but a rubber chicken? What do you do with that? Use it as some sort of club? As a missile weapon? It's elastic enough.

Do you need to act in character? What would a ninja character prefer?

It's time to make a decision. You have three choices. Do you:

Choose the water pistol? **P323**

Or

Choose the egg timer bomb? **P326**

Or

Choose the rubber chicken? **P332**

Choose the water pistol

You've chosen the water pistol loaded with red gunge. It might not be a traditional ninja weapon, but it will be effective. Also, it will give you the opportunity of another shot if you miss the first one.

Concealing the pistol amongst the folds of your ninja robe, you move through the doorway into the hall, then behind the stairs. This is the shortest way to the library, and you don't want to be seen. If you are seen, though, are you allowed to kill any witnesses? Your instructions don't say.

With one last look along the hallway running adjacent to the bathroom, the library and the ballroom, you ease the pistol out of its hiding place and peer around the doorway.

The library is carpeted, unlike the rest of the ground floor of the manor, probably to keep the noise level low for anyone reading in there. With your slipper-style ninja shoes, you'll be able to sneak in soundlessly.

In the nearest corner, the director gives you a thumbs-up and motions you forward. A camera operator has a camera trained on you. The sound recordist is ready too, though you don't plan on giving him much work

You're really in character now. This is something you could easily get used to.

Across the room, browsing the bookshelves, stands your victim—the wizard.

Presumably he won't cast any spells on you.

Silently, you tread across the room until you are standing behind the wizard at arm's length.

There's no indication he suspects anyone else is in the room. You truly are living up to your role as a stealthy killer.

You raise the pistol.

324

At that moment, the wizard farts loudly. *Phuuft*! You catch a lungful and almost give yourself away by choking. He's not casting spells—he's casting smells! What a fetid fug!

Time to perform the execution. You say ominously: "I knew I'd find you here."

The wizard turns to face you, a look of consternation visible above his lopsided beard. You make a double shot point-blank at his chest, assassin-style. Two red splotches of gunk spurt onto his costume. He groans, drops to his knees, then keels over and lies still.

Job done. You discard the pistol onto the nearest leather sofa and quickly make your way out of the library. The director gives you a thumbs-up as you exit, and the camera swivels to follow your progress.

No one's in the hallway. Where should you go now? You need to be well away when the body is found. The room furthest away from the library on the ground floor is the drawing room, so you go there, passing the dining room on the way.

The drawing room is pleasantly decorated and furnished with comfortable sofas. Refreshments stand on a side table. A camera operator on a Segway is crammed into one corner, panning the camera at you as you enter.

You take a glass of apple juice and join the nurse, who is enjoying the view of the gardens from the large bay window. Maybe she could be your alibi?

"It's so hot today," you say, making sure she knows you're there. "I needed a drink."

She faces you. "I didn't take one, in case it's poisoned. I guess they must be okay, though." She goes to help herself to an orange juice.

You sit on the arm of a sofa, sipping your drink, relaxing. The gardens look so peaceful …

After a few minutes, a wail comes from the direction of the library. It's the ghost's voice.

"Murder! There's a body in the library!"

You drain your glass. No point in wasting your drink, right? Killing is thirsty work.

You follow the nurse as she rushes out of the room. But, of course, the wizard is far beyond medical help now.

Go to: the body in the library. **P335**

326

Choose the egg timer bomb

You've chosen the egg timer bomb. It might not be a traditional ninja weapon, but it has the advantage that you don't have to be accurate. You'll only need to place it near your victim. Presumably, when the timer runs out, it'll "explode" with a boom or an alarm of some kind. But instead of it being a reminder to take the eggs out of the saucepan, it'll signify the demise of your unlucky victim.

You wonder what sound it will make. That's probably why you picked it. Also, guns are just awful. Even pretend guns. Ugh. You sigh; bombs aren't any better either. Maybe you should have gone with the rubber chicken? Too late now.

Concealing the egg timer bomb amongst the folds of your ninja robe, you move through the doorway into the hall, then behind the stairs. This is the shortest way to the library, and you don't want to be seen.

The hallway leading from the bathroom to the ballroom, past the library, is deserted. Just what you need. Walking as quietly as you can, you approach the library doorway and peer inside.

The library is carpeted, unlike the rest of the ground floor of the manor, probably to keep the noise level low for anyone reading in there. In the nearest corner, the director gives you a thumbs-up. A camera operator has a camera trained on you. The sound recordist is ready too, waiting for your move.

Your victim is on the other side of the room, his back to you while he browses the books on the shelves. It's the wizard. If you'd taken his envelope, that would be you.

No need to get any closer than the doorway. The camera operator has a good shot of you where you are. You withdraw the egg timer bomb from your robe with a flourish for the camera and set the timer to the minimum: two minutes. The timer is round, and you plan to roll it across the carpet to a point near the wizard. He'll never hear a thing.

But will you bolt for safety or wait to see the wizard's death enactment?

It's time to make a decision. Do you:

Roll the timer and get away? **P328**

Or

Roll the timer and watch? **P330**

Roll the timer and get away

You decide to deliver the egg timer bomb and get away as quickly as possible. That'll look best for the movie and mean you're less likely to be found at the scene of the crime.

Nothing obstructs the direct path between you and the book-browsing wizard. You bend down and roll the plastic egg timer across the carpet at a steady pace as if it's a tiny bowling ball. It comes to a stop a couple of paces behind the wizard, who's completely unaware of it.

That's your cue to leave. You duck out of the doorway and move behind the stairs.

Where should you go now? You need to be well away when the body is found. You head to the room furthest away from the library. The door has a little brass label:

DRAWING ROOM

When you look inside, you don't see anything to draw or paint with. There's just a bunch of sofas.

Across the room, there's a table with refreshments. You can never have enough free food. A camera operator on a Segway is crammed into one corner, panning the camera at you as you enter. The nurse is over by the bay windows, gazing out at the gardens.

"It's so hot today," you say, making sure she knows you're there, so she can be your alibi. She turns to face you and nods agreement. You chat away as you help yourself to a drink.

About two minutes later, a loud boom sounds from the library. Wow, that small egg timer must have been hacked to produce a noise like that.

"What was that?" you say innocently.

"Our murderer has been busy, perhaps?"

329

You follow the nurse as she rushes out of the room and joins the other kids running to the library. But, of course, the wizard is far beyond medical help now.

Go to: the body in the library. **P335**

Roll the timer and watch

You decide to deliver the egg timer bomb and stay to watch. You'd like to see how the wizard performs his movie death.

Nothing obstructs the direct path between you and the book-browsing wizard. You bend down and roll the plastic egg timer across the carpet like a tiny bowling ball. It comes to a stop a couple of paces behind the wizard, who's completely unaware of it.

Mwahahahaha! You grin malevolently, waiting for the "bomb" to detonate. That'll look awesome for the camera. You're really getting into this killer role.

After the two minutes is up, the little egg timer emits a loud boom. Wow, it must have been hacked to produce a noise like that. Usually they just buzz a little.

The wizard keels over onto the floor with a dull thud. His hat falls off.

The noise of the "explosion" alerts everyone in the house. Voices and footsteps are coming your way. Panicking, you start moving.

"Hey, Ninja!" A voice calls from further down the hallway. It's Alicia. You recognize her voice. Unfortunately, the star of the film has seen you.

You duck around the corner behind the stairs. If you can get away, maybe you'll be able to convince her it wasn't you whom she saw. However, dressed in the ninja outfit, that's unlikely.

The dining room is two strides away when the nurse character steps in front of you.

"Going somewhere?" she says, crossing her arms.

"Um … that explosion—"

"It was *that* way." She points behind you in the direction of the library. "You came from there."

Alicia comes around the corner at that point. You're trapped between them. There's no getting away, no chance of them believing you're not the murderer.

"Got you!" she says. "Mystery solved in record time."

Behind her, you see the camera man frowning. The director throws his hat on the floor. George stands there, his head in his hands.

Looks like they'll have to start the filming over again.

I'm sorry, this part of your story is over. You joined the film crew as an extra and discovered that most of the cast consisted of extras, such was the low budget of the movie. Having almost no script didn't help matters either. On the other hand, it presented you with the opportunity of stamping your mark on your pivotal role—that of the murderer. Shame you didn't get away with it, but no one thinks it's your fault that the mystery wasn't really a mystery at all. Film is art, and art is … well, vague. After a few minutes of shouting at you, the director laughs it off, decides to treat the morning as a rehearsal and sends everyone for a snack break. One thing about movie sets is that there's always plenty of food.

Perhaps you'd like to try murdering the wizard a different way? Or try another pathway in the book? What would it be like to be a production assistant, for instance?

It's time to make a decision. Do you:

Go to the big list of choices and start reading from another part of the story? **P366**

Or

Go back to the beginning of the story and try another path? **P253**

Choose the rubber chicken

You've chosen the rubber chicken. This is certainly the most unusual of the available murder weapons, but it's there … so you're going to use it. You're not a fan of guns or bombs.

The rubber chicken barely fits amongst the folds of your ninja robe, and it's a bit lumpy. Hopefully no one will see you. It'll be hard to explain why you have a rubber chicken stuffed down your front.

You move through the doorway into the hall, then behind the stairs. This is the shortest way to the library.

The hallway leading from the bathroom to the ballroom, past the library, is deserted. Just what you need. Walking as quietly as you can, you approach the library doorway and peer inside.

The library is carpeted, unlike the rest of the ground floor of the manor, probably to keep the noise level low for anyone reading in there. In the nearest corner, the director gives you a thumbs-up. A camera operator has a camera trained on you. The sound recordist is ready too, waiting for your move.

Your victim is on the other side of the room, his back to you while he browses the books on the shelves. It's the wizard.

With a little difficulty, you pull the rubber chicken free from your robes. In moments, you will execute your target. You feel yourself slipping into the mindset of a hardened assassin.

Now, how to deliver the killing blow? Try to sneak in and bludgeon the wizard with the rubber chicken? No, that's too clumsy. So, shall you throw it? But you might miss, and then what will you do?

You exhale softly, only just becoming aware that you were holding your breath. You don't want to waste time. Someone could come along at any moment.

Of course. You'll fling it like a giant rubber band. It's more accurate than throwing.

Out of the corner of your eye, you see the director grinning as you place the hollow head of the rubber chicken over one hand, then pull back on its legs with the other hand as if you're wielding a hand-held catapult. When it is stretched tightly, you aim … and then let go.

The rubber chicken sails across the room. For a moment, you think it's going to go well above the wizard's head, but then gravity does its work and pulls the missile down in a perfect attack parabola. It lands on the back of the wizard's head, sending his starred purple hat flying.

He's taken completely by surprise, but to his credit immediately plays the part of the unfortunate victim and falls to the ground, dramatically pulling a few books from the shelves as he does so. He comes to rest with the loose books scattered around his prone body.

Job done. The director gives you a thumbs-up, and the camera swivels to follow your progress as you leave the scene of the crime.

Where should you go now? You need to be well away when the body is found. The room furthest away from the library on the ground floor is the drawing room, so you go there, passing the dining room on the way.

You know it's the drawing room because it's labeled on the door, but there's no drawing stuff inside. There are some huge windows, though. The nurse is staring out of them at the garden.

"See anyone out there?"

The nurse turns, startled, then relaxes when she sees you mean her no harm.

"I wonder which of the party guests is the murder victim?" you say innocently.

"I hope it's Alicia," the nurse says. "Then the rest of us will get more of a role in the movie."

You shrug. "I think if the star of the movie got killed off, they'll want to start the filming over again."

"Have you seen anyone else since we left the dining room?"

Before you can answer, you hear a piercing wail. It's the ghost. "Murder! Murder most foul, as in the best it is, but this most foul, strange and unnatural!"

"The ghost has read Hamlet," the nurse says drily.

"Let's go and see what she's screaming about," you say, striding out of the room with the nurse at your heels. There'll be no surprises for you, of course.

Go to: the body in the library. **P335**

The body in the library

The cameras are still rolling. Literally rolling on their Segways, but also rolling in the sense that the director hasn't called "Cut!" The cameras are following you everywhere. You wonder how they don't get in each other's shots.

You and the nurse enter the library last except for Alicia, who is right behind you. Everyone's gaze is on the wizard, who lies on the floor in his death position, trying not to breathe too obviously. He doesn't look comfortable.

"What a way to die!" the superhero exclaims.

"Ooooh!" the knight says, as if she's a bit squeamish.

"A body in the library," Alicia says. "How … original."

No one says anything, but everyone looks at one another, as if a guilty expression will be evident on someone's face. Yours, however, is deadpan.

Then your heart skips a beat. The ghost knows you're the killer because she swapped envelopes with you! Unless she didn't read the contents first, but that wouldn't make sense. You have to hope she plays fair and doesn't ruin it by accusing you because she gave you the murderer's envelope.

The mother character comes into the room. "Oh, look, there's a body," she says, rather cheerily. "The murderer is one of you seven, and you have to deduce whom as a group. Now, there are rules to this game. You're each allowed to ask two questions. After all the questions, you can each make an accusation. Whoever correctly picks the murderer wins a prize. Okay?"

Everyone nods, including the dead wizard. That will have to be edited out of the final cut, you think.

"Have fun!" she says and leaves the room.

"So, where was everyone when I found the wizard's body?" the ghost asks.

"Does that count as a question?" the alien asks.

"Yes, it does," Alicia says. "And so does yours, Alien."

"Hey, that's not fair."

"Why do you think it's not fair?"

The alien laughs. "Got you. That's one of your questions gone now."

Alicia fumes. "Fine."

"Is anyone going to answer my question?" The ghost.

"And that's your second question," the alien says, giggling.

"But it's the same question as before!"

"No, it isn't," Alicia says. She and the alien have decided they're going to be the enforcers.

You speak up. "We need to answer the ghost's questions. We all have to say where we were when she found the wizard."

"I was sitting at the base of the stairs," the alien says.

"And I was in the ballroom, practicing my ballet." Alicia.

You think for a second. "I ate a couple of sandwiches in the dining room, then I went to the drawing room. The nurse was there, and we talked."

"Yes, we did," she confirms.

"I was in the bathroom the whole time," the knight says.

"Me too," says the superhero.

"Oh, so that was you I heard, then."

"Yeah. We have alibis. Each other."

"Ghost, you need to say where you were," Alicia prompts.

"I wandered about upstairs for a quick look around, then down again. I said hello to the alien, and I saw you in the ballroom, dancing."

"Hey, Alien, why didn't you say you saw the ghost wandering about?" Alicia asks.

"Because you didn't ask. That's your second question." the ghost giggles again.

"I'm going to sit down," the nurse says. "My head is spinning from all this." She sits on one of the worn brown leather sofas. One by one, everyone follows suit. You sit next to the nurse.

"Alien, did you see anyone else while you were sitting on the stairs? And yes, I know that counts as a question." That was the knight.

"I saw the nurse go into the drawing room almost straight away, and I saw the ninja go in there a few minutes later."

"Aha!" the superhero says. "Ninja, may I ask you two questions?"

"Sure," you say. "What's the other question?"

She groans, realizing that she's used one of them up. "What were you doing before you went to the drawing room?"

You shake your head as if it's a silly question. "I've already told you. I ate two more sandwiches in the dining room."

"Oh, yeah. I forgot."

"But can anyone corroborate that?" the knight asks.

"Second question," Alicia says, ever the rule minder.

Everyone shakes their head. No one saw you in the dining room because they weren't there themselves. And that, you realize, is fortunate, because if anyone had been there, they would have known that you weren't.

"It must be the ninja," the superhero whispers.

"Is that an accusation?" the nurse asks.

"First question." The alien.

"It's not an accusation. I'm just thinking out loud."

But it's enough to rouse the nurse's suspicions. More than anyone, she knows you would have had ample time to kill the wizard before joining her in the drawing room.

She turns to face you. "Ninja, did you do it?" Then she immediately rolls her eyes as she realizes she's used up her last question.

338

You know the cameras are zooming in on you, waiting for your answer. The nurse shrinks away from you on the sofa as if she might be your next victim.

It's time to make a decision. Do you:

Confess to murder? **P339**

Or

Say you are not the murderer? **P341**

Confess to murder

"Yeah, I did it," you say.

"Cut!" the director shouts. He smacks his forehead with the palm of his hand, knocking his yellow cap backward off his head. "What are you doing, Ninja? That was a question, not an accusation! You shouldn't have confessed! Now we have to shoot it all again from the beginning!"

George looks at you with a stony expression, his shoulders slumped. "Scooter, the whole point of the mystery game is the kids have to work it out. It needs to have more action and suspense than this. Don't confess. Just lie. Or think what a ninja would do. That's your character. Do something clever or dramatic."

It would have helped if there had been a script, or some direction from the directors, you think, but you keep those thoughts to yourself.

"Can I get up now?" the wizard asks. "I think my right arm has gone to sleep because I'm lying on it."

"If we're going to shoot again from the beginning, maybe we should replace the ninja. Do we have any other extras in the holding area?" the first assistant director asks.

"No," George snaps. "We used all of them to replace the actors you fired because of budget cuts."

The 1AD clicks her tongue. "Oh yeah."

"Okay," the director says. He's calmed down. "Everyone, back to the dining room. We'll go again. And I don't want any confessions this time."

I'm sorry, this part of your story is over. You joined the film crew as an extra and discovered that most of the cast consisted of extras, such was the low budget of the movie. Having almost no script didn't help matters either. On the other hand, it presented you with the opportunity of stamping your mark on your pivotal role—that of the murderer. But you unwisely confessed before the mystery had been solved—there were still ways to deflect suspicion from you, and you hadn't even used your own questions yet. But don't worry. This is a *You Say Which Way* book, and you can take that last decision again for a different outcome.

Or perhaps you'd like to try another pathway in the book? What would it be like to be a production assistant, for instance?

It's time to make a decision. You have three choices. Do you:

Retake that last decision and say you aren't the murderer? **P341**

Or

Go to the big list of choices and start reading from another part of the story? **P366**

Or

Go back to the beginning of the story and try another path? **P253**

Say you are not the murderer

"No, it wasn't me," you tell the nurse. "I had more of those little club sandwiches before I joined you in the drawing room. I've already told you that."

She nods and purses her lips. Maybe she's still unsure.

"Does anyone have any questions left?" the ghost asks.

"You can't ask that," Alicia says. "You've had your two questions already."

"Okay, then. It would be extremely helpful if anyone who still has questions left would say so."

"I have one question," the alien says. He's looking at you. At least you think so, but it's hard to tell.

"I have both of mine," you say.

"You go first."

"Okay, I'll ask one," you say. Some of the other kids probably suspect you're the murderer, so you decide to try to deflect their suspicions by casting doubt on what the others have claimed.

"Go for it," Alicia says.

You take a deep breath. "The knight said she was in the bathroom the whole time. So did the superhero. But then the knight said, 'Oh, so that was you I heard, then.' *Heard*, not *saw*. Knight, are you completely sure it was the superhero you heard?"

"Um … She said it was her. It can't be anyone else."

"Maybe, maybe not. As you didn't see her, there's no way to be sure," you say.

"Here's my last question, then," the alien says. "Superhero, did you see or hear the knight while you were in the bathroom? You didn't mention it."

The superhero shook her head. "No, I didn't, but I wasn't really listening, you know. I was struggling to get my costume off and on again in the cubicle."

"So, there it is," you say confidently. "We can't be sure the knight was in the bathroom. And even if she was, either she or the superhero could have snuck out, committed the murder and returned."

Some of the other kids look convinced. Some look dubious. "My last question now," you say. "Ghost, how many bedrooms are there upstairs?"

"I don't know," the ghost replies.

"But you said you went upstairs. Surely you know what you saw up there. Yet you say you don't know how many bedrooms there are."

"I wasn't counting. Besides, the alien saw me go upstairs. I went past him, and I came down again later. He knows I was up there."

"I know you went up there, yes," the alien says. "But I think the ninja has an idea."

"I do. There's a servants' staircase too, opposite the bathroom. You could have come straight down that way and into the library without being seen, killed the wizard, then back up the servants' staircase, and down the main one past the alien again."

"Wow. That's clever," the nurse says.

"That sounds like something the murderer would do to give themselves an alibi," you say, trying not to smile at the irony of you suggesting the ghost is the murderer when the ghost knows that you are because she swapped envelopes with you.

"We're all out of questions now," Alicia says. "It's time for some accusations."

"I think the murderer was the ghost," the nurse says.

"Me too." The alien.

"Same here." You add your vote. It's hard to keep a straight face.

"The ninja," the ghost says. The sheet over her head conceals her expression, but there's an edge to her voice.

"The knight," the superhero says.

"The ghost," the knight says.

"And I vote for the ghost too," says Alicia. "So that's a clear overall vote for the ghost. You're the murderer, Ghost."

"But … but …"

The mother character reappears. "Excellent game, everyone. I'm so glad it was a success. But let's find out who the real murderer is and if you're right. Wizard, you can get up now. Tell us who killed you."

The wizard stiffly gets to his feet. "It was the ninja."

The others gasp in astonishment.

You grin.

"Splendid!" the mother character says. "What fun! There'll be more party games later, and maybe even another murder. But it's back to the party food now."

"Cut!" the director shouts. "Ninja, that was ingenious! You're a natural! How do you feel about having a bigger role in the remainder of the movie? Maybe co-star with Alicia? We could write you into something—"

"Except we can't afford scriptwriters any longer," George reminds him.

The director is unperturbed. "Even better! The ninja's performance in this scene demonstrated that a script isn't required! Well done, Ninja! You're going to be a star!"

George mimes clapping.

Under the sheet, you're sure the ghost is scowling at you.

Congratulations, this part of your story is over. You joined the film crew as an extra, dressed as a ninja, and wound up performing a pivotal role in the murder mystery game in the movie—that of the murderer.

Furthermore, you managed to deflect suspicion away from yourself onto others and avoided being nominated as the killer by almost everyone. Well done!

What might have happened if you'd kept your original envelope or swapped with the wizard? Or maybe next time you'd like to be a production assistant and help with the movie production?

It's time to make a decision. Do you:

Go to the big list of choices? **P366**

Or

Go back to the beginning and try another path? **P253**

Keep your original envelope

"Thanks, but I'll keep my envelope," you say.

"Okay, I'll swap with someone else," the ghost says. You don't see who it is.

The wizard says nothing.

This will be fun. As a guest, you'll get to be part of solving the murder mystery. Much better than being the murderer, and a whole lot more preferable than being the unfortunate victim, who, you figure, will spend a lot of time lying on the floor pretending to be dead.

All around the table, kids covertly check their envelopes. You read more from the sheet of paper inside yours. There are further instructions telling you where to go and what to do when the game begins. You skim through them.

Well, this will be interesting, you think, and help yourself to another club sandwich and more fruit juice.

At one side of the room, the "parents" are talking together, a camera operator and a sound operator hovering nearby to catch what they say. The father character turns to face the table and speaks with his formal, grating voice. "Kids, it's time to start the murder mystery game. You've all got your instructions … and … and … um …"

Has he forgotten his lines? Or is this where the script runs out?

The mother character jumps in. "So, let's have fun! Remember to follow the instructions in your envelopes."

The other kids start filing out of the dining room. You join them. Your instructions said to wander freely around the downstairs parts of the house, but not to go to the library during the first ten minutes.

The more characters you see as you walk around the house, the better, you think. You can eliminate them as

346

suspects, making it easier for you to solve the mystery. Also, they can be your alibi for when the accusations fly.

It's time to make a decision. You have four choices. Do you:

Wander to the drawing room? **P347**

Or

Wander to the ballroom? **P349**

Or

Wander to the bathroom? **P350**

Or

Wander upstairs? **P351**

Wander to the drawing room

On the way to the drawing room, you see the alien sitting on the stairs. The nurse is standing by the bay windows in the drawing room, looking out at the garden. She startles and turns, gasping, when she hears your footsteps. A camera operator on a Segway films you entering the room.

"Don't worry," you say, helping yourself to a glass of apple juice from a side table. "I'm not the murderer."

"But the real murderer might say that."

You think about it. "True. But my task is to wander around the various rooms."

"Ah. I'm supposed to wait in here until something happens."

"Shouldn't there be some paints and easels in here?" you say, looking around.

The nurse sniggers. "You'd think so, wouldn't you? But the term 'drawing room' came from *with*drawing room, a room to withdraw to. It has nothing to do with artists."

You think about that while you drain your glass of apple juice. You needed that drink—something to wash down all the sandwiches you've eaten.

"How do you know I hadn't poisoned that before you came in here?" the nurse asks.

You freeze, the glass half way lowered to the table. "Poison it how?"

"With salt or something to make it taste different. I didn't, though."

"Ha ha. I'm not the victim. I'm an ordinary guest." You set the glass down and chat to the nurse for three or four minutes, before saying you should move on.

If you've been everywhere else, you should probably go to the library, but you can go there now if you want to.

348

It's time to make a decision. You have four choices. Do you:

Wander to the ballroom? **P349**

Or

Wander to the bathroom? **P350**

Or

Wander upstairs? **P351**

Or

Wander to the library? **P353**

Wander to the ballroom

On the way to the ballroom, you see the alien sitting on the stairs. The child star Alicia Tomova pirouettes on the polished wooden floor of the ballroom. You go inside and stand by the wall, watching, stunned at her graceful movements. This isn't just a role in the movie for her. She must have had years of training, and a camera operator on a Segway is there capturing it all.

She catches sight of you, overbalances, and topples onto her butt. Maybe her moves weren't so good after all.

"Oh, Ninja, I didn't see you there. Have you been here long?"

"Not long."

"I wonder what's going to happen." She gets up and starts dancing again.

After three or four minutes, you decide to move on.

If you've been everywhere else, you should probably go to the library, but you can go there now if you want to.

It's time to make a decision. You have four choices. Do you:

Wander to the drawing room? **P347**

Or

Wander to the bathroom? **P350**

Or

Wander upstairs? **P351**

Or

Wander to the library? **P353**

350

Wander to the bathroom

On the way to the bathroom, you see the alien sitting on the stairs. You make your way to the bathroom from the hallway running alongside the drawing room and dining room, so you can keep away from the library, and you pass behind the main staircase. The bathroom is a unisex one with three cubicles and a curtained-off shower space.

Odd, you think, if this is a family home, but perhaps it's a home that's been turned into a business. Or maybe tour groups visit. Who knows.

Two of the cubicles are occupied. From one, you hear the superhero say, "This damned costume!"

There's the sound of snapping spandex.

"Hey, Superhero," you call out.

"Who's there?"

"I'm the ninja."

"Oh, hi. I hope you have an easier time with your costume than I'm having with mine."

Time to find out. Lucky for you a ninja costume is not a problem in the bathroom. As you wash your hands, you notice the other two cubicles are still occupied. It's time to move on.

If you've been everywhere else, you should probably go to the library, but you can go there now if you want to.

It's time to make a decision. Do you:

Wander to the drawing room? **P347**

Or

Wander to the ballroom? **P349**

Or

Wander upstairs? **P351**

Or

Wander to the library? **P353**

Wander upstairs

You're not supposed to go upstairs, but you've got to kill some time (rather than another guest) and you're curious as to what you'll find up there. You make your way to the bottom of the main staircase. The alien is sitting on the red runner carpet, three steps up. It's almost impossible to read his expression because of his alien costume, but you get the feeling that he's sad.

A camera operator on a Segway hovers near the main entrance, right by your scooter, filming.

"What's going on, Alien?" You sit next to him.

"Nothing. I want to go home."

"What? Go home? Really?"

"Yeah, that's me. Homesick. Just waiting for the next flying saucer out of here."

You shake your head. "You're not making any sense."

The alien raises a long-fingered grey hand to the side of his mouth and whispers, "I'm playing in character, you dolt. Like we were told. Aliens either want to eat your brains, or they want to go home. I'm doing the latter."

"Ah. Gotcha." You get to your feet and take a few steps upstairs.

"You're not supposed to go up there."

"Maybe not, but I'm a ninja. I go wherever I want. You're lucky I let you see me. Normally I'm almost invisible."

The alien nods, his antennae wobbling. You continue up the stairs to a large landing. Several rooms come off it, most with the doors closed. Probably bedrooms. One room has an open door, with sunlight streaming through it onto the landing, glinting off the polished wooden floor.

You enter the room. It's an office, probably considered a small room in this manor, but it would be huge in an average

352

house. Files and bookcases line one wall, and a desk with a computer are on the other. Floor to ceiling glass sliding doors lead onto one of the balconies.

For a minute or two, you stand in the doorway, in the warmth of the streaming sun, enjoying the vista through the windows. Then you decide you should return downstairs.

If you've been everywhere else, you should probably go to the library, but you can go there now if you want to.

It's time to make a decision. Do you:

Wander to the drawing room? **P347**

Or

Wander to the ballroom? **P349**

Or

Wander to the bathroom? **P350**

Or

Wander to the library? **P353**

Wander to the library

You make your way to the library. When you open the door, you stop and stare.

It's stunning. Wooden shelving fills three-quarters of the room from the floor to the mural-covered ceiling. Muted light passes through fancy net curtains over the windows opposite you.

Two aged leather sofas, comfortable stuffed chairs and coffee tables are dotted around the room. There's even a portable stepladder to help readers reach books on the higher shelves.

The library is carpeted, unlike the rest of the ground floor of the manor, probably to keep the noise level low for anyone reading in there.

But walking into the room, you discover something that makes you draw your breath in sharply.

The wizard is lying on the floor. A sticky red substance mars his purple starred costume. A few paces away, a pistol lies discarded.

You've found the murder victim!

"There's a body in the library!" you turn and shout out of the doorway. As you turn back, you catch sight of the camera operator, sound engineer and the director crowded in the nearest corner of the room. The director gives you a thumbs-up.

The sound of running footsteps comes from around the house, and the other party guests pour into the library.

"Oooh!" the ghost says.

"Did you see anyone?" the knight asks you.

Before you can answer, the mother character comes into the room. "Oh, look, there's a body," she says, rather cheerily. "The murderer is one of you seven, and you have to figure out who. Here are rules: You're each allowed two questions. After all the questions, you can each make an accusation. Whoever correctly picks the murderer wins a prize. Okay?"

Everyone nods, including the dead wizard.

"Have fun!" she says and leaves the room.

"I didn't see anyone when I found the wizard here," you say.

"Then how do we know that you're not the murderer, and you shouted out that you'd found the body after killing the wizard yourself?" the knight asks.

"That's your two questions," the alien said.

"Hey! I asked one of those before we were even told the rules."

"It still counts."

"I have an alibi," you say. "Other people saw me."

The people who saw you nod their heads.

"I guess we can eliminate the ninja from the investigation, then," Alicia says. "So, where was everyone else?"

"I was sitting on the stairs the whole time," the alien says. "And that's your first question."

"And I was in the ballroom," Alicia says.

"I was in the bathroom the entire time," offers the superhero.

"Me too. I heard you." That was the ghost.

"Well, it's hard to get that spandex costume off quietly."

"I was in the bathroom too," the knight says quickly. "I heard you as well."

"I was in the drawing room." The nurse chimes in.

Alicia scratches her head. "Alien, did you see anyone else while you were sitting on the stairs?"

"Yes." The alien giggles. "That's your second question."

"But you didn't say who you saw!"

"You didn't ask who I saw. You only asked if I saw anyone."

Alicia fumes. "Fine. Maybe someone else can ask."

The superhero asks. "Alien, did you see the ballerina go into the ballroom?"

"Yes." The alien sticks to his monosyllabic answers.

"Well, did you see her come out again?" the superhero presses.

"No. She was in there the whole time. And that's your second question."

"I could see the alien on the stairs while I was spinning around," Alicia said.

You're not going to make the same mistake of asking separate questions about entering and leaving a room. "What about the nurse? Was she in the drawing room the entire time?"

Dang. You realize you asked two questions anyway.

"That's two questions," confirms the alien, giggling. "Are you asking me?"

"Yes, and that's your first question," you shoot back.

The alien might be frowning, but you really can't tell. Perhaps his mask is bending a little bit. "Yes, the nurse was in the drawing room the whole time."

"Superhero, did you hear or see the ghost or the knight in the bathroom?" the nurse asks.

"No, but I wasn't listening much. I had to concentrate on getting this damn costume off before I peed myself."

"Then how can we know you were really there, Ghost?" the alien says.

"That's your second question," Alicia says.

The ghost holds up the end of her sheet. "My costume's wet. You think it's easy to sit on the toilet with a sheet over you?"

Ooo. You hope that's water and not … something else.

356

"And that's your first question, Ghost," Alicia says.

"But that was a rhetorical question. Why should that count?"

"All questions count. That's your two, now."

"I did hear the door open once, just after I entered the cubicle," said the superhero.

Only the nurse has a question left. "Knight, how many cubicles were occupied when you were in the bathroom?"

The knight hesitates a moment. "Two, I think. Maybe one. I didn't really look."

That's not helpful, you think.

"We're all out of questions now," Alicia says. "It's time for some accusations."

You think hard. Who killed the wizard? You know you can solve this mystery.

It's time to make a decision. Do you:

Accuse the superhero? **P357**

Or

Accuse the ghost? **P358**

Or

Accuse the knight? **P359**

Or

Accuse the alien? **P361**

Accuse the superhero

You decide the superhero must have slipped out of the bathroom, killed the wizard, and returned.

"I think the murderer was the superhero," you say.

Everyone else makes their accusation. Most of them disagree with you.

You're wrong.

Where did you go wrong with your thinking?

The ghost must be telling the truth about being in the bathroom because her costume got wet. She heard the superhero in there, struggling with her costume, the entire time.

I'm sorry, this part of your story is over. You joined the film crew as an extra and discovered that most of the cast consisted of extras, such was the low budget of the movie. The main focus of the movie (so far) was the murder mystery game, and you played the role of one of the guests.

Unfortunately, you didn't solve the mystery, though you did well in front of the cameras, so at the end of the day, George says he wants you back the next day. But if you want to try to solve the mystery, you can take that last decision again for a different outcome. Or perhaps you'd like to try another pathway in the book? What would it be like to be a production assistant, for instance?

It's time to make a decision. Do you:

Take that last decision again? **P356**

Or

Go to the list of choices and start reading from another part of the story? **P366**

Or

Go to the beginning and try another path? **P362**

Accuse the ghost

You decide the ghost must have slipped out of the bathroom,` killed the wizard, and returned.

"I think the murderer was the ghost," you say.

Everyone else makes their accusation. Most of them disagree with you.

You're wrong. Where did you go wrong with your thinking?

The ghost must be telling the truth about being in the bathroom because her costume got wet. However, the superhero said she heard the bathroom door open once, not twice, so the ghost must have entered and not slipped out to kill the wizard.

I'm sorry, this part of your story is over. You joined the film crew as an extra and discovered that most of the cast consisted of extras, such was the low budget of the movie. The main focus of the movie (so far) was the murder mystery game, and you played the role of one of the guests. Unfortunately, you didn't solve the mystery, though you did well in front of the cameras, so at the end of the day, George says he wants you back the next day. But if you want to try to solve the mystery, you can take that last decision again for a different outcome. Or perhaps you'd like to try another pathway in the book? What would it be like to be a production assistant, for instance?

It's time to make a decision. Do you:

Take that last decision again for a different outcome. **P356**

Go to the big list of choices? **P366**

Or

Go back to the beginning of the story and try another path? **P362**

Accuse the knight

By process of elimination, or very good guesswork that is usually called intuition, you've determined that the knight is the murderer.

The ballerina and the alien provide alibis for each other. Therefore, you know the alien was on the stairs the whole time, and he said the nurse never left the drawing room. So, none of those three can be the murderer.

The ghost was evidently in the bathroom at some time because her costume was wet. While in there, she heard the superhero in another cubicle, and the superhero said she only heard the bathroom door open once, so you know the ghost came in and did not leave.

That only leaves the knight, who also said she was in the bathroom, but no one saw her or heard her in there. Furthermore, if she was in there, the superhero would have heard the door opening twice for the ghost and knight to enter, then again for the knight to leave. That didn't happen.

The knight is the only person who doesn't have a real alibi.

"I'm sure the murderer was the knight," you say.

Everyone else makes their accusation. Most of them agree with you.

You were right.

Well done! You've solved the murder mystery!

Congratulations, this part of your story is over. You joined the film crew as an extra and discovered that most of the cast consisted of extras, such was the low budget of the movie. The main focus of the movie (so far) was the murder mystery game, and you played the role of one of the guests, dressed as a ninja. Through clever deduction, you managed

360

to solve the mystery and catch the murderer. Even better, you did well in front of the cameras, so George wants you back the next day for more filming. That means more free food and another day's pay. Then the director adds that he's so pleased with your acting skills and your powers of deduction that he's chosen you as the 'extra' to be given a much greater role in the rest of the film. You're going to co-star! It's the start of a movie career for you! Congratulations!

But what might have happened if you'd swapped your original envelope? As this is a *You Say Which Way* book, you can change your previous decision. Or maybe you'd like to try another pathway in the book? What would it be like to be a production assistant and help with the movie production?

It's time to make a decision. Do you:

Go to the list of choices and start reading from another part of the story? **P366**

Or

Go back to the beginning of the story and try another path? **P362**

Accuse the alien

You decide the alien must have slipped away from the stairs, killed the wizard, and returned.

"I think the murderer was the alien," you say.

Everyone else makes their accusation. None of them agree with you. You're wrong. Where did you go wrong with your thinking?

You saw the alien on the stairs yourself, and Alicia, the ballerina, confirmed she saw the alien on the stairs while she was dancing. He couldn't have gone anywhere without her noticing.

I'm sorry, this part of your story is over. You joined the film crew as an extra and discovered that most of the cast consisted of extras, such was the low budget of the movie. The main focus of the movie (so far) was the murder mystery game, and you played the role of one of the guests. Unfortunately, you didn't solve the mystery, though you did well in front of the cameras, so George wants you back the next day. But if you want to try to solve the mystery, you can take that last decision again for a different outcome.

Or perhaps you'd like to try another path? What would it be like to be a production assistant, for instance?

It's time to make a decision. Do you:

Go to the big list of choices? **P366**

Or

Go to the beginning and try another path? **P362**

362

Back at the beginning

So, as you know, you start the story scooting through the wealthy part of town. It's early morning and you aren't expecting any traffic or people—but instead you come across a lot of action as a film crew is setting up for the day. It turns out they could do with a hand, and you get taken on. Your first choice is to be an extra or a production assistant.

It's time to make a decision. Do you:

Choose to be an extra? **P311**

Or

Choose to be a production assistant? **P257**

Glossary

Call Time: when everyone is required to be on set, e.g. 7:00 a.m.
Check the gate: check the camera to see if it got the shot.
Cut: stop filming this sequence.
Extra: someone who (usually) may have a bit part in a movie.
Flushing: transporting people or equipment across an active film set.
Gator: an all-terrain vehicle (ATV).
Holding area: where the extras wait before being called.
Honeybadger: a tiny cart that contains all the batteries needed for the set.
Honeywagon: toilet
Hot brick: a charged walkie-talkie battery.
In the can: filming completed or "wrapped".
Landed: arrived on set.
Quiet on the set: everyone needs to be quiet because filming is about to start.
Rolling: currently filming
Script: the dialogue and other information comprising the movie's contents.
Set box: accordion file containing the most-frequently-asked-for paperwork, e.g. Script, revisions, time cards, schedule, crew lists, vouchers etc. Set PAs have them.
Setup: the positioning of equipment for the filming of a scene. May be many setups for a scene.
Sides: the pages of the script being shot that day.
Take: a continuous filming sequence. May be many takes in a setup.
Ten-O-One: I need to use the toilet.
That's a take: they got the shot and are ready to move on to the next one.
Three-banger: a trailer with compartments for three actors.
Wrap: filming completed for the day or a scene or a setup.

BIG LIST OF CHOICES

DUNGEON OF DOOM

Secret Bonus Level 1
The Goblins 7
Invisibly Sneak Past the Goblins 10
Chop the Ivy 14
Follow the Ivy 15
Run for It 19
Break the Spell 20
The Narrow Doorway 28
The White Door 31
Don't Open the Purple Door 34
The White Door 35
The Yellow Door 36
Throw the egg to the Dwarves 42
Throw the egg to the Shark 44
The Purple Door 46
The Yellow Door 50
The Purple Door 51
Ogres, Rock and Roll 54
Dark Room 56
Stabby Stabby 57
Tickly Tickly 59
So Cool 61
Swimming Pool (or is it?) 65
Help Zim 67
Don't Help Zim 71
Sorry, Your Majesty 73
So Hot 76
Down the Stairs 79
Leave Them and Escape 84
Keep Running 85
The Zenobian Snapper 87
The Nammering 89
Open Both Doors 91
Ogres Again 94
Back at the Beginning 95

SECRETS OF THE SINGING CAVE

The stronghold 98
The hunt 101
The ceremony 105
The chase 110
The ambush 112
Throw the spear at the vootbeest's neck 118
Run towards the hunt master 123
Tell Zenan about your plan to protect hunters from shredders 130
Talk to Thamus about your shredder protection plan first 135
Go and collect thorns from the nearest thorn bush 137
Help Rooth 140
Keep running and let Rooth fend for herself 142
Agree to travel home with the girl 144
Stay with the strangers until after the migration 149
Stay seated and allow Zenan to be caged 159
Support Zenan 163
Wait for head protection 165
Flee the stronghold to find a new tribe 171
Go with Rooth to tell the prime guardian your side of the story 175
Go riding right now 178
Enter the slippery passage with Thamus 181
Don't risk the slippery passage, get captured instead 190
Hide in the stronghold 191
Go hunting with Zenan 194
Go with Thamus to the chamber of interesting things 199
Try to move the rock 204
Exit the stronghold 205
Keep going down the passage 207
Go check out some unexplored tunnels 210
Go hunting on your own 214
Go tell the prime guardian what you've discovered 220
Climb up to the cave in the cliff 223
Complain about the hunt master 229
Agree to keep quiet 231
Keep moving and look for somewhere else to hole up 235
Keep shouting to be released 237
Try to find another way out of the chamber of light 239
Enjoy the feast 245
Use your legs to move the rock 247
Find Zenan and tell him your problem 250
Use your shoulder to move the rock 252

366

MOVIE MYSTERY MADNESS

Movie crew at the manor 253
Choose to be a production assistant 257
Order beans 260
Order mushrooms 263
Fetch a brick from the garden 266
Ask someone what a 'hot brick' is 268
Do the flushing 270
Leave Alicia alone and tell George that she's upset 273
Tell George that you couldn't find Alicia 275
Knock on Alicia's door 277
Deliver the sides 281
Get rid of the set box and get out 283
Deliver the sides, seriously 285
Wait outside until scene one is filmed 288
Bluff your way inside 290
Make the alien stay inside 294
Stay in your lockdown post 295
Leave your lockdown post and get some food 297
Let the alien out 299
Search around the trailers 301
Search amongst the trees 307
Choose to be an extra 311
Swap envelopes with the wizard 317
Swap envelopes with the ghost 321
Choose the water pistol 323
Choose the egg timer bomb 326
Roll the timer and get away 328
Roll the timer and watch 330
Choose the rubber chicken 332
The body in the library 335
Confess to murder 339
Say you are not the murderer 341
Keep your original envelope 345
Wander to the drawing room 347
Wander to the ballroom 349
Wander to the bathroom 350
Wander upstairs 351
Wander to the library 353
Accuse the superhero 357
Accuse the ghost 358
Accuse the knight 359
Accuse the alien 361

Please leave a review of this book on Amazon

Reviews help others know if this book is right for them.
It only takes a moment.
Thanks from the You Say Which Way team.

YouSayWhichWay.com

Printed in Great Britain
by Amazon